ROMANTIC TIMES PRAISES *NEW YORK TIMES* BESTSELLING AUTHOR NORAH HESS!

LARK

"As with all Ms. Hess's books, the ending is joyous for everyone. The road to happiness is filled with wonderful characters, surprises, passion, pathos and plot twists and turns as only the inimitable Norah Hess can create."

LACEY

"Emotions leap off the pages and right into the reader's heart. You'll savor every word."

FLINT

"Ms. Hess has once again created a memorable love story with characters who find a place in readers' hearts."

FANCY

"The lively action…from the talented Ms. Hess is sure to catch your FANCY."

SNOW FIRE

"Ms. Hess fills…each page with excitement and twists. This warm and sultry romance is a perfect dessert for a cold winter day."

RAVEN

"Ms. Hess has again written a steamy love story [that] moves along as fast as a herd of buffalo. There's evil, laughter, sexy romance, earthy delights and a cast of characters to keep the reader turning the pages."

MORE *ROMANTIC TIMES* RAVES FOR CAREER ACHIEVEMENT NOMINEE NORAH HESS!

TANNER

"Ms. Hess certainly knows how to write a romance...the characters are wonderful and find a way to sneak into your heart."

WILLOW

"Again Norah Hess gives readers a story of a woman who learns to take care of herself, and fills her tale with interesting, well-developed characters and a plot full of twists and turns, passion and humor. This is another page-turner."

JADE

"Ms. Hess continues to write page-turners with wonderful characters described in depth. This is a wonderful romance complete with surprising plot twists...plenty of action and sensuality. Another great read from a great writer."

DEVIL IN SPURS

"Norah Hess is a superb Western romance writer.... *Devil in Spurs* is an entertaining read!"

KENTUCKY BRIDE

"Marvelous...a treasure for those who savor frontier love stories!"

MOUNTAIN ROSE

"Another delightful, tender and heartwarming read from a special storyteller!"

Other books by Norah Hess:

LARK
LACEY
TENNESSEE MOON
FLINT
SNOW FIRE
RAVEN
SAGE
DEVIL IN SPURS
TANNER
KENTUCKY BRIDE
WILLOW
JADE
BLAZE
KENTUCKY WOMAN
HAWKE'S PRIDE
MOUNTAIN ROSE
FANCY
WINTER LOVE
FOREVER THE FLAME
WILDFIRE
STORM

Dylan

NORAH HESS

LEISURE BOOKS NEW YORK CITY

A LEISURE BOOK®

March 2005

Published by

Dorchester Publishing Co., Inc.
200 Madison Avenue
New York, NY 10016

ISBN 0-8439-5058-7

The name "Leisure Books" and the stylized "L" with design are trademarks of Dorchester Publishing Co., Inc.

Printed in the United States of America.

Dylan

Chapter One

Rachel awakened to angry voices in the gray morning light. She lay a moment, thinking. She knew that this day was going to be different, but just how didn't come to her right away. Then she heard her father-in-law swearing at his wife, Edna, in the kitchen below, and the woman's cry of pain, the thud of her falling body, and everything that had passed yesterday came back to her in an instant.

At first, an almost indescribable gladness surged over her. Her bridegroom of two short hours was dead. An outraged husband had shot him down as he traveled homeward from the church where he'd promised to cherish and protect her all the days of their lives.

Although she'd been married such a short time, she had already learned what kind of life she would have led with Homer Quade. She shuddered as she recalled those short hours of married life.

They had been only a few miles from the church

when Homer pulled her down off the palomino mare she was riding. He was unbuckling his wide leather belt before she hit the ground.

As she stared at him, her eyes wide with fright, he said, "Well, Miss High-and-Mighty Rachel, you're gonna learn right now how to be a good wife. When I tell you to do something, you'd better jump to do it, or you'll get this."

With those words he started striking her with the belt. She threw up her arms to protect her face, but soon she had long, angry-looking welts all over her arms and legs and down her back. He hadn't stopped wielding the belt until she was beaten to the ground, nearly unconscious.

She lay there helplessly, bitter tears soaking the ground beneath her cheek. How could she bear being married to such an animal? She wouldn't live long, that was for sure. Homer would eventually beat her to death.

But God was with her. Before she could even drag herself to her feet, her husband was dead.

For years, Homer had been avoided by all the women on the mountain. They knew he would force himself upon any unprotected female, married or not. Hearing of his wedding, one of his unfortunate victims had finally found the courage to tell her husband what the new bridegroom had done to her. The man had lit out for the church with his rifle in hand. He'd shot Homer down in plain sight of his battered bride.

Rachel's mother-in-law was the only one in the

family who had shed any tears over the loss of Homer. Her father-in-law, Silas, had only sworn that it wasn't fair he had another mouth to feed. Her three sisters-in-law had looked at the welts on her arms and legs with satisfaction. One smirkingly said, "He got to give it to you good before he died, didn't he?"

Rachel wasn't surprised that Jenny would say such mean things to her. It was well known in the mountains that Jenny had wanted to marry Homer, and that she spent most of her time at night in his bed. Everyone knew that the black eyes she often wore didn't come from her husband.

The Quade brother Jenny had married was on the dim side. He didn't know what went on between his wife and brother. As she lay there in bed, Rachel wondered which of the brothers Jenny would go after next.

Rachel painfully dressed herself and was debating about going into the kitchen for a cup of coffee. She was hungry this morning, but she could hear Silas carrying on again about the extra mouth to feed, and she didn't know if she dared.

A couple minutes later, however, Edna, her mother-in-law, brought her a cup of chicory coffee and a piece of day-old wedding cake. She accepted the offering, thinking that the kind woman didn't deserve the life she had to live with people like the Quades. She would love to kiss the big bruise on Edna's thin cheek that had been put there just minutes ago by her husband. She knew, however, if she showed the woman any kindness, it would only make things worse for Edna.

Rachel was barely finished eating the tasteless cake and drinking the bitter chicory coffee when Silas called her down to the kitchen. As she entered, he pulled a chair away from the table and sat down. Frowning at her, he said coldly, "I talked to your pa yesterday. He don't want you back. In fact he flat-out refused to let you come home. Taig says he has too many mouths to feed as it is.

"And that brings us to the Quades. With Homer not here to provide for you, I can't feed you either." Silas paused a moment then continued. "Of course, we can't just turn you out, so me and my kinfolk had a talk last night and we come to this decision. Homer's cousin Dylan will have to take you in. He's got plenty of money and can feed and clothe you real good."

Rachel stared at Silas a moment, then protested, "But he's no relative of mine. I hardly know him!"

"You'll get to know him after a few days." Silas gave her a stern look. "You just be good to him. Do you know what I mean? If you ain't, he'll take you down to the trading post, where you can take care of the trappers' needs."

A cold uneasiness swept through Rachel. Did this awful old man know what he was talking about? Could she just be handed over to any man who came along?

Silas rose from the table. "Be ready to catch the

coach down at the grocery store in about an hour. We took up a collection to pay for your ticket. You'll arrive in Jackson Hole somewhere around dark. I'm goin' to let my nephew know to expect you."

He laid some coins on the table in front of Rachel, then without another word, left her sitting alone in the kitchen, staring blankly out the window. What was she to do? she asked herself. She remembered seeing Dylan Quade a couple times several years back. He had struck her as being an arrogant man, one who thought he was better than the rest of them because he owned a ranch down in the valley.

He certainly looked better than the mountain men, she remembered. He was clean and handsome, and his hair, though a little long, was neatly trimmed and as black as a crow's wing.

She recalled how smitten all the girls and young women were with him, twittering and giggling and making eyes at him. She had been taken with him herself, but she hadn't done any of those things. She hated the way he was so stuck on himself, acting like he was above them. She had ignored him completely.

Her lips twisted wryly. Now she might have to live with him . . . if he would have her. Would he remember how she had snubbed him? If he did let her live with him, what would he demand of her? He couldn't be worse than Homer.

Thunder began to rumble in the mountains, and

Rachel prayed that the rain would hold off until she got to Jackson Hole. She had made up her mind that her clothes were too ragged to be seen by passengers in the coach. She was going to ride her mare to Jackson Hole.

The young mare she had been riding from the church was Rachel's prize possession, a beautiful animal named Goldie. Rachel had caught and tamed her all by herself.

Neither the Quades nor the Sutters would want her to have the golden palomino, so she would have to take her on the sneak.

She went up to the loft room to get her few clothes together and wait until everyone left the shack to do the chores. When all was quiet, Rachel picked up her small bundle of clothes and slipped softly out of the shack.

Goldie whiffled softly when Rachel entered her stall, and Rachel quickly cupped her palm over the mare's nostrils. Sounds carried in the clear mountain air.

As she saddled the mare, Rachel thought how much she was going to miss her mother. But, she added as she fastened her bundle of clothes on the cantle, she would not miss any of the Sutters. Nor would she miss most of the other mountain folk, except for her cousin Jassy and Granny Hawkins.

She led Goldie out into the cool, windy morning and climbed into the saddle. No matter what lay ahead, it had to be better than what she was leaving behind.

Chapter Two

Although it was nearly spring, the early March wind was cold and raw as it swept down from the mountains.

Standing on the edge of the cabin porch, Dylan Quade lifted his head and sniffed the air. Damm, he thought with a frown, it's going to rain. He hoped he could make it to the trading post before the downpour arrived.

It had been a good winter for trapping, and he had many fine pelts to sell. He didn't want to arrive at the post with the furs soaking wet. But he felt he had them well-wrapped in oilskin and need not worry about their condition when he reached the post.

A crooked grin stirred his lips. He was more than ready to get off the mountain and spend the summer months in the lowlands. He would thaw out there and tend to his herd again. Round up the wild mustangs. And how pleasant it would be to feel the soft, warm body of a woman again after all these months.

He hadn't had a woman since he rode up the mountains last fall to set out his traps. "Almost six months with no one but you for company, Shadow," he muttered to his dog. He dragged a comb through the thick black hair that hung to his shoulders, then shook his head. That was quite a dry spell for a man in his early thirties.

But all that was about to change, he thought, and picking up the straight-edged razor lying beside a shaving mug of lather, he began scraping away a winter's growth of beard. When he had finished, he felt his face, nodded his satisfaction, then tossed the pan of soapy water and stubble over the edge of the porch. When he had wiped the pan dry with the towel he had dried his face on, he entered the kitchen to prepare his breakfast.

He took a heavy frying skillet off the wall and placed it on the small cast-iron stove. When he had laid his last two strips of salt pork in the pan, he set about peeling the three potatoes left in his larder. Half an hour later Dylan had finished eating and had washed the dishes he'd used.

He went into his bedroom and began sorting through his clothes, deciding which to take down the mountain and which to leave behind. He laid to one side several pairs of denim pants, as well as shirts and underclothing. These articles would be worn on the range when driving the cattle out of the brush and gullies. The buckskins, such as those he wore now, would be mostly used in the rainy season. The fringe on the shirts and trousers drained the water off a man when he was caught out in the rain. Most folks didn't know that.

After Dylan had shoved everything into a saddlebag, he checked his Colt. He would be traveling through some outlaw country as well as land inhabited by scattered bunches of renegade Indians. His gun must be in perfect working order. When he found it so, he hung it on the foot of the bed.

He next laid his hand to gathering up his trapping gear and carrying it to the sturdy little storage shed. There the traps would stay until the next freezing frost, when they would be set out again. Slamming the door shut, he clicked the heavy lock in place. The lock was there mainly to keep out the Sutter clan. It was claimed that the Sutter men would steal anything they could get their hands on. By and large, they were a lazy bunch; it was mostly the women who provided the food for their tables.

That task finished, Dylan went back to the cabin. It was time he started putting together those supplies he would take with him to his ranch five miles out of Jackson Hole. He wouldn't need to take much—just a few days' supply of grub, small cloth bags of flour, coffee, and sugar. He didn't want to ride to town right away for supplies. When he first returned to the Bar X, what he most liked to do was to ride over the range, checking how the cattle had fared over the winter. He was always anxious to see how many new calves had been dropped.

He only had a couple hundred head of cattle, but they were special. They were Brahmas crossbred with longhorns. Their offspring would carry more meat than ordinary cattle and would consequently bring more money.

But separate from his prize herd, Dylan also had thirty head of longhorns. These he kept out of affection for the dying breed. Some of the old mossyhorns weighed close to thirteen, fourteen hundred pounds, and they were as mean as the devil himself. They were always ready to take out after a man if they caught him on foot.

As Dylan walked back to the cabin, he thought it strange how he was always drawn between two worlds. When the autumn wind blew from the mountains, cool and bracing, a longing for the wilderness descended on him. Then the sun of the lowlands seemed to shine too hot on his head, and as soon as the cottonwood and aspen leaves began to fall, he headed for the high country, where nobody but eagles and mountain sheep went. His grandfather had always said that he was like an Indian, that he had a love for the wild and lonely. He half suspected that was true.

But then again, every year around this time, when the leaves began to bud out on the trees and the grass started to green up a bit, he heard the silent call of the valley coaxing him from his high lonesome, hinting that he should find a wife, start a family.

Dylan shook his head with a wry smile. What

woman in her right mind would want to live the way he did, caught between two very different worlds? It was a good thing he never wanted to get married.

Dylan had made up his bed and swept all the floors when he heard the distant rumble of thunder. His brow darkened. That rain was getting closer. He would never make it to the trading post without being drenched.

He was putting his shaving paraphernalia in the saddlebag when Shadow began barking. Dylan glanced out the window and saw an elderly man coming down the ridge behind his cabin. He recognized his uncle, and from the old man's hunched posture he guessed that something bad had happened at the Quade place.

His old relative had no sooner climbed off his mule than he was crying out in his cracked voice, "My Homer's dead, nephew! Shot down in cold blood comin' home from church yesterday when he warn't carryin' no gun."

"I'm sorry to hear that, Uncle Silas." Dylan turned his head so that the old man couldn't see that he felt no sorrow to hear of his cousin's death. If ever there was a mean bastard, it was his cousin Homer.

"I'm sorry I missed his funeral," Dylan lied again. "I guess there was a big turnout for his wake."

Silas frowned and looked off through the trees. His voice was gruff when he said, "Most all the folks had excuses why they couldn't make it." He paused, then added, "A lot of people didn't like my Homer. They wuz jealous of him. You remember how good-lookin' he wuz, what a good fighter he wuz."

Yeah, like hell jealousy was what kept folks away, Dylan thought to himself. *They didn't come because they couldn't stand the bastard. I doubt that I would have gone even if I'd known about it in time*. The folks living on Tulane Ridge could now walk about the mountain in peace. The men and teenagers would no longer be badgered to fight with him.

And the women, single and married alike, would no longer have to fight off his advances. They would no longer have to keep silent about what Homer did when he found them out alone. They were aware that if they told their menfolk about the things he did to them, their male relatives would be forced to fight the big bully. And Homer Quade had never fought a fair fight in his life.

Yes, the womenfolk would sleep deeply tonight. They would no longer have to live in fear of Homer Quade.

Dylan's lips tightened. With the exception of himself, he'd thought all the men living in the mountains were afraid of Homer. He wondered what had provoked Homer's killer. It must have been something terrible for the man to shoot him down in cold blood. Mountain people didn't tolerate that sort of killing. But the mean bastard must have deserved it.

While Silas dabbed at his teary eyes with a dirty rag, Dylan admitted to himself that he was doubly glad Homer was dead. He had known for a long time that some day Homer would go too far and he'd be forced to kill the man. That would start a feud the likes of which hadn't been seen in the mountains for many years.

When Silas began to complain again, Dylan made himself listen to the old man's grumbling.

"It wasn't bad enough that my boy was struck down at such a young age," Silas was complaining, "but he had tied a girl in wedlock only a couple hours before."

For a long minute Dylan could only stare at his uncle in disbelief. What girl in her right mind would be foolish enough to marry Homer Quade? Every female for miles around knew what kind of beast he was.

Dylan was finally able to ask, "Who did Homer marry? Is it anyone I know?"

Silas nodded. "You know her. She's Taig Sutter's daughter. The white-haired one. You know, the one with the long legs."

Dylan knew which girl the old man was talking of. Everybody whispered about Rachel Sutter. With the exception of having long legs, she didn't look like her siblings. They resembled their father, dark-skinned, with hair as black as an Indian's.

It was rumored that Rachel didn't belong to Taig. It was whispered among the mountain people that she'd been sired by a schoolteacher who had taught in the mountains eighteen years ago. He had been seen often keeping company with Rachel's mother. When school had let out for the summer, he had left, promising to be back by fall. He had never returned.

And to add to the people's suspicions, Taig didn't treat Rachel the way he did his other children. He never missed an opportunity to cuff the girl on the ears, or take a stick to her. Everyone felt sorry for Rachel and said it was wrong that she should be slapped, have her hair pulled, be made to work like a slave. It was not unusual for the girl to still be working in the fields while the rest of the family were sitting down to supper.

But no one interfered in Rachel's treatment. It was a mountain law that everyone turned a blind eye to what went on in his neighbor's home, so Rachel continued to lead a hellish life.

She was rarely seen at gatherings of the mountain folk. The girl always hung on the fringe of the family when company came to visit. She was very shy and tended to roam the mountains alone.

Dylan remembered with a hidden smile how Homer had come upon Rachel one day on the mountain and tried to have his way with her. The story was that she'd fought the bully off. She had a fighting spirit he hadn't suspected. She'd grabbed up a heavy stick and hit him alongside his head. He had bled like a stuck pig. From then on, Homer had stayed clear of Rachel Sutter.

Come to think about it, so did the other males on Tulane Ridge. He recalled that he, himself, had been snubbed by her more than once.

A grim look came over Dylan's face. There was only one reason Homer would marry the girl. For revenge. As her husband, he could get even with her for striking him that day. He could beat her when he pleased, and use her like she was a whore.

Did Rachel know how lucky she was that her husband had been shot dead on their wedding day? He felt sure that in her heart she was celebrating.

Dylan looked at Silas and said, "I'm surprised the girl would marry Homer after clobbering him on the head that day."

"Oh, that warn't nothin'." Silas made a dismissive wave of his hand. "It just showed that the girl had spirit. Homer would have knocked that out of her if'n he'd had the time. Besides, her pa ordered her to marry Homer. I'm tellin' you, there was quite a to-do up at their place that day."

Silas shook his head. "There was Rachel acryin' she didn't want to marry Homer, and her ma tryin' to make Taig stop hitting the girl with a stick. Ida ended up with two black eyes."

Silas snorted a tittering laugh. "While everyone was catching their breath, Homer grabbed Rachel and flung her on his horse and hightailed it out of there."

Dylan frowned at Silas. "I know that Preacher Robison has his faults, but I'm surprised he married them, what with Rachel claiming that she didn't want anything to do with Homer."

"That son of mine was a corker," Silas guffawed. "He told Rachel that if she opened her mouth to the preacher, her ma would meet with an accident. It worked. The girl didn't say nary a word except 'I do.' "

Dylan crushed the desire to smash his fist into his uncle's mouth. Instead, he asked, "Will the girl be going back to her folks, or will she stay with you and Aunt Edna?"

Silas shifted a chaw of tobbacco from the right side of his mouth to the left. He spat a mouthful of brown juice at a bee in the center of a flower, then, avoiding eye contact with Dylan, said, "Now, that's a worrisome question, and part of the reason I've come down to see you.

"You see, Rachel's pa won't take her back. He claims that since she married Homer, she is now a Quade and it's up to us to take her in. As you know, our shack is bustin' at the seams what with my other three boys, their wives, and all the young-uns. We just ain't got the room for one more person."

Silas paused and shifted his tobacco again before saying, "All us kinfolk had a meetin' last night. You're not goin' to like this, Dylan, but we decided that you wuz the most likely one to take her in."

He rushed on before Dylan could speak.

"You've got that big place down in the valley. You got a passel of rooms and you got no wife to take care of them. Rachel is a hard worker and a good cook." He gave a sly, cackling laugh. "You might even want to marry up with her some day."

"Now, just a damn minute!" Dylan burst out when his shock faded enough to allow him to speak. "I'm not having anything to do with that Sutter outfit on Tulane Ridge. They're shiftless and no-account and no kin of mine. I'm not obligated to that girl in any way."

"You're kind of shirt-tail cousins," Silas persisted. "Your pappy wuz a seventh cousin to Taig Sutter's seventh cousin."

"Man! If that's not scraping the bottom of the barrel!" Dylan exploded. "You go back up the mountain and have another meeting with your kin and tell them that I won't take the girl in. They'll have to make other arrangements for her."

Again Silas shifted his wad of tobacco and, as before, without looking at Dylan, muttered, "It's too late to do that. Rachel is already on her way to Jackson Hole by coach. She'll arrive there sometime this afternoon."

While Dylan stared at him in disbelief, Silas climbed up on his mule. He hit the animal across the rump with a short switch that sent the mule galloping up the ridge.

"You old bastard!" Dylan called after him. "I'll send her back up the mountain first thing in the morning."

He watched the mule disappear up the mountain and sighed. He hated sending the girl back to a life of misery, but he couldn't imagine her living with him. People would talk, and the first thing he knew, they'd have him marrying the girl. He might feel the urge to marry every spring, but it wouldn't be to a Sutter woman. He had too much pride for that, he thought as he went back into the cabin.

Dylan took a last look around the cabin, then strapped on his Colt and stepped out onto the porch. As he closed the door behind him, he swore softly. A wall of rain was coming toward him. He had a wet trip ahead, all right. He picked up the large bundle of furs off the porch and whistled to Shadow. He'd have to put off his trip to the post. Instead he'd have to detour to the stagecoach office in Jackson Hole to meet Rachel Sutter.

As he walked toward the barn, a large drop of cold water fell from a tree and ran down his neck. With an impatient oath, he pulled the collar of his slicker up above his chin.

Chapter Three

Rachel was cantering down the river road when suddenly through the gray mist of rain she saw the buildings of Jackson Hole. She slowed the mare to a walk when she caught sight of passengers a couple blocks away descending from the coach. When she came to the alley of the station building, she turned Goldie's head toward its entrance. Midway down the narrow passage, she reined the mare in. She sat a moment, her body sore and weary from the beating she'd suffered the day before and the long hours in the saddle.

Finally she told herself that she couldn't sit here all night and, dismounting, she walked to the end of the alley and peered through the rain.

She spotted Dylan right away. She would know that tall figure anywhere. He was as handsome as ever, she thought, studying him as he stood beneath the light of a lantern hanging on the station wall. And just as arrogant looking, she added. Even in buckskins, with water dripping from the fringes of his pants and jacket, he stood tall, his pride in himself evident.

What should she do now? Rachel asked herself as the last passenger left the coach and hurried inside the station. She stepped back into the shadows when she saw Dylan turn his head and look in her direction.

"I've got to make myself known to him," she muttered to herself. "If he sees me lurking out here in the dark and rain, he'll think I'm woods-queer for sure."

She was ready to step out into view when Dylan hopped down from the porch and splashed through the mud and water to stand before her.

His eyes were level and hard beneath the rim of his hat as he asked coldly, "You're Rachel Sutter, aren't you?"

Rachel swallowed and answered through chattering teeth, "Yes, I am."

"Why are you standing out here in the rain? Why aren't you inside with the others?"

Rachel shrugged and looked at the ground.

Dylan cast a glance over her soaked body and decided that he knew why she stood outside. She was embarrassed to be seen by the other passengers because of her clothes.

After a pause of a few seconds he said gruffly, "Uncle Silas told me what happened to you, but I don't know where he got the idea that I could take you in."

Rachel lifted a surprised gaze to him. "But he told me it was all settled."

"The old buzzard!" Dylan swore savagely. "He just wanted to get you out of his shack. He should have known a bachelor like me couldn't take you in."

When Rachel made no response to his anger, only kept her gaze on the ground, Dylan peered closer at her. But what with the rain and her soaked hair hanging in her face, he couldn't see much of her. He skimmed his gaze over her body and thought that she certainly was shapely.

What in the hell was he to do with her tonight, though? he asked himself. He couldn't just ride off and leave her standing in the rain.

Dylan looked at her again, saw the pitiful sight she made and came to a quick decision. At his ranch there was a cot in the tack room where the teenage stable boy sometimes napped. There was also a stack of horse blankets for covers. She could sleep there tonight, and tomorrow he would take her down to the trading post and see if the new owner, John Jacob Andrews, could give her a job of some kind. He would make it clear that Rachel was a decent girl, that she was not the kind of woman to service the trappers. If there was no work for her at the post, she'd just have to ride back up the mountain.

"Get your horse and we'll ride out to my ranch," Dylan said and stepped up on the porch to wait for her.

His eyes opened wide when she led the golden palomino out of the alley. Never had he seen a more beautiful animal. It was perfect in all ways: color, limbs and arched neck.

"Does that animal belong to you?" he asked suspiciously.

"Yes, she does." Rachel answered so sharply Dylan stared at her. "I caught her when she was a filly. I tamed her, and nobody but me can ride her."

"You mean you won't let anyone else ride her," Dillon said with dry amusement.

"I mean she won't let anyone else ride her," Rachel answered curtly.

Dylan gave her a curious look. Maybe she had more spunk than he'd thought, he told himself, watching her throw a long, shapely leg over the back of the mare. Without another word, he mounted his own horse, whistled for Shadow, and headed down the street with Rachel following him.

As Dylan and Rachel traveled down the river road, the rain slackened and by the time they rode into the ranch barnyard it was only a drizzle. Rachel threw him a surprised look when Dylan dismounted and said, "The tack room is this way." Why did she need a tack room? she asked herself as she followed him into the barn.

In the dry, warm darkness of the barn, which smelled like new hay, she heard a match scratch against wood, then blinked when a light flared up. She watched Dylan lift the chimney of a lantern and hold the flame to the wick. When it was lit, he told her to dismount, and when he had done the same, he gathered up their reins in one hand, and with the lantern swinging from the other, started walking down the wide aisle.

"You'll be warm and dry in here for tonight," he said, pushing open a narrow door. "Tomorrow I'll take you down the river to the trading post. The owner is a decent man, I hear. I'm pretty sure he'll give you a job."

The trading post! Rachel thought, appalled. She didn't want to end up there. Silas Quade had warned her about that place and the kind of work she'd be forced to do there. "Maybe I could find work on a ranch, cooking or doing housework," Rachel suggested as she followed Dylan into a small room.

"That's very doubtful," he said gruffly. "Housewives around here do their own cooking and household chores. Your best bet is waiting on customers at the post."

He placed the lantern on a feed box that had been turned upside down, then pulled some blankets off a shelf. Tossing them on the narrow cot, he said, "We eat breakfast around eight o'clock. We'll go down the river as soon as you finish eating."

"It's plain that you can't wait to get rid of me," Rachel accused as Dylan turned to leave. "Why can't I do *your* cooking and cleaning? You don't have a wife."

"And that's the way I want to keep it," he shot back, turning to face her. "If I had a young girl like you working in the house, folks hereabouts would have us married in no time. You'll be better off at the post," he said with finality and stalked out the door.

"Arrogant beast," Rachel muttered, then decided she'd do better to think about getting out of her wet clothes. But what would she put on? she worried as she sneezed three times in a row.

She hurriedly spread three blankets over the cot, then stripped off her soaked clothes. She wondered why her body could feel so hot even though she was shivering so hard her teeth were chattering.

She crawled onto the cot and, lying on one blanket, pulled the other two up over her shoulders. She drifted into a sleep of delirium, moaning and muttering.

Monty Hale first noticed the rain when he stepped outside the trading post. By the vivid streaks of lightning, it was a frightful storm. Anyway, that was the way it looked to his fuzzy brain. He had been in the post all afternoon drinking John Jacob's corn whiskey. He staggered to the long row of open-ended stalls that had been built to shelter the patrons' horses when the weather turned bad. He struggled onto the back of his roan and, gathering up the reins, left the post and cut across country. He wanted to get to the Bar X ranch just as soon as he could.

To Monty's disappointment, the shortcut did him little good. Within minutes he was soaked to the skin. He had sobered considerably by the time he rode up to the ranch house.

"Son of a gun, Dylan's back," he muttered, noting a light in a bedroom window. Dismounting, he led his horse into the barn, stripped the gear off and wiped it down with a piece of blanket, then started to leave the barn.

As he walked past the tack room, Monty paused and strained his ears toward the small room. Was he mistaken, or had he heard a whimpering sound coming from it?

When the sound came again, he pulled his Colt, sidled up to the tack-room door and eased it open.

"Good Lord!" he exclaimed when he saw the figure of a woman lying on the narrow cot. He walked across the floor and stared down at her. Her face was as white as the pillow her blond head lay on. He cautiously picked up her wrist. Her pulse was beating frantically. He laid his palm on her forehead and found it red-hot.

"She's awfully ill," he whispered and wondered who she was and what she was doing in a room full of saddles, reins and such. "I've got to let Dylan know she's in here," he muttered and stepped back into the rain.

Dylan heard a pounding on the kitchen door.

He scrambled out of bed and yelled loudly, "Settle down, whoever you are. I'm coming."

He swept open the door and swore when he saw his foreman and best friend staring at him with glazed eyes. "Dammit to hell, Monty," he swore, "don't you know it's raining like the very devil? You'd better get to bed and sober up."

"Dammit to hell to you too, Dylan. And welcome back. Did you know there's a sick woman in the tack room? I think she may have pneumony. She's shivering and talking out of her head."

Damnation, Dylan thought as he swung his feet to the floor. He hadn't known the girl was sick when he'd banished her to the tack room.

As he stumbled his way across the pitch-black yard with Monty fumbling along behind him, Dylan regretted his earlier decision to keep her out of the ranch house. He'd wanted to make it clear to both the girl and the local gossips that she would not be living with him.

He entered the tack room, where the lamp still burned. Its yellow light shone softly on the girl's face. This was the first good look he'd got of Rachel since she'd arrived.

Monty had smoothed the white-blond hair off her forehead, and, looking down at her fair, unblemished face, Dylan thought that never had he seen a lovelier woman in his life.

"We've got to get her to the house and warmed up," Dylan said, looking up at Monty with worried concern. When Monty asked him how the girl had got into his tack room, Dylan pretended not to hear him. He was too ashamed and embarrassed to tell the truth of it.

Gathering Rachel up in his arms, blankets and all, he said to Monty, "Grab her things, then go on ahead and lay some more logs on the fire. We can get her warmed up faster in front of the fireplace."

Monty left at a run, suddenly very sober. By the time Dylan got to the ranch house, Monty had flames leaping up the chimney and had put a pot of coffee on to brew in the kitchen. "Where do you suppose she came from?" he asked as Dylan gently placed his unconscious burden on the settee in front of the fire.

"She came down from the mountain," Dylan explained reluctantly. "She's one of the Sutters from Tulane Ridge."

Monty was filled with curiosity at this news, but decided it was best not to press his friend for all the details just yet. "We need to get some clothes on her so she's decent. Have you got a shirt she can wear?"

Dylan frowned. "I'll find something." He didn't like the idea of dressing Rachel in front of another man. It was up to him to do what he could to preserve her modesty. He looked at Monty and said gruffly, "You can go to the bunkhouse now."

Monty sat down in a rocking chair close to the fire and, with amusement glinting in his eyes, said, "I'll just stay a bit longer, see if the girl comes around alright."

Dylan gave the other man a dirty look but didn't argue with him. Monty was more friend than hired hand. They had known each other since they were youngsters. "Do as you please," he muttered and went up to his bedroom, leaving Monty to keep an eye on Rachel. As he searched for a clean shirt, he cursed himself for the uncaring way he had put her in the tack room. He had told himself he was doing it to protect her reputation, but now he realized it was mostly because he'd been afraid of being stuck with her.

But what if he did get stuck with her? he asked himself. What harm could it do? He could afford to give the girl a home. So what if the local gossips thought the arrangement improper? He had never cared much what others said of him.

Returning to Rachel with a clean linen shirt draped over his arm, Dylan moved toward the hearth wondering what would be the best way to put it on their patient. "I'll hold her up with the blanket covering her front while you put the shirt on her," he suggested to Monty. When a moment later his friend exclaimed in horror, he frowned.

"What is it?" he demanded.

"Dylan, look at her poor back and arms. She's been beaten!"

Dylan's stomach turned over when he looked down at the white flesh marked with angry-looking red welts. Savage oaths ripped out of his throat. "I'll kill the bastard who did this to her."

"Whoever did it used a wide leather belt,"

Monty observed. "Find the man who wears such and you will have her beater."

"Homer Quade!" Dylan exclaimed, swearing again.

His cousin was well known for the four-inch belt he wore. He used it in fights and was very adept at wielding it like a whip. He had maimed many men with it.

"Your cousin Homer?" Monty said, his fists clenched. "Let's go get him."

"Hell!" Dylan gave the hearth a savage kick. "The bastard's already dead. My Uncle Silas came and told me about it this morning. He's the one who sent the girl down here."

Dylan sighed. He might as well tell what he knew of Rachel and Homer's marriage. It would all come out sooner or later.

He cleared his throat and said, "This girl, Rachel Sutter, was married to Homer a couple hours before he was shot and killed. The marks on her back were probably his wedding gift to her."

"I wonder if she realizes how lucky she is that Homer Quade is dead," Monty said, then, looking at Dylan, he added, "We'll need a basin of warm, soapy water to bathe the cuts that are bleeding. They may have dirt in them. In the top right-hand kitchen cabinet you'll find a jar of Balm of Gilead salve. It's real good for healing cuts and burns and such."

When Dylan had brought the water and salve,

the two men turned Rachel onto her stomach and set about treating her cuts.

While they worked, Monty asked, "Why did Silas send the girl to you? You're not related to her."

Dylan gave a short laugh. "It seems that my kinfolk got together to decide what was to be her fate. None of them wanted her, and it was decided that since I have a ranch and earn a decent living, I should take her in."

"You fell for that bull!" Monty snorted.

"Hell, no, I didn't," Dylan denied vehemently. "But the old reprobate had already told her that she'd be welcomed by me and had sent her on."

Dylan looked away from Monty and said with some shame in his voice, "I shouldn't have put her in the tack room. She was soaking wet and shivering. It was just that I was so mad at Silas, I took it out on her. And I didn't want the gossips to get going about an unwed girl staying in my house."

"Let's hope that she don't come down with pneumony and die," Monty said morosely. "She's the prettiest little thing I ever did see." He looked at Dylan. "Don't you think so?'

Dylan reluctantly agreed, but added, "I wouldn't want her to die if she was as ugly as a mud fence."

"Well, yeah, me neither," Monty hurried to agree. With that, Dylan poured them each a cup of coffee, and they settled down in front of the fire to watch over their patient. They had bandaged her wounds and managed to put Dylan's shirt on her, but she continued to toss restlessly. "I'm afraid she may have lung fever." Monty said half an hour later, breaking the silence that had fallen between them. "I think you should go fetch the doctor."

Dylan groaned inwardly. It was just as he had feared. And if the girl died, it would be his fault. He clenched his fists. He didn't think he could live with that on his conscience. Dylan splashed his way to the barn and walked down the wide aisle to the last stall on his right. It held the fastest horse on the ranch. It took but a few minutes to saddle the animal and lead him outside.

As Dylan rode through the wet night, he wondered if Homer had slept with his new bride before he was shot to death. He found himself wishing that his cousin hadn't. The girl was too beautiful, too fine-boned to have mated with such an animal.

When Dylan arrived at the doctor's office, he pounded so hard on the door that the middle-aged man awakened immediately. Dressed in his red longjohns, he threw open the door and stared at Dylan. "What in tarnation are you trying to do, Dylan?" he demanded in a rough voice. "Are you trying to break my door down?"

"Sorry, Dr. Johnson, but I have a very sick woman out at the ranch. I think she may have pneumonia. I wish you'd come and have a look at her."

"And catch pneumonia myself," the doctor

complained. He sighed and said, "While I get dressed, you go to the livery stable and have the teenager there hitch up my buggy."

Fifteen minutes later Dylan led the way out of Jackson Hole, the buggy wheels whirring along behind him.

When Dylan and the doctor arrived at the Bar X ranch, they turned the buggy and horses over to Monty, who was waiting for them anxiously.

Dr. Johnson grabbed the small bag from the seat beside him and sprang nimbly to the ground despite his age and considerable girth.

In Dylan's absence Monty had built a fire in a potbelly stove in one of the bedrooms, spread Rachel's things out to dry before it and tucked the girl into bed. They found the girl tossing and turning beneath the covers, her face flushed with fever.

Monty joined them as the doctor took off his wet coat and unwound a scarf from his neck.

"Do you think it's pneumony, doc?" Monty asked worriedly. "She is burning up with the heat."

The doctor sat down on the edge of the bed. He took Rachel's limp wrist in his hand and while he felt her pulse said gruffly, "You two men can leave the room now."

Both men blushed. They weren't hanging around in hopes of seeing some bare flesh, and Dylan angrily told the doctor so. "We've done what we could to make her decent," he said defensively.

"I'm sure you have," Dr. Johnson replied, hiding his amusement. "I just thought that maybe I should remind you."

Dylan's only response was a loud snort as he and Monty walked down the hall to the kitchen.

"What do you think? Does she have pneumony?" Monty repeated as Dylan placed two cups on the table, then filled them with coffee that had been keeping warm on the back of the range.

"I hope not," Dylan answered, a serious note in his voice. Monty gave him a quick, searching look. Had his friend finally fallen for a woman?

When Monty had drunk half his coffee, he said in slightly chastising tones, "You shouldn't have put her in the tack room, wet and all."

"I told you why I did it!" Dylan shot back. "I was mad at old Silas. I wasn't thinking straight."

"Are you gonna give her a home now?"

"Hell, I don't know," Dylan said in frustrated tones. "I feel I ought to—she's got nowhere else to go. When she's feeling better, I may make that old bastard find her a husband up there in the mountains."

There was a long pause, then Monty shook his head saying, "If you think about it, it would be a shame for such a beauty to be married to one of your uncle's kin. She'd be old and worn out from having younguns by her early thirties. It was God's mercy that Homer was killed before he could do any worse to her."

Monty waited a minute for Dylan to make a response. When his friend didn't answer, he asked gruffly, "Don't you think so?"

"Yes, dammit, I do," Dylan said impatiently. "Can we stop talking about it now?"

Monty's answer was a disgruntled grunt. Several seconds went by, and then he said, "I'd marry her myself before I'd let that happen to her."

Dylan was too stunned to respond to that remark for a second, then he gave a short, disdainful laugh. "How would you take care of her? You can only halfway take care of yourself."

"That's true," Monty agreed. "I don't have anything but my gun and horse, but I'd work myself to the bone to take care of her."

"Let's don't argue about it," Dylan said, surprised at the jealousy sparking in him. "Why would she want to marry a cowpoke anyway?"

"I'll bet she'd take me over them wife-beatin' mountain men," Monty said, becoming a little heated. When Dylan only shrugged his shoulders indifferently, Monty announced that he was going to bed. After he left for the bunkhouse, Dylan walked back down the hall to talk to the doctor.

"Come on in," Dr. Johnson responded to his knock on the door.

"How is she, doc?" Dylan asked, seeing that the doctor was closing his bag.

"Looks like pneumonia," the doctor said. "I've given her medicine to bring down the fever. You let me know how she's doing in the morning."

* * *

Dylan sat in front of the fireplace, wide awake. His conversation with Monty kept running through his mind. Was he going to give the girl a home? He felt obligated to do so. She was seriously ill because of him. If she did stay, how would it work out? he wondered. She was so damn beautiful. Would he be able to keep his hands off her? A decent man didn't play fast and loose with a woman like her, and he wasn't about to settle down with a wife and children . . . even if she would have him. Which he doubted, after the way he had treated her.

A picture of his handsome friend Monty flashed before him. Monty was quite smitten with Rachel. How would he feel if his long-time friend started courting her? What if Monty asked her to marry him and she said yes? Would that bother him? He told himself no, but he knew that he lied. It would bother the hell out of him.

It was midnight according to the chiming of a clock in a distant room when Rachel came awake. She only listened and counted with half her attention. She was trying to figure out where she was and how she'd got there.

Then the name Homer Quade came to mind and every nerve in her body came alive, as well as a flood of memories.

Foremost was the horror of her forced marriage to Homer. Then hard on the heels of that was the travesty of a wedding party outside in the churchyard. She shuddered, remembering the drunken relatives snickering and making rude remarks, describing in detail what would go on in the wedding bed that night.

When Edna Quade tried to hush everyone up so the handsome young preacher wouldn't hear, her father-in-law hit his wife with the back of his hand. As Edna tried to hide her tears, Silas looked at Homer and sneered, "You got to take the frost out of them, Homer. Show them who's boss from the start."

"I intend to, Pa," Homer said. "I'll learn her just like my brothers learned their wives."

"Just don't beat her unconscious, Homer," Silas cautioned in an undertone. "You want her to have enough wits to do everything you tell her to do."

"You're right, Pa. I'm gettin' hot just thinking about it. Let me get my jug and we'll be off."

Rachel remembered Homer picking up a jug, then jerking her to her feet and tossing her up on Goldie. As soon as they were out of earshot of the others, the beating had started. From then on everything was blurry. She recalled vaguely a man stepping from behind a tree and accusing Homer of raping his wife.

She remembered there was the retort of a gunshot and the smell of gunpowder. Then had come the sound of running feet and Silas and Homer's brothers arrived on the scene. The man had watched them with rifle in hand as they carried her new husband to the house. She could only think how glad she was that he was dead.

As she stared into the darkness, she remembered the following morning, the way Silas had ordered her off to meet Dylan, the endless ride through the storm, Dylan's cool reception.

Rachel eased over on her back. She realized now that the old devil had lied to her. Dylan Quade had no intention of giving her a home. He had barely allowed her to sleep in his tack room overnight.

But this was the strangest tack room she had ever seen. There was no ranch equipment that she could make out in the dim light, and the bed she lay on was warm and soft, something she had never experienced before.

Rachel started to turn over on her side and winced with pain. She felt her back and wondered a moment at the bandages her fingers encountered. She couldn't remember anyone treating her cuts, but Dylan must have doctored her while she was unconscious. She blushed at the thought of his big, strong fingers touching her bare skin.

She sat up in bed and stayed there a moment until her head stopped spinning. She slowly stood up then and became so dizzy she almost fell. Her head hurt something awful, and she felt hot.

Even so, she walked slowly, hunting for her coat. She found it hanging before the stove. She was thankful that it was only a little damp as she pulled it on, over an oversized shirt that was not hers. Had Dylan put it on her, seen her naked?

She shivered. Her shoes were still soaking wet when she pulled them on.

Very quietly then, she left the room and slipped down the hall. She paused a moment when she saw Dylan asleep in front of the fireplace. When he didn't stir, she continued on. She carefully opened the kitchen door and stepped out into the damp, cold night. On cold and clammy feet she made her way across the dim yard to the barn.

Goldie whinnied softly to Rachel as she struggled to heave the saddle onto her back. She winced with the pain of her clothes rubbing against the cuts and welts on her back and arms.

She silently bore the discomfort as she mounted the mare and rode out of the barn.

Rachel looked often over her shoulder at her back trail. She'd heard stories of how outlaws roamed the territory, the mountains their refuge. *I don't want to run into any of them,* she thought as she rode on in the piercing cold.

When Rachel came to a much-used trail that followed the river, her spirits lifted. In the distance she spotted a twinkling light. She squared her shoulders, and, so weary she was swaying in the saddle, she rode toward it.

Chapter Four

John Jacob Andrews followed his last customer outside. When the man climbed on his horse and rode down the river road, John Jacob stood on the narrow porch sniffing the air. It had finally stopped raining, and he breathed deep of the fresh, crisp air.

John Jacob was still getting used to this country; it was so different from the place he had left behind three months ago. Missouri was hot and humid by this time of the year, and got more so when summer came along. He hadn't meant to settle in Wyoming. His plan was to travel to Montana. But there had been a fierce fight between a bunch of trappers and buffalo hunters the night he stopped in for a drink at the Grizzly Bear saloon here at the trading post. In the melee the owner of the place was shot and killed. The heir to the place was the owner's nephew.

The young man was a spineless sort who hated the saloon and was afraid of the rough men who patronized the place. He knew that he would never be able to control them.

And that young man's weakness is the reason I have a good-paying business now, John Jacob thought.

He had been like a tumbleweed all his life, blowing from one place to another as an itinerant teacher. He had grabbed at the chance to settle down when the young nephew offered to sell him the saloon at a ridiculously low price.

When he was asked if he thought he could handle the carousers who gathered there, he only laughed. He was an old wolf from Nebraska, rough and wild as an unbroken mustang. It was known in most parts that a man would do well to leave John Jacob Andrews alone.

The skin around his eyes crinkled in amusement. In the few weeks he'd owned the post, he had already demonstrated that to his customers, He was a big man, six foot tall and weighing close to two hundred pounds. Those who challenged him had ended with black eyes, cut lips, sometimes a broken nose and a few cracked ribs. Consequently, the almost constant brawling that had gone on before was slowly tapering off.

There were still fights, off and on, usually over one of the saloon girls. He didn't allow the men to fight inside, to break up his tables and chairs. They could kill each other outside if they wanted to.

John Jacob yawned and stretched his powerful

body. Rosie was waiting for him and it was time he got to bed. Four women had come with the business, and he could have his pick of them. Rosie, however, suited him. She was older than the others, and she realized that he was no spring chicken himself. She didn't make any fancy demands of him.

He was ready to return inside and lock up for the night when he saw a horse coming slowly down the river road. Its rider was either a woman or a teenager. Whichever one, the rider was having a hard time staying in the saddle. He stepped off the porch just in time to catch the slender figure that slid out of the saddle. He held the woman against his chest as he climbed the two porch steps. When he stepped into the saloon and the light from a wall lamp fell on long, white-blond hair, his heart gave a lurch.

He was still standing beneath the light, staring down at Rachel's face when Rosie entered the saloon from their living quarters.

"Where did she come from, John Jacob?" Rosie asked as she came close and looked down at Rachel. "She looks half dead."

Rosie gave him a curious look when he muttered, "Oh, God, don't say that."

Rosie laid her hand on Rachel's forehead. "She's burning up with fever, John Jacob!" she exclaimed. "Let's get her to bed and do what doctoring we can for her."

"Yes, we must do that right away," John Jacob said and started walking toward the door that led to their quarters behind the bar.

"Why are you taking her to our room?" Rosie asked then, but he made no response.

She was leery of breaking his purposeful stride and perplexed by the strange look on his face. *He's probably not thinking straight*, she thought, making an excuse for his strange behavior. But she really didn't believe it. There was something about the girl that had hit him hard.

When John Jacob laid Rachel down on his bed and Rosie had a close look at her, she understood better her lover's strange reaction to the girl. Everyone in the mountains talked about Rachel Sutter's beauty. Rosie had also heard that she was to marry that brute Homer Quade. Had he beaten her already? Had she run away from him?

Rosie decided that she'd best tell John the girl was a married woman. If he had any romantic notions about her, he'd better forget them. Otherwise, Homer Quade would hide behind a tree and shoot him dead.

As she followed John Jacob into their bedroom, she said, "I recognize the girl."

"You did?" John Jacob straightened up from laying Rachel down. "Who is she?"

"She used to be Rachel Sutter. But I heard from one of the girls that she was to marry Homer Quade. I guess that makes her Rachel Quade."

John Jacob shook his head. "It's strange that

she would be out alone on a night like this. You'd think she would be with him."

"Maybe," Rosie said. "Let's take a look at her back."

"Why should we do that?" John Jacob frowned.

"Homer Quade is noted for his brutal treatment of women," Rosie began, then exclaimed, "Would you look at this!"

When John saw the bandages on Rachel's back and the welts beneath them, he exclaimed hoarsely, "My lord, she's been beaten! Could Homer Quade do this to his new bride?"

"He could and he did," Rosie said, fire in her eyes. "She's not the first woman he ever beat. And he would have especially enjoyed beating Rachel."

"Why do you say that?" John pulled the blanket up over Rachel's back.

"She once whacked him on the head with a tree branch when he tried to have his way with her."

"Why in the world would she marry him, then?" John gently smoothed a hand over Rachel's back.

"The folks on the mountain think that Taig Sutter made Rachel marry Homer."

"What sort of man is Taig Sutter to force his daughter to marry such a man?" John Jacob asked in anger and disbelief.

"You see, Rachel is the only one of eight younguns to have that white-blond hair. Taig thinks she's not his. He always treated the girl badly. He'd jump at the chance to be rid of her. He wouldn't care if Homer beat her to death."

John Jacob didn't speak for a minute. He had gone strangely still. He said then, "That bastard is as guilty as Homer Quade."

"Yes, he is, in a manner of speaking."

"By God!" John Jacob hit the wall with his fist. "Those two men will answer to me."

"What are you going to do with the girl?" Rosie asked. "Will you find some family to take her in? I'd hate to see her go back to either one of those men."

"Don't worry about that happening, Rosie," John Jacob said, an angry glint in his eyes. "She's staying right here with me. If either of those men come around, I'll put a bullet through his heart.

"Right now I'm going down to the Indian village to talk to the medicine man. He'll give me something that will perk Rachel right up."

Rosie gave him a surprised look. "I never knew you were acquainted with that old redskin."

"It's been years since we saw each other, but our friendship will still be as strong as when I last saw him."

John Jacob settled his hat on his head and, saying he wouldn't be gone long, walked outside.

John Jacob loped his stallion over the well-trodden path leading to the Indian village where he had spent many pleasant hours when he was a teacher in a one-room mountain schoolhouse eighteen years ago. He thought back over those years.

Strangely, upon his arrival in the area to take up his first teaching job, it was a nearby tribe of Indians he'd initially become friends with. He had become especially close to a young brave called Yellow Feather.

The two young men hunted and fished and roamed the mountains together. Evenings were spent sitting around a large fire listening to the elders tell stories of their youth.

John Jacob smiled. Yellow Feather was in love with a pretty little maid. He had confided that when they were a couple years older, they would wed. John Jacob wondered if the two had married each other. He smiled again. He couldn't picture his wild friend being a father.

A somberness came over John Jacob. That summer he had fallen in love himself.

Ida Hawkins was a lovely young woman, shy and sweet with curly black hair. She hadn't been one of his students, though. She'd already had two years of schooling, and her parents thought that was enough book-learning for a girl. Especially since she would be getting married soon.

But Ida hadn't cared for the thin, tobacco-chewing man she'd been promised to and didn't want to marry him. Still, the parents kept on insisting. Ida's grandmother favored John Jacob but the rest of her kin didn't look on the schoolteacher as a suitable husband. He was a "furriner," they claimed, with different ways from theirs.

John Jacob and Ida had been meeting secretly for months before they made love. They were so wrapped up in each other then, the days slid into weeks and months, and before they knew it, school was out. They spent the lazy, sunny days of summer in the mountains or walking along the river.

One day in August John Jacob received a letter offering him a teaching job in Nebraska, his home state. He and Ida had spent a tearful night together in her grandmother's cabin. He had promised that as soon as he found a place for them to live, he would come back for her and they would marry.

He had honestly meant to come back for her. But the deaths of his parents that fall in Nebraska had delayed his return. When he'd finally come back to Tulane Ridge, his heart had been broken when he learned that Ida had married Taig Sutter.

He had drifted for years after that, teaching sometimes, gambling, sometimes working on ranches or at any job that turned up. He had been a solitary man, a drifter, with no more home than a tumbleweed until the day he drifted into Jackson Hole, Wyoming.

But all that changed tonight when he looked down on his daughter's lovely face. Rachel didn't look like him, but she was the image of his mother, her grandmother, dead now for eighteen years.

John Jacob might not be able to do anything for the woman he'd once loved, but he was determined to protect his daughter. Just then, a half-dozen rib-thin dogs came charging out of a stand of pines. His lips spread in a wide smile. In a matter of a few minutes he would see his old friend.

He pulled the stallion up in front of the largest tepee in the village, but he remained in the saddle. He would stay there until Yellow Feather opened the leather door flap and quieted the dogs.

It was but a short time before a stern masculine voice hushed the clamoring animals.

He has not changed much, John Jacob thought of his friend when Yellow Feather stepped outside. He had put on some weight, and there were streaks of gray in his long hair. Otherwise he was the same, even to the smile that lit up his black eyes.

"So, my brother, you have come back at last." The big Indian moved forward to grasp the hand John Jacob held down to him.

"Yes, friend. But as I'm sure you know, not soon enough."

Yellow Feather nodded solemnly as he released John Jacob's hand. "The little white-haired one has had it hard, living with the Sutters, taking Taig's abuse. He, like everyone else in the mountains, doesn't believe the girl is his."

John Jacob avoided Yellow Feather's eye as he asked, "Who do they think the father is?"

Yellow Feather was silent for a moment; then with a trace of sorrow in his voice he answered, "Some have guessed the truth, that a young schoolteacher fathered the child when he was teaching in the mountain schoolhouse."

John Jacob brought his gaze back to Yellow Feather. "How is Ida? Is she well?"

"What is your opinion of that, friend? You know what kind of young man Taig Sutter was. Time hasn't softened him. Poor Ida has lived a life of hell, along with her firstborn. He works her like a horse, and she's worn out from having a baby every year."

John Jacob sighed deeply. He understood now why Ida had not been able to wait for him. She had needed a father for her baby. He had ruined a young girl's life. He looked at Yellow Feather and asked, "Did you know that Rachel has married Homer Quade?"

"I know. I also know that Quade was shot and killed by an outraged husband a couple hours later."

What else does Yellow Feather know? John Jacob wondered. It seemed he had a way of knowing about everything that happened in the area. John Jacob looked at his friend and asked gravely, "Do you know what happened to Rachel, then?"

Yellow Feather shook his head. "One of my braves saw the girl riding down from the mountain yesterday. He didn't know where she was headed."

"That's why I'm here at this hour, Yellow Feather. Rachel is at my place, and she's very ill. I'm afraid she has pneumonia. She has a very high fever and she's wheezing. I've come to you for help, friend."

"Let me get my blanket and we'll go talk to the medicine man. He knows how to treat the lungs."

When John Jacob left the medicine man's lodge a half hour later, he carried with him two leather pouches. There was a large-sized one that held roots, barks and dried berries. In another pouch, much smaller, was a brownish powder. He'd told John Jacob that he was to make tea from each bag. The roots and berries would break up the congestion in Rachel's lungs, and the ground powder would lower her fever.

John Jacob thanked the medicine man and said to Yellow Feather, "As soon as Rachel is better, I would like to go hunting with you again."

The Indian nodded and said quietly, "Just like it used to be."

When John Jacob reached the post and entered through the back door leading into the kitchen, he laid the bags on the table and hurried to where Rosie sat at Rachel's head, sponging her forehead with cold water.

"She is no better," Rosie said in answer to the question in John Jacob's eyes. "She's been talking a lot, but it doesn't make much sense."

"She is delirious from her fever. There are two bags on the kitchen table. I got them from the medicine man in Yellow Feather's village. He said she should be feeling better tomorrow. I will sit with Rachel while you make the tea."

"It won't take me long," Rosie said, relinquishing her seat to John Jacob. "I've had a kettle of water boiling ever since you left."

Chapter Five

A log in the fireplace burned through and fell into the grate. Its noise awakened Dylan, who had fallen asleep on the leather couch that had been placed before the fire.

He immediately thought of Rachel and jumped to his feet. He hadn't meant to fall asleep, but it had been a long, worrisome night.

In the dim light of early morning he made his way to the hall that led to the bedrooms.

He couldn't believe it when he came to Rachel's room and found her bed empty.

He hurried down the hall, opening all the bedroom doors. Rachel was in none of them. Maybe she'd been hungry and had gone to get something to eat, he thought.

The kitchen was empty also. He became panic-stricken. Where could she be? He half ran back to his room and stamped his feet into his boots. He shrugged into his jacket and slapped a Stetson on his head. He left the house, running to the barn and stables.

He entered the big building and paused a moment to check the tack room. It, too, was empty. Next he checked all the stalls and found them holding only his own stock. The golden palomino Rachel had been riding was gone.

His heart sank. Where had she gone in her feverish state? If anything happened to her, it would be his fault. If he had done the humane thing and brought her straight into the house, let her sleep in a warm, dry bed, he wouldn't be feeling like a low-down snake now.

How long had she been gone? he asked himself as he saddled his stallion. He hoped it wasn't still raining when she'd left, or the horse's tracks would be washed away.

Luckily, he spotted the tracks as soon as he left the barn. They were going in the direction of the trading post. He prayed that the customers had already left the post by the time she'd come by, that she hadn't run into any of them. Or come across any renegade Indians, for that matter. The new owner of the post was said to be an honorable man. Dylan hoped that the man wouldn't let any of his customers insult Rachel, or take advantage of her.

A few stars still hung in the sky when Dylan drew rein in front of the post. All was dark inside, except for a dim light in the back of the building which he assumed was the owner's living quarters.

Dylan swung out of the saddle and climbing up on the narrow porch, rapped sharply on the door. There was no answer. He was about to knock again when the door opened.

A big man, looking tough as rawhide, stared at him out of cold gray eyes.

"What do you want?" he demanded. "Can't you see that I am closed for the night?"

"I wouldn't be knocking at your door at this ungodly hour if it wasn't important," Dylan replied in an equally hard voice.

"Alright, what brings you here?" John Jacob's voice softened a bit.

"A young woman was spending the night with me. She is very ill. The doctor thinks she probably has pneumonia. Sometime during the night, in her delirium, she slipped out of the house, and now I'm hunting for her. I have traced her horse's tracks here to the post."

The silence grew between the two hard-mouthed men. John Jacob spoke first. "Rachel is here," he admitted. "But she is not leaving with you. I have given her a warm bed, and she will have a home here as long as she wants it."

Dylan took a step inside the door but paused when the man's hand dropped to the gun strapped at his waist. His eyes narrowed to hard slits, Dylan asked, "Is it her wish to stay here with you, or have you sweet-talked her into it?"

John Jacob took a step toward Dylan. "I ought to shoot you where you stand," he gritted out.

"But I'm going to let you ride out of here. However, if I see you around the post again, I swear I'll shoot you."

Before Dylan could make a response, the door was being slammed in his face. He caught hold of the door and holding it steady, demanded to know how Rachel was faring. "Is she still feverish?" he asked. "I have some medicine the doctor left at the house. I will give it to her."

"There's no need for that. I have medicine for her," John Jacob said coolly, and this time he was successful in closing the door in Dylan's face.

Outraged at the insult, Dylan slammed his fist against the heavy wood. All he got for his angry action was a badly swollen fist an hour or so later.

He fumed all the way back to his ranch. John Jacob Andrews was old enough to be Rachel's father, but it was obvious he had fallen hard for her. Dylan could tell by the way the man's voice softened when he spoke of her, by his protective manner. The man was devilishly handsome and would probably be able to sweet-talk Rachel into most anything he wanted.

When Dylan entered the house, he walked over to the fireplace and kicked off his boots. He stretched out on the leather couch, his hard body relaxing. He would rest there a minute before changing clothes and eating a bite of breakfast.

Trying to put Rachel Sutter out of his mind, he focused on the ranch. He wanted to get an early start gathering up the cattle. Many of them had taken to the brush because of the flies. It would take some hard riding to get them out into the open. Because of Rachel, he hadn't even gone out to check on them yet.

The fire sank low and Dylan slept. His cattle were forgotten as a slender, white-haired girl, flitted through his dreams.

When Dylan awakened, the sun shone quite bright, even though it had to fight its way through windowpanes that hadn't been washed as long as he could remember.

He stretched and grunted at the pain of sore muscles. He sat up, then slowly stood. He frowned down at his wrinkled and soiled clothes. It took him a while to recall why he was still dressed in yesterday's clothes. As he built a fire in the kitchen stove and set a pot of coffee to brewing, yesterday's events came back to him, his shame over the way he'd acted, his need to know that Rachel was really alright. He decided that he must go back to the trading post and demand that the owner let him talk to Rachel; he had to explain to her that he had acted in anger.

As he searched through dresser drawers for clean clothing, he recalled the shirt he and Monty had dressed her in. The recollection of the terrible welts on her back made him frown. Poor kid. She had deserved better treatment at his hands. If only he'd known that she was sick and battered.

She certainly hadn't let on. Dylan's lips spread into an amused grin. Rachel was a feisty one, all right. He remembered her remark about her mare, that no one but she could ride the beautiful palomino. He remembered her demand to know why she couldn't keep house for him. Obviously, Rachel had a lot of pride despite the hard life she'd led. Dylan found himself wishing he could make her life a little easier. He realized he was looking forward to seeing Rachel again, even if it meant he'd be making her an awkward apology.

Catching the aroma of the pot of coffee he had set to brewing, Dylan returned to the kitchen and took a cup out of the cupboard. He filled it with the strong brew and walked out on the porch to drink. As he sipped it, curling his lips away from its heat, he watched a deer come down from the mountain. He would have to keep his eyes on his cattle. When the deer came down, the cougars followed. He'd have to see about buying another dog. Shadow did the work of three men, driving cattle out of the brush and chasing away cougars and wolves.

But all that would have to wait. First he was going to see Rachel Sutter.

Dylan tied his bundle of furs down securely, then swung into the saddle and cut across country, headed in the direction of the trading post. He could smell spring in the air, as well as see it. Groves of aspens were putting out new light green leaves, and patches of snow had melted on the sunny side of the mountain and hills.

When his stallion Devil snorted and shook his handsome head, Dylan looked up and saw a thin trail of smoke reaching beyond the pines. The trading post was just a few yards ahead.

There were no horses tied to the hitching rack as Dylan approached the long, low building. He was grateful for that. He didn't know Andrews and had no idea what kind of greeting he would receive this morning. The new owner of the post had ordered him to stay away, and he looked quite capable of taking care of himself in a fistfight. Had Andrews really meant it when he'd said he'd shoot Dylan if he returned? The Colt he wore strapped at his waist certainly looked as if it had been used often.

As Dylan drew near the log building, he checked his own Colt and eased his gun belt a little. When he stepped up on the porch, he made sure he made plenty of noise stamping the mud off his boots. He didn't want it to appear that he was trying to slip up on anyone.

He swung open the heavy door and was greeted by the aroma of freshly brewed coffee.

"That surely smells good," he said, grinning at the big man who turned away from the stove.

It seemed for a while that Dylan's friendly greeting wasn't going to be returned. Finally, Andrews said gruffly, "You're welcome to a cup."

"That would sure hit the spot," Dylan said, shedding his jacket. "The mornings are still quite chilly," he added, accepting the cup of steaming coffee handed to him.

"What brings you back here again this morning?" Andrews demanded, pouring himself a cup of coffee and carrying it to where Dylan had seated himself at the table.

"I just came from the mountains yesterday where I had spent the winter trapping. I've got a bundle of furs to trade, and I need to pick up some supplies."

There was silence for a while as the two men sipped their coffee. Dylan grew uneasy at the narrow-eyed look Andrews shot him. It wasn't at all a friendly look. Dylan gave a jerk when the post owner slammed his cup down on the table.

"You bastard." He glared at Dylan. "I've spoken to Rachel this morning and she told me what happened. Why wouldn't you let that poor girl sleep in a bed? Why did you put her in a tack room like you would a mangy dog?"

Dylan looked down at his cup. He turned it around and around as he asked himself what answer he could possibly give. Every word the man had spoken was true. He heaved a heavy sigh. If only this angry-looking man knew how much he regretted his actions, he might soften toward him.

He looked up at Andrews, swallowed, then said, "Everything you accuse me of is true. But you don't know the whole story. In my mind, it wasn't the girl I was treating so shabbily, it was my Uncle Silas. He tricked me, put me in an impossible position when he asked me to take her in. I have very little to do with that branch of the Quades. They are a shiftless bunch of no-accounts.

"Anyhow, old Silas lied to Rachel; told her I would welcome her. I was spittin' mad, and it was Silas I was striking out at."

John Jacob Andrews shook his head. "No! It was Rachel you struck out at, and you almost caused her death."

"I realized that this morning," Dylan said ruefully. "That's the other reason I came back. I would like to speak to her, tell her how sorry I am, and that she is welcome to make her home with me."

"Hah!" Andrews snorted. "Now that you've seen how nice she dried out, how beautiful she is, you're willing to let her live with you."

"That's not true!" Dylan slammed his cup down, hot coffee splashing all over the table and onto his hand. "I'd give her a home if she was as ugly as a spotted toad. I only want to talk to her, ask her forgiveness for the way I treated her."

"Well, you're not going to see her. Not today anyhow. She's sleeping. She needs a lot of rest to recover from this pneumonia. When she's up and around, she can visit you if she wants to."

Dylan saw the determination in the firm set of the man's lips and knew it would be a waste of breath to argue further. All he would probably get would be a bullet somewhere. But it was all he could do not to accuse the older man of wanting Rachel for himself.

He heaved a sigh. He had a long ride ahead of him. He'd have to ride to Jackson Hole to sell his furs and get his supplies. He was damned if he'd buy as much as a potato from this bastard.

"Thanks for the coffee," he said and, rising, strode out of the kitchen.

He did not see the door to the back rooms, which had been open a crack, close softly as he left. Rachel Quade had heard every word he'd spoken.

Riding along at a fast lope, Dylan spotted thin trails of smoke rising from several chimneys. It was nearing noon, and the wives of Jackson Hole were cooking dinner.

He swallowed the saliva that came into his mouth. He hadn't eaten any breakfast.

As he rode down the street toward the livery, he anticipated a good meal at one of the restaurants in town. He'd sell his furs, order his supplies, then sit down to a dinner he hadn't cooked himself.

Dylan rode Devil into the livery. Swinging down to the straw-covered floor, he nudged his booted toe into the hostler who sat napping against a wall, a blanket around his shoulders.

When the man came awake, startled and wide-eyed, Dylan said, "Take care of my horse, would you? And be careful of him. He bites and kicks if he gets the chance."

His stomach was rumbling loudly by the time

Dylan sold his furs and walked outside. He strode down the wooden sidewalk, his spurs clinking as he made his way to the small café of his choice.

The two waitresses moving between the tables, heavy-laden trays in their hands, recognized him immediately. They collided as they raced to get to him first. Mrs. Bevens, the owner and cook of the neat little café, snapped a towel at their rear ends and ordered them to behave themselves.

"Are you leading those poor simpletons on, Dylan Quade?" Mrs. Bevens scolded, a twinkle in her eyes as she led him to a corner table. When he was seated, she said, "Our special today is steak. Will you have that?"

"Sounds great. I've eaten wild game all winter, and I don't mind telling you, I've had enough of that fare."

"When are you going to stop spending the winters up in the mountains like a wild man? Don't you think it's time you settled down in the valley? Every spring when you come down you look more and more like a mountain man."

"I like the mountains, Ruthie. I like the solitude there, the stillness. The snow-covered earth lets a man think when he's sitting before his fire on a cold winter's night."

"When you're doing all that thinking, do you ever think of women?" Ruthie teased.

"In what way do you mean, Ruthie?" Dylan asked, a grin lifting his lips.

"Not the way you're thinking." Ruthie slapped the back of his head. "I mean like getting married, having some youngsters."

"Naw." Dylan shook his head. "A crazy thought like that never enters my mind."

"You mean to tell me that you ain't never seen a woman that made you think of marriage just a little bit?"

"Nope." Dylan avoided Ruthie's eyes.

"Liar," she grunted and went into the kitchen.

Ten minutes later as she came back into the dining room, carrying a tray that held a steaming steak and baked potato, the door opened and John Jacob Andrews walked inside.

"Good afternoon, John Jacob," Ruthie greeted him and pulled a chair away from a table. "Sit down and I'll bring you a cup of coffee while you decide what you want to eat."

"How come you didn't bring me a cup of coffee?" Dylan scowled at Ruthie as she placed his food before him.

"You never have your coffee until after you've eaten, that's why. If you've changed your eating habits, I'll bring you a cup of coffre."

"Never mind," Dylan said stiffly. "You can bring it later."

Ruthie gave him an amused look and moved to the table where John Jacob had sat down.

"I hear you have a young lady staying with you, John Jacob," she said. "Your swamper, old Jasper, said she was in bad shape when she showed up at your post."

"Yes, she was," John Jacob said shortly, "but she's going to be alright. In fact, when I leave here I want to take her some soup. She's hungry, and that's a good sign."

"Yes, it is. I have some beef broth I made yesterday. I'll put some herbs and vegetables in it and have it ready by the time you leave."

"Thank you, Ruthie. I don't think the women at the post know much about making soup. And I certainly don't know how to."

Dylan was about to say he knew all about herbs and soup, but he didn't think his comment would be appreciated.

"Where is the girl going to stay when she gets her health back?" Ruthie asked.

"She'll be staying with me," John Jacob answered as though that was a foregone conclusion. "There will be lots of little things she can do around the post."

"Like serving drinks to the drunken trappers who hang around your place," Dylan sneered, forgetting that he'd originally thought of finding work for her at the post himself.

"No, by God, I won't have her doing that!" John Jacob thundered. "Anyway, I don't know what business it is of yours what's to become of her. Her welfare certainly wasn't on your mind when you put her in your tack room to spend the night."

"I didn't know her condition then."

"And you didn't care to find out."

"Alright, you two, settle down," Ruthie ordered when she saw that the men were ready to come to blows. "After you've eaten you can go outside and kill each other if you want to."

She looked at Andrews. "John Jacob, have you decided what you'll have?"

"The steak looks good," he said after a minute.

The two men ate in silence, and Ruthie heaved a sigh of relief twenty minutes later when Dylan pushed back his chair and left the café.

There would be no fight between the two big men today, she thought, but there would be some day.

A broad smile curved her lips as she carried Dylan's dirty dishes to the kitchen. That young man had finally found a filly he liked, Ruthie guessed, and an older, more experienced stallion also wanted her. It would be interesting to see who won the little white-haired beauty.

Chapter Six

Rachel stood on the porch of the trading post, gazing down at the lazy river. The sun was just beginning to rise and everything was quiet except for the occasional soft wind that fluttered through the cottonwood trees that had only recently budded out.

A week had passed since the night her horse brought her to the post, unconscious and burning up with fever. If not for John Jacob, she would have died that night.

Although her arrival at the post was fuzzy in her mind, she remembered being fussed over, talked to kindly.

Her fever had broken the next morning, and for the following week John Jacob and his friend Rosie had coaxed so much soup and stew into her, she sometimes feared she might burst open.

Rachel grinned and took a long sip from the coffee cup she had carried outside. She had gained so much weight, her raggedy old brown dress was threatening to burst its seams. John Jacob had noticed its condition and had remarked this morning on how she must get some new duds before that rag split open and showed her hiney. If any other man had made that remark, she would have been up in arms. But she knew that John Jacob meant no disrespect when he referred to her rear as her hiney.

Rachel leaned against a supporting post. John Jacob was a gentleman, no matter how rough his exterior. He was always gentle and respectful to her, but she knew he could be quite different when some of his customers acted up. He was a tall man, and big, too. Any man who fought John Jacob soon found himself flat on his back, with the senses knocked out of him. John Jacob had been tested but three times before word spread that it was best to leave the new post owner alone.

Rachel knew that it was fear of John Jacob's fists that made the men who came to the post show her respect. They knew they could look, but they mustn't touch. She thanked God for that. For the most part, the men who came here were a mean, shifty lot, not unlike the men who lived in the mountains where she came from. One of them had made the mistake of laying his hand on her hip one night. John Jacob had practically beaten him to death for the act. She was thankful for John Jacob's protection, but she didn't want a man killed because of her.

The ring of a horseshoe on a rock caused

Rachel to turn her head and look down the river road. A young woman, seated bareback on a bony old mule, rode toward her. The mountain woman's feet and legs were bare and none too clean as they swung alongside the gray flanks.

Rachel frowned when she recognized the female who had been her sister-in-law for a few hours. What was Jenny Quade doing here? she asked herself. Come to cause some kind of trouble, she answered herself.

Jenny had hated her since the day it was decided Rachel was to marry Homer Quade. Jenny had never made it a secret that she had a hankering for Homer. Only her simpleminded husband was ignorant of the fact that she'd shared her brother-in-law's bed.

Her enemy pulled the old mule to a stop in front of the post. She stared down at Rachel for some time, then, giving her an ugly sort of smile, she swung to the ground.

"Well, Miss High-and-Mighty," she sneered, "ain't you gonna offer your poor relative somethin' to eat and drink?"

Rachel shook her head and answered coolly, "The post isn't open for business yet."

"I wasn't thinkin' of doin' any business," Jenny whined. "I was thinkin' of visitin' and havin' a cup of coffee and a bite of somethin' to eat."

"I'm sorry, but the breakfast things have all been put away."

Jenny gave Rachel a threatening look. A look

that promised retaliation. "You mean to say you ain't got a pot of coffee keepin' warm on the stove?" she demanded, putting a foot onto the bottom porch step.

There was a crunch of gravel, and a cold male voice said, "If Rachel says there's no coffee, then there's no coffee." John Jacob stepped from behind the post and walked toward them.

"Who are you?" Jenny demanded gruffly as she stepped back to the ground.

"What difference does it make who I am? The place is closed."

Jenny gave him a brazen smile that revealed several teeth missing. "I bet you're that John Jacob feller what owns the post now," she said.

John Jacob stepped up beside Rachel. "That's right," he said shortly. "You might as well leave. We're not going to open the post for some time. Rachel is going to Jackson Hole this morning to buy some new clothes."

Jealousy and hatred flashed in Jenny's slitted black eyes. "She ain't got no money." Venom dripped from her words. "How is she gonna buy new duds?"

"She's got money," John Jacob lied. "She's been helping my cook in the kitchen."

Jenny curled her lips and sneered, "I just bet that's not all she does. I bet she—"

John Jacob's words cut like ice into what Jenny was about to say. "I said that Rachel helps my cook and that's all she does. In case you haven't noticed, Rachel is a lady. I would never let her work around my rowdy customers."

"Hah!" Jenny snorted, flinging a bare leg over the old mule's bare back with a complete lack of modesty. As she kicked the animal in the sides and it went trotting away, Rachel blushed for Jenny, but John Jacob roared with laughter.

"Did you ever see anything that ugly in your life, Rachel?" He could hardly get the words out over his mirth.

Rachel didn't want to laugh, but she couldn't help it, so she covered her mouth. She felt sorry for the old mule, though. He was the recipient of Jenny's anger as she switched his bony old rump.

"She's going to hate me all the more now," Rachel said as she managed to stop laughing.

"Why does she hate you?" John Jacob asked.

"Because she wanted my husband. She often lay with Homer."

"Did you mind?"

"Heavens, no! I wasn't married to him then, and I never dreamed that I'd be forced to marry him. As for that, I wouldn't have cared even if I had been."

"Why did you marry him if you didn't care for him?"

"My father, Taig Sutter, made me marry him. And Homer said that if I didn't, he'd hurt my mama. He would have too."

John Jacob swore a savage oath. "I'll take care of that bastard Sutter some day. He'll pay for every wrong he's done you."

Rachel grabbed the big man's arm. "Please don't say anything to him. He'll beat my mama real bad."

"Does he beat her?" John Jacob's hand unconsciously tightened on Rachel's arm.

"Sometimes he does. When she's taking up for me, trying to stop him hitting me. He beat her real hard when she insisted that I not marry Homer Quade."

John Jacob said no more about the Quades or the Sutters. He knew that if he heard any more about them he would be in danger of climbing the mountain and shooting the whole tribe.

"You about ready to go to Jackson Hole, honey?" he asked, changing the subject.

"Anytime you are," Rachel said and hopped off the porch. She followed John Jacob into the stables his customers could use in bad weather. She smiled when Goldie whinnied a greeting. It would be the first time she'd taken the mare out since her illness.

There was a dampness in the air as Rachel and John Jacob rode along the river. Rachel sniffed the air. It smelled like spring. Her mother would be working the garden patch by now.

She felt a stab to her heart. She was going to miss her mama. She wondered how long it would be before she saw her again. Her mother was never allowed to go to Jackson Hole, and as for herself, she was a little afraid to climb the mountain to visit her mother. She had no idea how Taig Sutter would receive her.

But as sad as that realization was, she wouldn't leave John Jacob and his girls for anything in the world. She had never know such kindness in her life. John Jacob was like a father to her, the kind she had always wished for. And the women who entertained men in their rooms treated her like loving sisters.

John Jacob drew his horse in and pointed downward. "There lies Jackson Hole," he said.

Rachel followed the direction of his pointing finger. All she could see was spirals of smoke rising over the treetops. John Jacob lifted his reins, and Rachel urged her mare to follow his sorrel as it started down the gentle slope. In just minutes they entered Jackson Hole's wide main street.

Horses dozed at the hitching post, swishing their tails at flies. Rachel noticed that John Jacob lifted his Colt, checked the loads, then slipped it back in its holster. Was he expecting trouble? she worried.

She kneed Goldie to follow John's sorrel to the hitching post. She sat and watched him swing down from the saddle, then tie his horse alongside the three others there. Her eyes widened in surprise when he lifted his arms to help her dismount.

"Come on, girl, don't be shy," he coaxed.

"You mean you want me to go into those stores with you?" she asked as she slid down when he gripped her waist.

"Of course, I want you to come with me," he chuckled. "You're gonna have to pick out what you want. I don't even know what colors you like."

Rachel looked down at the dress she wore. It was so faded, she had no idea what color it might have been originally. Mountain women wore mostly gray and brown. Their clothes were homemade and home-dyed from roots and walnut shells.

And the shoes she wore made her blush with shame. They were an old worn-out pair of her father's. In fact, the only shoes she had ever owned had been his castoffs.

John Jacob took her hand and patted it before tucking it under his arm. "Don't you go worrying about anything, honey," he said gently. "You're going to have the fanciest dresses and bonnets this town has to offer. If we don't find what you want here, I'll hire a dressmaker to sew you some."

"You can't do that, can you, John Jacob?" Rachel looked at him with wide, doubtful eyes.

"You just wait and see if I can't. I've had some luck over the years, what with one thing and another," he said, not bothering to explain that his luck had come at the gambling table. "Never had much to spend my money on before, though."

Rachel hung back behind John Jacob when they walked into Jackson Hole's largest and finest mercantile. Her gaze flew around the large room. Never had she seen anything like it. Behind glass there were shelves and shelves of underclothing of fine cotton, and even a material she thought might be silk. Beneath the shelves, lined up on the floor, were shoes that laced and had high heels, and boots of the finest leather.

Then her eyes caught sight of dresses hanging in a row on a long rod. She actually gasped in awe.

They were of colors that delighted the eye. They were made of materials she had never seen before. They were trimmed in ruffles and lace. Along with the dresses were warm shawls of fine wool with long fringes.

From the corner of her eye she glimpsed shelves of bed linens that no woman in the mountains had ever seen the likes of. But her attention didn't linger on sheets and blankets and such. Her gaze was drawn back to the row of dresses.

"Come on, child." John Jacob reached behind him and took her hand. "Let's go over by the dresses. This fine woman will help you find your size, won't you, missus?" He smiled his beautiful smile at the woman.

"Of course, sir," the woman said, coming from behind the counter. "I would be pleased to help her."

"She knows the colors and styles she likes," John Jacob lied, "but we're not sure of her size. She's been growing like a weed."

The woman was friendly and sympathetic to the shy young girl, and John Jacob leaned against a counter and smiled his appreciation and approval.

A couple hours were spent as day dresses and fancy gowns were tried on, then boots, underclothing and stockings so thin Rachel could see through them. They would never keep a body warm, she thought.

Another hour was spent on bonnets, scarves and gloves. Rachel had never even realized such items existed. *Where will I ever wear them?* she wondered, then wished that her mother could see them.

"If you're finished here," John Jacob said when the pile of merchandise was stacked a foot high on the counter, "we've still got to buy some grub. Especially some air tights."

"What are air tights?" Rachel whispered at his side.

"Air tights are fruits and vegetables that are sealed in tin cans. Things like tomatoes and peaches."

Rachel thought that over for a minute, trying to imagine fruit and vegetables in tin cans. But if John Jacob said there were such, it must be true. She had found him to be very wise.

While the clerk was totaling up the cost of Rachel's purchases, John noticed her chewing on her bottom lip. "Is anything wrong, honey?" he asked gently. "Was there something else you wanted?"

"Oh, no, you have bought me more than I can ever wear. If it's alright with you, I'd like to buy the girls something."

"That's a good idea, Rachel. What would you like to get them?"

"Would some of those silk stockings cost too much money?"

"I think I could swing that," John said, hiding his amusement. "What color do you want?"

"I think red. They like bright colors."

John Jacob and the clerk looked at each other and grinned. Rachel, in her innocence, had chosen the color that advertised the women's trade.

When the stockings were added to the items on the counter, John said to the lady clerk, "While you tote this all up and wrap it, Rachel and I will go to the Red Rooster next door. I'll have a drink of red-eye while Rachel has a sarsaparilla. Did you ever have a sarsaparilla, Rachel?" he asked as they went out the door.

Rachel shook her head, then stopped short when she and John Jacob entered the fancy saloon. She'd never been in such a place. Well-dressed men and women walked about on thick carpeting, going from game to game, trying their luck at poker, faro or monte.

Rachel noticed there were saloon girls here like those at the Grizzly Bear, but these women looked different. John Jacob's girls were older and looked worn out compared to the young, fresh faces she saw here. These girls wore dresses of silk and satin that showed most of their bosoms.

Rachel didn't notice the looks of admiration the men cast her way, but John Jacob did. Even in her old worn dress, she was a beauty. He was practically strutting when they left the saloon, Rachel holding his arm.

He was guiding her across the street back toward the mercantile when Jenny Quade sidled up to her. Apparently, she had not gone back up the mountain after leaving the post, but had come into town instead.

"You're quite the lady now, ain't you?" She curled her upper lip.

When Rachel ignored her, she said spitefully, "Enjoy yourself while you can. Your pa is gonna make you come home."

"Like hell he will!" John Jacob brought them to a stop in front of the store. "I'll blow the bastard's brains out before I see Rachel go back to his abuse."

"He's got the law on his side," Jenny claimed. "A young'un belongs with her family."

"From what I hear, Taig Sutter never claimed Rachel as part of his family."

Jenny looked away from John Jacob. "I ain't never heard anything about that," she mumbled.

"You lie, Jenny Quade!" Rachel's eyes blazed with anger. "You've called me Taig Sutter's white-haired bastard more times than I can remember."

Jenny's face turned beet red with guilt. "I didn't mean it," she whined. "I just wanted to make you mad."

John Jacob took Rachel's arm again and guided

her to the store. "Just be thankful, honey, that you aren't a Sutter or a Quade." He said it loud enough for Jenny to hear him.

Without a look or word of farewell to Jenny, they entered the store.

The forest was still and lonely as Rachel and John Jacob, their horses laden with packages, hit the timberline. There was a sharp smell of spruce and pine as a cool wind blew down the slopes of the mountain. When she heard the faint murmur of running water, Rachel smiled. The post was just beyond the next bend in the trail. Already the long, rugged log building seemed like home to her.

The horses stepped up their pace. They knew that hay and rest awaited them.

The first three days Rachel spent there, she had been afraid, almost terrified of the men who visited the large building that sprawled along the river. Then the tavern women, who were rough but very kind, had taken her under their wings. If any man stepped out of line with her, the women immediately reported it to John Jacob. Those men were roughed up, thrown out the door and told never to show their face in the Grizzly Bear again.

That was enough to make the other men think twice about what they said to her.

Rachel knew the men thought she was John Jacob's woman. She didn't care what they said. Let them say all they wanted to. For the first time she could remember, she felt safe and loved. Besides, she knew that John Jacob looked on her like a daughter.

When they arrived at the post, Rachel went on inside while John Jacob took the horses to their stalls. The four tavern women, Wilma, Gracie, Iva and Rosie, sat in front of the fireplace, their feet propped up on the hearth.

"You look frozen, honey." Wilma, a pretty woman with red hair, looked at Rachel and smiled. "Come sit by the fire and get the chill out of you."

Rachel took off her lightweight jacket, and Wilma and Gracie scooted apart to make room for her. Sitting down between them, she took off her boots.

"Did you girls have any company while I was gone?" Rachel asked, stretching her feet to the leaping flames.

Iva gave a bored yawn. "I did. Preacher Robison stopped by."

"The preacher?" Rachel repeated, shocked.

"Yeah, he comes in the afternoon when no one will see him." Rosie explained. Her eyes twinkling, she added, "The way them bed boards were popping, he sure wanted his money's worth."

"Doesn't he always, the ruttin' bastard? I knew that by the time he got his fill, I wouldn't be able to work tonight, so I charged him double."

The girls laughed, then Gracie laughingly said, "He sure looked satisfied when he strutted out of here."

"What a hypocrite he is!" Rachel exclaimed.

"Yeah." Iva sounded tired. "He spouts one thing from the pulpit, but his actions are something else again. I feel sorry for those two orphans he took in."

"Why?" Gracie asked.

Iva looked at Gracie. "Did you ever sleep with that fancy man?"

Gracie shook her head. "Can't say I've had the pleasure."

"Pleasure, hell. He may be handsome, but there's no pleasure in it. It's a rough experience. He's hung like a horse and never seems to get enough. I wonder how long he'll keep his hands off those girls."

After a moment Iva said, "I've been thinking about moving on, just to get away from him."

"Oh, no, Iva, you don't want to do that," the women cried out in one voice. "How come you've never complained to John Jacob about the old reprobate?" Gracie asked. "John would tell him to leave you alone."

"Maybe I will talk to him," Iva said, "I've got my two young'uns to think of. I'd just as soon stay put if I can."

Iva had two little boys who shared her room at the post. They were grimy little urchins who were often to be seen playing barefoot in the yard while their mother slept the day away.

Iva coughed, her chest rattling. "I'm just so tired," she said. "If only I could get rid of this cough."

John Jacob entered the saloon then, with four

trappers following behind him. The men spotted the women and made straight for them. John Jacob looked at Rachel and said, "Let's go put your things away."

Rachel readily agreed, and followed John Jacob into the large back room that had been allotted to her. As she went through the door, she glanced over her shoulder. Her friends and the four men were going through the hall door that led to the bedrooms in the back. She wasn't as innocent as John Jacob imagined. She well knew what would happen behind the doors in the back rooms.

The Sutter family of two adults and eight children all slept in one bedroom, the three youngest in the same bed with their parents. The act of procreation was no mystery to Rachel.

But despite the fact that she was a widow, she had no actual experience of it. She had always kept her distance from the mountain boys who pursued her, and thank God, Homer Quade had never had the opportunity to get her into his bed.

There was only one man who'd ever caught her eye. But Dylan Quade seemed to think he was too good for the likes of her. Just the same, as she began putting her purchases away in the wardrobe in her room, she couldn't help wondering how he would go about pleasuring a woman. She felt sure that he suffered from no lack of experience.

Chapter Seven

Dylan stood in the quiet of the early evening. His whole being urged him to ride down to the trading post. In the warm, still air he mopped his forehead with a handkerchief and silently cursed. He was bone tired. He had chased cattle out of the brush all day. He would no sooner drive a bunch out of the thickets than they'd turn around and run right back in. He'd be glad when he got the lot of them into one herd and could drive them to market.

Horses had more sense than to run through thorny brush.

Dylan dropped his cigarette into the dirt, then ground it out with his booted foot. He swung onto Devil's back and headed him down the river road toward the post.

"Damm fool," he mumbled to himself, "you knew all along that you'd be going there. You just can't get those long legs out of your mind."

As he rode through the willows, he kept his right hand on his thigh. It was only inches from the heavy Colt stuck in his belt. Not only were there renegade Indians roaming the mountains, but also outlaws. And that was to say nothing of the mean drunks riding home from the Grizzly Bear saloon.

Finally an illuminated window appeared in the gathering darkness. Dylan nudged the stallion into a trot. He pulled up in front of the hitching rail and swung to the ground. A moment later he pushed through the bat-wing doors into the Grizzly Bear saloon. He stepped to one side of the door and stood waiting for his eyes to adjust to the brightness inside the room.

An excited cry rang from the lips of three saloon women when they spotted him. They almost knocked each other over in their rush to get to him first.

"When did you come down from the mountains?" they wanted to know, grabbing him by the arms and squeezing them against their scarcely covered breasts.

"Girls, turn him loose!" John Jacob bellowed. "The man can't walk with you hanging on him like a bunch of monkeys."

The women loosened their holds somewhat, but still kept step with Dylan. It was easy to see that he was a favorite of theirs. If they were asked whether he paid them extra, they would vehemently deny the charge. When pressed to say why they all wanted his company, their answer was a sly grin that played havoc with a person's imagination.

Dylan and the three women were crowded up against the bar, and Dylan had just ordered John Jacob to bring him a bottle when he felt an intense gaze on his back. He lifted his head and looked into the mirror over the bar and straight into Rachel's face. His face grew fiery red at the contempt in her gray eyes. At that moment one of the women slid her hand down the front of his buckskins. He jerked her hand away so fast, she let out an angry squeal.

"What's wrong with you, Dylan?" she exclaimed. "You've never objected to my hands down your pants before."

The few men in the saloon guffawed. "Tell him, Gracie. We've seen you do that lots of times."

"Go to hell, all of you," Dylan grated, and flinging some money on the bar, he stepped into the next room to play poker.

He hardly knew what cards he held in his hand. His mind was on how he'd like to break Gracie's neck.

He remembered then the many times the girl had done the same thing before. He had never objected. He had only followed her to her room. It wasn't right for him to suddenly act as if her touch was poison. He'd have to apologize to her the next time he got a chance.

After losing several hands, he threw down his

cards. There was no point hanging around any longer. He'd hoped to get a chance to talk to Rachel, but after the incident in the bar, she'd want nothing to do with him. And somehow, the other women held no appeal for him tonight.

Dylan walked toward the door. He was about to step outside when he saw a fat man waddle past the window. Dylan didn't know him and paid him little attention.

Dylan was nearing the spot where Devil was hitched when he heard the soft voice of a woman talking to the stallion. Alarm jumped in his chest. Devil was a mean one who wouldn't let anyone but his owner approach him. Dylan was afraid to think how Devil would react to a stranger, and a woman at that.

He stopped suddenly when he was a few feet away from the horse and just stared. It was Rachel speaking to the stallion. And Devil, that scamp, was nudging his head into her shoulder as if he had known and loved her all his life.

Dylan slid his hat to the back of his head and asked himself what he should do. Should he just stand here in the shadows and wait for the girl to leave? If he walked up to them, he might startle Devil, and Lord knew what the testy animal might do.

Dylan decided that he would sit down under a tree and wait out of the pair. He was just about to turn away when from the corner of his eye he saw the shadowy figure of a man slipping up on

Rachel and the stallion. He recognized the rounded shape of the fat man he'd seen out of the saloon window. Dylan had already taken a step forward when he realized by the man's furtiveness that he was up to no good. He opened his mouth to shout a warning to Rachel, but a split second before he could utter a sound, the man had grabbed her and clamped his hand over her mouth. Dylan let loose a thunderous yell, which startled the stallion. He reared up on his hind legs, screaming his fury.

Rachel was no passive victim. She was kicking her assailant in the legs, aiming for his crotch and clawing her nails at his face. Dylan sprinted across the short distance to where they struggled. He lunged at a broad back that looked the size of a small mountain.

The man was driven to his knees by Dylan's charge. He scrambled to his feet and Dylan waded into him. His fists battered the fat face until the man's lips were cut and one eye swollen shut.

The fat man was blubbering and begging for mercy when the post door flew open and John Jacob came flying down the path, roaring like a mad bull.

"Did I hear Rachel cry out?" he puffed, out of breath.

Dylan had just caught Rachel in his arms to steady her, and he didn't know how Andrews would take it. He eased her to her feet, and she went flying into John Jacob's arms. Dylan frowned when the post owner clasped her tight against his chest and pressed her face against his shoulder. He stroked her back as he whispered to her.

So that's how it is, Dylan thought bitterly. He'd never have a chance in hell against Andrews. The older man obviously had money, and he'd taken Rachel in when she was sick, been kind to her. No doubt she thought Dylan a beast for the way he'd treated her, and tonight he'd appeared the worst kind of woman chaser.

He was about to climb into the saddle when he saw John Jacob and Rachel coming toward him. He paused and waited, wondering what was on the man's mind.

"Quade," John Jacob began, his arm still around Rachel's waist, "I want to thank you for what you did for Rachel. I only wish you'd shot the bastard."

Dylan shrugged and drawled, "I was having too much fun beating the hell out of him."

John Jacob grinned. "I can understand that. I feel like throwing a bucket of water on him so that I can beat the hell out of him, too."

The big man held his hand out to Dylan. "Maybe I've been too hard on you. What do you say we let bygones be bygones?"

"Sounds good to me," Dylan said and glanced covertly at Rachel. His heart lurched a bit when she smiled shyly at him. Maybe all wasn't lost after all.

"Will you come back to the post and have a drink with me?" John Jacob asked.

Nothing would have suited Dylan better, but he didn't want to press his luck with Rachel. She had given him a smile; he'd better be satisfied with that.

"Thank you, John, but I'll take you up on that another time. I have a mare ready to foal at any time," he lied. "I want to be close by in case she has any trouble dropping her baby."

"The offer stands," John Jacob said, and taking Rachel by the arm, he led her toward the post.

With a bleak sigh, Dylan mounted the stallion and headed for the ranch. He was so deep in thoughts of Rachel, asking himself if she would ever care for him, that he was nearly thrown from the saddle when an owl swooped by the stallion's head.

When Dylan had calmed the animal, he sat Devil awhile, catching his breath and telling himself what a damn fool he was to go mooning over a female who cared nothing for him. He was going to stop it right now. Dylan Quade didn't have to beg any woman for anything.

He picked up the reins and nudged Devil on down the trail.

Chapter Eight

Rachel stood looking out the window, watching Dylan ride away. She had laughed out loud when she'd seen Devil rear up, startled by the owl.

"What's so funny?" John Jacob asked.

"Our arrogant neighbor was almost tossed on his rump just now when an owl spooked his stallion. It was all he could do to bring the animal down on his feet."

"I would have liked to see that." John Jacob grinned. "That rooster needs to be brought down a bit. But you know, I can't help liking him. He's rough and tough, but he's an honest man. He sincerely regrets the way he treated you when you first arrived in Jackson Hole. Have you forgiven him for letting his temper get the best of him that night?"

When she nodded blushingly but failed to say anything about her feelings for the rancher, John Jacob thought he knew which way the wind blew.

"A woman could do worse than be married to him," he commented.

"How can you say that, John?" Rachel asked, surprised. "What girl in her right mind would want to be married to a woman chaser like him? She'd have to worry every night about who he was sleeping with."

"She'd never have to worry about that," John Jacob said as he shrugged into his jacket. "Once a man like Dylan picks a woman he wants to spend the rest of his life with, he'll never look at another woman with the thought of taking her to bed. He'd be true blue to the woman he loves."

"Do you honestly think that a man like Dylan Quade could love one woman, be true to her?"

John Jacob did not miss the hopeful look in her eye. "I certainly do. I've seen it happen time and time again. The one thing a man like that cherishes above everything else is a wife who loves only him. He will love and protect her, fight to the death for her."

Rachel shook her head doubtfully. She just couldn't visualize Dylan Quade being all of that. As she turned from the window, she found herself wishing that she could.

John Jacob left the trading post and went to the long storage building where he kept his extra supplies and the grain and hay for his horses. Now that he was feeding Rachel's golden palomino as well, he wanted to check whether he needed to buy more feed. Goldie was the most magnicent piece of horseflesh he had ever seen, with the exception of Dylan Quade's black stallion. He smiled at the recollection of the way the horse had almost thrown Dylan. Like its rider, it was half wild, but John Jacob had a hunch Rachel could tame them both.

He was about ready to leave for the barn when the door opened and Rosie stepped inside. She gave him a tentative smile. "I've been wanting to talk to you about the new clothes you bought Rachel last week. You got her some lovely clothing, but where do you think she's going to wear such finery? There're no fancy places around here. And don't you think she's rather young to be wearing silk stockings and pantaloons?"

If Rosie had been paying any attention to John Jacob's face, she would have seen that her words weren't sitting well with him. She blinked when he said coldly, "Rachel is seventeen. How old were you, Rosie, when you wore your first pair of silk bloomers and stockings?"

"Around that age, I guess," Rosie stuttered, her face growing red.

"As for where Rachel will wear her finery," John continued, "I intend to send her back East to school."

"Do you really think that's a good idea, John? I doubt she's had much schooling. She wouldn't fit in with those stuck-up folk."

John Jacob looked thoughtful. "I just want to do

the right thing by that little girl. Rachel is like the daughter I've never had. I intend to help her all I can." For some reason, he didn't want to admit even to Rosie that he was Rachel's father.

"I understand that, John, I do," Rosie hurried to say. "It's just that there've been a few remarks made."

When John Jacob made no response to her remark she said after a minute, "I'm going back to the post now. I just thought you should know." John Jacob made no response, and she closed the door softly behind her.

John Jacob knew remarks were being made about his and Rachel's relationship. The men knew better than to invite themselves to her room. Was it because they thought only he had that privilege?

He decided he would talk to her about going to school back East. If Rachel didn't like that idea, he would have to make a position for her at the post. Maybe he could claim that she was his niece. People might not believe his story, but none would dare say so to his face.

As he stepped out of the storage house, he was nearly knocked over by Iva's two little boys. He stared after them, shaking his head. Their mother was entertaining a man in her room, and the poor little fellows had been sent out to the barn to sleep. He stood a moment looking after them. They were both dirty, their hair snarled. Was it ever brushed? he wondered. And their clothes were practically nothing but a bunch of rags. And they shouldn't be going barefoot. The days were still quite cool.

He thought of their mother. Iva's cough was no better, and she seemed to sleep most of the time when she wasn't working, leaving the boys to run wild. What was to become of them?

John Jacob shook his head. If someone had told him a few months ago that he would take on the care of a seventeen-year-old girl and worry about the welfare of various other waifs, he would have burst out laughing. He'd lived his life as a bachelor, with no ties to anyone. But Rachel had changed him, showed him the joys of caring for someone else.

His head full of plans for her future, John Jacob hurried inside the post, calling Rachel's name as he went through the door.

"What is it, John?" Rachel smiled at him. "You look ready to burst to tell me something."

"Come into the kitchen, honey, and I'll tell you." John Jacob pulled a chair away from the rough plank table for her and she sat down.

"I've been thinking about your future," John Jacob began. After a slight pause he asked, "How would you like to go back East to school?"

Rachel stared at him as if he were joking. "Me? Go to a fancy school back East?" she finally got out. "I wouldn't know what to do."

"You can read and write and do sums, can't you? Maybe your mother taught you."

"Yes, she did. She is very smart," Rachel said proudly. "She has a lot of school books that she used to teach us children." Rachel warmed to John's idea. She'd always enjoyed book learning. And maybe if she was educated, Dylan Quade wouldn't look down on her so. "I'm sure she'd let me have them so I could begin studying again to prepare myself. I'll go up the mountain tomorrow and visit her. I've been misssing her a lot."

John Jacob frowned. "Do you think it's wise for you to go up there alone? You should take someone with you. I'd go with you myself but I'd be robbed blind in my absence."

"I'll be alright," Rachel asserted, ignoring her own misgivings. "The people up there will be too afraid of you to harm me." She just hoped Taig Sutter would also be intimidated by the news of her new guardian.

"I hope you're right, girl," John Jacob said, doubt in his voice. "Just make sure you get off that mountain before dark."

"I will. I promise. I'll just visit awhile with my mama, then I'll leave."

"When will you be going?"

"I think tomorrow morning. I want to get there when Mama will be doing her chores. We can have a little privacy while she's milking the cow, then begin working in the garden.

"Oh, I've missed her so."

Chapter Nine

Rachel set out on Goldie bright and early the following morning. As she rode away from John Jacob, she asked herself what it was about this stranger she had known for only a few weeks that made her feel such a strong kinship to him. She had never before felt this way toward any man.

She certainly had never felt so close to the man she had called Pa ever since she could remember.

She had been around four when she began to realize that Taig Sutter was not her father. He had never been affectionate with her; nearly every day he cuffed her little curly blond head. And though she didn't know what the word meant, he often called her a bastard. She recalled that by the time she was seven, all the children on the mountain teased her and called her names.

One day she had asked an old man who spent most of his time whittling what the word bastard meant. The old fellow had hesitated a moment, then said reluctantly. "A bastard child is, a young'un without a father."

"But I have a father," she had answered. "Taig is my pa."

After a while the old man shook his head. "No, child," he said solemnly, "he is not."

She had been overwhelmed with happiness at learning that Taig Sutter was not her father. "Who is my father, then?" she had asked eagerly.

The old mountain man made no answer for several seconds, then said, "Nobody but your ma knows."

She had rushed home, her heart pounding. But when questioned about her parentage, her mother had only shaken her head and said, "What difference does it make, Rachel? He lives a long way from these mountains, and you will never see him."

Many times, as she wiped away tears from a beating doled out by Taig, she had wondered about the man who had fathered her. Probably she would never know who he was.

As Rachel rode along, a soft wind blew through the aspen leaves, fanning her face. Her heart began to beat faster as she neared the timberline. This was the wildest, loneliest country a person could ever see, yet she loved these old mountains. She loved the stillness of them, the solitude. And above all, she loved the frail woman who lived there, among the rocks, boulders and ravines.

Would the tiny woman's face be bruised today as usual? She hoped that her absence from the dilapidated cabin had eased things for her mother somewhat.

The little mare, Goldie, lunged up a rocky ridge to where the Sutter shack sat. Rachel's heart leapt and beat a little faster when she saw her mother working in the rocky garden patch.

Ida's frail body and bent back brought tears glimmering in Rachel's eyes. Her mother was only in her late thirties, but already she looked like an old woman. Hard work, child-bearing and abuse from her husband had aged her far beyond her years.

The small woman looked up and, seeing her daughter, cried happily, "Rachel!" and started running toward her. They met at the edge of the field and clasped each other tightly.

"I was beginning to think I would never see you again." Ida wiped her tearing eyes on her apron. "I've missed you so."

"I've missed you, too, Mama." Rachel put her arm around Ida's shoulders and wanted to cry at how thin they were. "So much has happened to me. Some things bad, but mostly good."

Ida put her arm around Rachel's waist. "Let's go into the cabin and you can tell me all about it while we have a cup of sassafras tea. I dug up the roots yesterday. You know how Taig likes sassafras tea."

Rachel looked at Ida's freshly blackened eye and wanted to ask *Is that how he thanked you, Mama?* But that would only embarrass the gentle woman, so she silently followed Ida into the old cabin.

For once her siblings were out somewhere and Rachel and her mother had the place to themselves. As they drank the fragrant tea, Rachel related to Ida all the things she had experienced, dwelling especially on the good parts, the lovely clothes John Jacob had bought her, how kind he was to her. She spoke then of how he wanted to send her back East to school.

In her excitement Rachel didn't notice how quiet her mother had grown when she mentioned John Jacob.

She talked on about her mixed feelings at the idea of attending a fancy school, her excitement about the opportunity to better herself, her reluctance to travel so far from home. "I remember, Mama, that you have some schoolbooks. I wonder if you would loan them to me. I promised John Jacob I would begin studying."

"I'd be proud to loan them to you, child." Ida jumped to her feet. "I will give them to you to keep. Taig doesn't want me to teach the other children how to read and write. He said it would make them 'uppity,'" she laughed. She knelt down in front of a rough-board cupboard and started pulling out some books.

"I don't have many," she said, "but enough to get you started. I imagine if you go to a store in Jackson Hole, they could order you more when you need them."

Rachel was leafing through the tattered books, remembering passages her mother had taught her as a little girl, when the outside door slammed open. Her heart began to beat with anxious thumps. She'd know those heavy footsteps anywhere.

When Taig Sutter stopped in the kitchen door, she lifted nervous eyes to him. "I didn't believe it when my neighbors said you'd dared to come to my home," he said in a whiskey-sodden voice.

"I got lonely to see you and Mama, Pa," Rachel said in a quivery voice.

Taig crossed the room to stand in front of Rachel. "Don't ever call me that again, you little bastard," he said through gritted teeth.

Rachel opened her mouth to protest, and without warning he hit her in the mouth with his fist. Ida screamed as her daughter fell off the chair, blood running down her chin.

Ida flew at Taig, beating him with her meager fists. Savage oaths ripped from his lips as he backhanded the little woman. She landed in a crumpled heap in the corner of the kitchen. When Rachel struggled to her feet to go help her mother, Taig turned to her again.

In a rage he knocked her back to the floor, then began hitting her repeatedly in the face. When she lay motionless, he kicked her in the legs a few times before picking her up and carrying her outside to fling her across the mare's back. He gave Goldie a sharp slap on the rump and she started to run farther up the mountain. He turned back into the cabin then to finish beating his wife.

Dylan sat on his front porch, having a smoke and watching the sun move slowly toward the mountains. It would be dark in another couple hours. After a while he stretched his long body, then rose to his feet. He might as well make himself some supper before he and Monty headed down to the post. Now that he was on better terms with Andrews, he was eager to see if he could make any headway with Rachel.

He had just finished eating a large steak and was rubbing his full stomach with satisfaction when he was hailed from outside. He went to the door and was surprised to see John Jacob Andrews astride his sorrel. Monty Hale was just coming out of the bunkhouse.

"John Jacob," Dylan called. "Get down and come in the house and have a drink with Monty and me."

"I don't have the time, Dylan." John Jacob said, a grim look on his face. "I'm looking for Rachel. She left home this morning and still hasn't come back. I'm worried about her."

"Was she going anywhere in particular?" Monty asked as he joined them.

John Jacob nodded. "She was going to visit

her mother. She said she wanted to see if she was alright."

"Oh, Lord," Dylan swore, rolling down his shirtsleeves and slapping his hat on his head. "You should never have let her go there alone. You should have gone with her."

"I tried to talk her out of going, but she insisted she would be alright. She said the mountain people liked her, and that Taig would be afraid that I would beat him up if he touched her."

"That foolish girl," Dylan groaned. "Doesn't she realize yet that Taig Sutter is crazier than a March hare in his normal state, and liquored up, he's got no sense at all. The man is sick with hatred. I'm afraid of what he may do to Rachel."

Dylan grabbed his Colt and holster from the back of his chair. Strapping it around his lean waist, he said, "I'm going after her, but there's not much daylight left."

"I'm going with you," John Jacob said as Dylan hurried toward the barn.

"I think you and Monty should search the area around the post in case she shows up there."

The two men agreed that was a good idea and took off together. "Good luck, Dylan," Monty called back as they rode away.

Dylan rode along at a fast lope until he came to the narrow trail that led up into the mountains. As he urged Devil upward, an owl glided past on great slow wings. Dylan ducked his head and swore. The last thing he needed was for the stallion to shy again. It wasn't like Dylan to be so nervous. No, he wasn't really nervous, he thought, just worried sick about what might have happened to Rachel. John Jacob didn't know it, but Taig Sutter was capable of killing Rachel in one of his crazy rages.

Fortunately, there was a full moon and Devil was able to pick his way up the trail until the Sutter shack loomed ahead. It leaned precariously to the right, and he imagined that a strong wind would send it tumbling to the ground.

He lifted the reins slightly and Devil lunged up the rock-strewn path. He brought the stallion to a stop at the edge of a weedy yard that was in no better shape than the shack.

Dylan remained in the saddle as the barking of several coon hounds announced his arrival. He might have to ride away in a hurry. If Taig was drunk, he could very well take a shot at him.

He saw the blur of a face through a grimy window. He thought it was a man. He straightened up and moved his hand a little closer to the Colt's handle when the sagging door creaked open.

Taig Sutter stood there, barefoot. He was dressed in grimy longjohhs and homespun pants held up by one suspender.

Sutter stepped out on the porch, his wife just behind him. He ordered her to get back inside, but she only moved one step back.

"What do you want?" Sutter asked with a curl of his lips.

"I'm looking for your daughter Rachel," he said. "John Jacob Andrews told me that she was coming up here to visit her mother. She hasn't returned to the post yet and he's worried. Has she been here?"

"Well, you're wrong on two counts. She's not my daughter and she hasn't been here."

"Oh, but, Taig, you forget. She was here," Ida said in a frightened voice and received a glaring look from Taig.

"How long did she stay, Mrs. Sutter?" Dylan asked softly.

"Not long," Ida answered. "We had a cup of tea and then she was going to look over my schoolbooks. I'd say she was here not more than twenty minutes."

"You shut your mouth," Taig cut in.

"Well," Dylan said impatiently, "which was it? Was she here or not?"

"I told you. She hasn't been here." Taig bristled. He turned on Ida and growled, "Get back inside."

Ida cringed, but she stood her ground.

Dylan was fast growing alarmed. Rachel had been here; he felt sure of that from Ida's words. Had this crazy man harmed her in any way? God forbid, but could he have killed her?

His hand dropped to his Colt, palming the handle. "Look, you sorry excuse for a man, tell me straight. Did you lay a hand on Rachel?"

Taig shrugged. "I might have," he answered contemptuously. "She was sassin' me. She had no right to talk back to the man who fed and clothed her all these years. I gave her a little slap."

Dylan looked at Ida and saw on her thin face that Rachel had received more than a slap. "Which way did she go?" he asked, a dark threat in his eyes.

Taig didn't answer, but stared at him sullenly. Dylan shifted his gaze to Ida.

She pointed up the mountain.

Dylan said no more. He rode the stallion up close to the porch where Taig stood and, lifting his foot, he kicked the man hard in the face. Taig went over backwards, blood and teeth flying. Before Dylan rode away he looked down at Taig and said through gritted teeth, "If I find that you beat Rachel, I'll come back and kill you."

Taig lay cowering on his back, staring up at Dylan, his hand over his mouth. Dylan looked at Ida before he rode away. Her poor bruised face wore a look of supreme satisfaction.

Chapter Ten

The moon provided barely enough light for Dylan to see the dim deer trail he was following. The only sounds were the tramping of his horse's hooves and the chirping of crickets.

He must find Rachel soon or she'd have to spend the night on the mountain at the mercy of bears and cougars.

He reined in suddenly. He had heard the striking of a hoof on stone. He leaned forward and peered ahead. A horse was coming down the trail, its reins dragging on the ground. With an in-drawn breath he recognized Goldie, but couldn't make out the bundle lying across the mare's back.

A savage oath ripped from his throat when the horse drew near and he recognized the bundle as a body and that the body was Rachel's. A dull fury built inside him mixed with terrible fear as he swung from the saddle and ran to her.

He lifted her head and could hardly recognize her, her face was so badly bruised. When he gently pulled her off the mare, she let loose a cry of pain. It told him that she had bruises on her body, possibly some broken bones.

She moaned a few times as he awkwardly climbed into his own saddle while cradling her in his arms. When he turned Devil's head back down the mountain, Goldie followed him.

It was almost midnight when John Jacob saw two horses coming up the river road. He and Monty had given up their search an hour ago. He had been sitting on the narrow porch ever since, waiting for Dylan's return.

A cold chill slithered down his spine when he saw that one of the horses was riderless, and that the single rider was carrying a body. He couldn't clearly see the body, but in his heart he knew the rider was Dylan and that he held Rachel in his arms.

John Jacob jumped off the porch and reached Devil in two long strides. "Is she alive?" He looked anxiously at Dylan.

"She is, John, but barely. That bastard has beaten the hell out of her." He gently lifted Rachel down into John Jacob's waiting arms.

"I'll blow his brains out!" John Jacob gritted through his teeth as he carried Rachel into the post.

"You'll have to beat me to it," Dylan growled under his breath as he followed the other man inside.

Rosie and the other girls crowded into Rachel's

room as John Jacob laid her down on the bed. The half-dozen patrons in the place would have done the same if Rosie hadn't blocked their entrance.

"You know you men don't belong in here," she snapped, "but one of you go to the Indian village and bring back some medicine."

"Rosie," John Jacob called, "come and strip Rachel down and get her in a gown."

He and Dylan started pacing the floor as they waited for the medicine, sometimes bumping into each other.

Dylan stopped once to ask, "Have you felt her pulse, Rosie?"

"Yes, I did that right away. Her pulse is strong."

It seemed but a short time before there came the sound of hooves pounding down the river road. "I sent Monty to the Indian village," Rosie said. "He's made the trip in record time."

John Jacob sighed his relief. "The old medicine man will send something to help Rachel. He knows how to heal battered bodies."

The bedroom door opened and Monty stepped inside. "Chief Yellow Feather sends a message to you, John Jacob. He says this Taig Sutter must be stopped before his evil can do more harm," Monty explained, holding out a pouch. "His medicine man sent this for Rachel."

John Jacob and Dylan looked at each other, their eyes bleak. "What are we going to do, Dylan?" he asked.

"I'll go after him," Dylan said. "But first I want to know Rachel is going to be alright."

"Then let's mix up this medicine," Rosie suggested.

"The medicine man said it will ease her pain," Monty said.

"I hope he's right," John Jacob said, and Rosie left the room to gather bandages and boil water.

When she returned to where Rachel lay, she ushered all but one of the women from the room. She asked Iva to bring her a basin of warm water, soap, a washcloth and a towel.

As soon as Iva returned, Rosie made a tea from the medicine man's powder and carefully spooned it down Rachel's throat. Next she turned to the basin of water and the washcloth.

As Rosie rolled up her sleeves, she looked at the two men and ordered, "John, you and Dylan can leave now. I won't be needing you to help me bathe Rachel."

Both men blushed.

Rosie and Iva looked at each other and smiled. Then they started to do what they could for Rachel.

The younger woman gasped when she saw the condition of Rachel's body. "How could a man do this to a woman?" She looked at Rosie with wide, unbelieving eyes. "I've had a few rough customers, but they never beat me like this."

"You've been lucky that you had men like John

Jacob to look after you. If you're wise, Iva, you'll stay here with John. You may not make as much money as you would in a fancy place, but you'll have protection."

When Rosie had done everything she could for Rachel, she went into the kitchen to report to John Jacob and Dylan.

"She looks bad, John Jacob," she said. "One eyelid is almost closed, and her whole face is swollen from cuts and a split lip. She has bruises all over her body where she was hit and kicked.

"And I think she has some broken ribs. She's going to suffer some, but I believe she's going to be alright. The medicine man's tea seems to be helping the pain. She should sleep through the night. If she does rouse, I'll give her some more."

"Thank you, Rosie." John Jacob hugged her shoulders and added, "I'll be sitting up with Rachel the rest of the night. I'm going to look in on her now."

Dylan followed John Jacob into Rachel's room. Her face was bruised and battered, but her breathing was even and she seemed to be resting more comfortably.

"Thank God, she's going to make it," Dylan murmured. "Now I'm ready to go after the bastard who did this to her."

Rosie caught his arm at the door. "Dylan," she said, "I don't blame you for wanting to kill the man, but at least have a cup of coffee before you start out. You must be exhausted by now. It will steady your nerves." Dylan took the cup of coffee Rosie handed him and drank it in two swift swallows.

Devil was still tied and saddled outside the post and Dylan mounted, then touched the stallion with his spurs. The black quivered and bunched its muscles, then sprang forward.

When Dylan hit the narrow path to the Sutter shack, the freshness of the mountain air was like a tonic to him. His fatigue fell away. He thought of only one thing now. Getting his hands around Taig Sutter's throat.

When he heard the long howl of a coon hound, he knew he was near the Sutter shack.

Four hounds came bounding out to meet him. They looked half starved. They kept their distance from Devil, knowing to stay clear of his hooves.

As Dylan reined Devil in, he thought it strange that all the barking and baying hadn't brought Taig out to investigate the racket. He cupped his hands around his mouth and hailed the house.

He frowned when after a few minutes, no one came to the door. He called out again, this time calling Taig's name. When the skinny mountain man still didn't make an appearance and all continued to be silent, Dylan dismounted and rapped on the sagging door. No one called out to him to enter, and a chill ran down his spine. It was ominously quiet inside.

He cautiously pushed the door open. Taig could

be waiting in the darkness, a rifle trained on the door.

Dylan could see by the pale light of the moon that the kitchen was empty. He carefully made his way to the next room, and there he stopped short in the doorway. The body of a woman lay sprawled on the floor in front of the fireplace. Still careful to keep an eye on the dark corners, he went and knelt down beside Ida Sutter's still body. He knew without turning her over that she was dead. The darkening stain of her blood had spread all around her.

When Dylan did turn her over, he found that she had died from a bullet between the eyes. But before that she had been brutally beaten. He went into the bedroom and pulled a tattered quilt off the sagging bed.

"You have gone to a better place, Ida Sutter," he said softly and spread the cover over her face.

Dylan stepped outside and breathed deeply of the fresh air in order to chase away the foul odor of death. He stood at his horse's head a moment in thought. Should he set out after Taig, or return to the post and alert everyone to what had happened in this dilapidated shack?

His mind made up, Dylan swung onto Devil's back and turned in the direction of the post. A posse should go after the killer. It was claimed that Taig wasn't Rachel's father, and Lord knew he didn't like to think of Taig Sutter's blood flowing in her veins, but all the same, he wouldn't take the chance of maybe killing her father.

Rachel was going to take the death of her mother hard, of that he was sure. She must have loved her mother deeply to risk Taig's wrath by visiting her.

Dylan found John Jacob sitting in the darkness of the porch, waiting for him. "Well, what did the bastard have to say for himself?" the big man asked as he stood up. "I hope you beat the hell out of him."

"I didn't see the polecat." Dylan stepped up on the porch and sank down in a chair. He sat a moment, then said, "I'm afraid I have some news that is going to upset Rachel mightily."

John Jacob narrowed his eyes at Dylan. "The no-good bastard beat the hell out of Ida, didn't he?"

"Yes, he did," Dylan said solemnly.

"Will she be alright?"

"She's dead, John. After nearly beating her to death, he put a bullet in her head."

"Oh, Lord, no!" John Jacob exclaimed hoarsely. He walked to the edge of the porch and stared out into the darkness, remembering the young Ida he had loved so many years ago. Guilt and remorse overwhelmed him. If only he had been able to come back for her before she'd married Taig Sutter. Her life would have been so different.

"How is Rachel?" Dylan asked softly.

"She rallied a couple times. I think she's going to be alright," John Jacob answered after a while.

"I expect the death of her mother is going to hit her hard," Dylan said.

"I'd rather be beat with a blacksnake whip than to have to tell her the news."

Dylan sympathized with Andrews but didn't offer to break the distressing news to Rachel. He said instead, "I expect we should start notifying the people up on Tulane Ridge. We'll need some womenfolk to lay Mrs. Sutter out." He paused a moment before pointing out, "We must get a posse together and track Sutter down before he escapes."

John Jacob nodded his agreement; then Dylan added with a small, humorless laugh, "We'll use his hounds to track him down."

John Jacob stepped off the porch then and went to saddle his horse. When he returned from the barn leading his sorrel, he said, "It'll be dawn soon. I don't think we'll have any trouble rounding up some men to hunt Taig Sutter. I've never heard any of my customers speak a good word about him." He returned inside the post and started taking ammunition off a shelf. "Help yourself to some shells for your Colt, Dylan," he invited.

Dylan hesitated a minute, remembering that he didn't want to have any part in killing a man who might be Rachel's father. He said finally, "I'm pretty beat from climbing the mountains. I want to rest awhile before I join you."

"I expect you are a little tired," John Jacob said with a smile. "Why don't you stay here and keep an eye on Rachel. The girl's going to need a friend when she wakes up. You can use my bed to grab forty winks."

As the big man hurried out, Dylan found Rosie closing up the saloon. "Can, you tell me where John Jacob beds down?" he asked.

"Next door." Rosie jerked a thumb toward the door next to the kitchen. Dylan had his hand on the latch when Rosie darted forward and got in front of him. Her face red, she said hurriedly, "I have to straighten up his bed. You stay here."

It was only minutes before she was back in the kitchen, some rolled-up clothing under her arm. "You can go in now," she said, smiling widely at him.

Dylan entered the room and closed the door behind him. He glanced at the bed and was surprised. It was made up so nicely there was no way Rosie could have done it in the few seconds she had been in there.

A look of confusion spread across his face when he turned back the bed quilt and saw beneath the pillow a woman's folded nightgown. John Jacob did not sleep alone.

Dylan was surprised. Rosie was a fine-looking woman, but not nearly as beautiful as Rachel.

Dylan took off his boots, slid out of his pants. As he stretched out, he heard the galloping hooves of John Jacob's sorrel racing down the river road, and he wondered what kind of man would bed a saloon wench like Rosie when he could have a girl like Rachel?

Chapter Eleven

The posse, led by John Jacob, wound up the rocky mountain trail that led to Taig Sutter's shack. Everyone knew that the man they sought wouldn't be there. They wanted Sutter's hounds. The men would give them a whiff of something that had the man's scent on it, then send them off searching for Sutter.

The men's wives, walking some distance behind their husbands, were coming to dress Ida Sutter in her burial clothes.

When the posse arrived at the weed-choked yard of the Sutter shack, all was silent. Apparently, the children had run off, probably to nearby kin. Even the bravest man among them felt a cold shiver run down his spine as he thought of frail little Ida, battered and bruised, lying alone in death.

The posse was soon greeted with the howls of Taig's hounds. There was hunger as well as threat in their barking.

"They probably haven't been fed," one of the men remarked.

John Jacob swung out of the saddle and entered the kitchen. He saw in the semigloom a man's shirt hanging on the back of a chair. He had no doubt it belonged to Taig. He jerked it up and hurried outside. He couldn't bear to go into the next room and look upon Ida's dead, battered face. He preferred to remember her as the beautiful woman he'd loved, young and trusting and so full of life.

He mounted up, and as he and the men followed the baying hounds, they heard the women coming up the trail.

The ten men hadn't gone far when the hounds suddenly cut across country. "Why would he go in that direction?" one of the men asked. "There's nothing there but a bluff that drops straight down."

"He's probably making for a cave higher up the mountain," another man answered.

"Yeah," another agreed. "There's a whole passel of Sutters living up there. That's where he's headed, I betcha."

Taig had been riding for about an hour, always climbing, when he spotted in the distance the cave he was looking for. Very few people knew about this cave. None knew that it ran back under the mountain for at least a mile. Once he got there he would be safe. After all the commotion died down, he'd sneak out to one of his relatives. His kin would help him get away.

He pulled his horse in. There was a small creek nearby, and before he continued on he must let his horse have some water. *Better quench my own thirst, too*, he thought.

When he came to the stream of clear water, he swung to the ground. Throwing aside his hat, he stretched out on the ground and drank deeply.

He was wiping his mouth with the back of his hand when his horse lifted its head, ears up and nostrils flared. What had the animal seen or heard? Taig asked himself.

He listened intently. All was eerily quiet. Then he froze. He had heard the whisper of a moccasin in the brush. He trembled with fear. How many were out there? He knew that the Indians of Yellow Feather's band roamed these mountains.

Taig stood up and, leading his horse, slipped from tree to tree, his scalp pricking with every step.

He felt that he was giving the Indians the slip when suddenly there sounded a blood-curdling yell and red men seemed to rise out of the ground all around him. He swung into the saddle and brought his quirt down across the horse's rump.

Within moments, the Indians were close on his heels, their arrows whizzing past his head, their shrill yells falling painfully on his ears. He could almost feel a knife making a circuit around his scalp.

Taig soon realized that the Indians were driving him away from the safety of the cave. He swore angrily. The heathens had guessed what his plans were. A bleakness came into his eyes when he saw that they were crowding him toward a line of deep bluffs. They meant to force him over one of them.

Taig's pulse leapt with relief when he saw a stand of aspen trees a few yards ahead. There would be no bluffs there.

He soon learned that his assumption was wrong. Suddenly there was a narrow avenue opening up between the trees. Before him loomed a wide bluff. He looked over his shoulder. The Indians were pressing at his horse's heels.

The animal screamed when a deep chasm opened up under its feet. Taig joined his horrified cry to the horse's as down, down they went into a mass of coiling rattlesnakes.

The Indians circled their ponies alongside the bluff, watching impassively as Taig screamed and screamed.

When all was quiet below, the red men kicked their shaggy ponies in the flanks and rode off in the direction they had come from. After a mile or so they came across the posse. Yellow Feather raised his hand palm up as both sides reined in.

"You search for Taig Sutter, my friend?" he asked.

"That is so." John Jacob nodded. "Have you seen him?"

"Yes," the Indian nodded. "He is now lying with the snakes at the bottom of a bluff about a mile back. His cruelty to his wife and daughter had to end." A grim smile creased his face. "Sutter will kill no more."

John Jacob studied the stern face a moment, then said, "I don't know how I can ever repay you, Yellow Feather."

"There is no payment between friends," the chief replied.

Dylan had slept only one hour before taking up his vigil in a chair at Rachel's head. He gazed sadly at her face. There was no beauty in it now. It was bruised and swollen beyond recognition. But he remembered every detail of her countenance and he knew that it would be the same again.

But it wasn't just her beauty that attracted him to her so. Yes, at first he had been drawn to her pale loveliness, her long, long legs, but he had come to realize that she had an inner beauty as well.

Dylan stood up to stretch his long legs. He walked to the window and stared out. John Jacob had recognized her courage and sweetness. The owner of the trading post loved Rachel as well. It was as if he wore a map on his face that declared it to the world.

Dylan shook his head in confusion. But the older man was sleeping with Rosie. And often enough that the saloon girl kept her clothes in his room, her nightgown in his bed.

Was it possible that Andrews had a different sort of relationship with Rachel? Could his feelings for her be fatherly rather than sexual?

He wished he could ask Rachel how she felt about the older man. He wished still more that he knew how she felt about him.

Dylan suddenly felt eyes upon him. He looked over his shoulder and saw that Rachel had woken. She was staring at him, looking confused and afraid.

"Don't be frightened, Rachel," he said gently, walking back to the bed and resuming his seat in the chair. "You're back at the post, honey. You'll be safe here. I found you on the mountain, half dead from the beating Taig gave you."

Dylan saw her brow crease as she tried to remember. Then a look of pain entered her eyes as everything came back to her.

Rachel's voice was flat and expressionless as she began talking. "Taig, as usual, was drunk, and as usual he was being very nasty to me. My poor little mother intervened and he turned on her. He hit her hard and she fell to the floor."

Rachel's voice began to rise. "I ran to help her and he went crazy. He beat me in the face and kicked my body when I fell to the floor. Thank God I finally fainted.

"That's all I remember until now." Her voice dropped again. "I pray Mama is alright."

She looked up at Dylan's face and saw the pity there. She struggled into an upright position and grabbed his arm so hard her nails bit into his flesh. "Is my mother alright, Dylan?" she cried. "Did he beat her bad?"

With a low, pitying sound, Dylan pulled her onto his lap and pressed her head down on his shoulder. "Be brave, little girl," he murmured. "Your mother has had her last beating from that bastard."

Rachel pulled away from Dylan and looked up at him with wide, suffering eyes. "Do you mean that she . . ."

"Yes, honey." Gently Dylan pushed her head back onto his shoulder and with infinite tenderness stroked her hair. "She has gone to a better place."

Rachel was sobbing hysterically when John Jacob burst into the room. He looked questioningly at Dylan.

"She knows about her mother, John," Dylan said quietly.

John Jacob sat down on the edge of the bed and lifted Rachel out of Dylan's arms. And though Dylan didn't like the big man's action, he didn't say or do anything about it. He couldn't for the life of him understand what was going on between the pair. He did know that Rachel hadn't protested at being taken away from him, and that she seemed quite content cuddled in John Jacob's arms, her head nestled on his shoulder.

He sat a moment, feeling very much a third wheel, then decided that he would go ask some of the men if they had found Taig.

When he heard the story of how Yellow Feather's band of Indians had chased Taig over a bluff into a nest of rattlers, he agreed to go to

Jackson Hole with the posse to celebrate.

"We deserve a poke after chasing that bastard all over the mountain," one man laughed.

However, when they came to a break in the trail that led to his ranch, Dylan silently fell behind his companions and took it. He had no desire to take a whore to bed.

Chapter Twelve

The mountain women were in a quandary. What were they to lay Ida Sutter out in? Besides the ragged dress she had died in, there was only one other hanging on a peg in the wall. It was more ragged than the one she wore.

"I can't find no petticoat or bloomers," one woman complained. "It don't seem decent that she should go to meet the Lord without any underwear on."

"I can't find no shoes or stockings either," another woman said. "Now that I think on it, she always wore Taig's old castaway shoes."

"Her daughter Rachel has plenty of nice clothes now. I saw that John Jacob man buy them for her," Jenny Quade said spitefully. "Someone should go down there and demand that she give one of them fancy dresses for her poor mother to be buried in."

"Hesh up your mouth, Jenny Quade," Ida's old grandmother ordered. "We all know how my

Rachel and Ida loved each other. Rachel wouldn't hesitate a minute to give everything she owns to her ma."

The old woman looked at her sixteen-year-old great-granddaughter. "Jassy, go down to the post and tell that Andrews man that we need clothes to bury Ida in."

"What if he won't give me anything?"

"He'll give 'em to you," the old woman said, a wise look in her eyes. "He'll be glad to do it."

Rachel had eaten a light supper of stewed chicken and was sleeping again when a soft knock sounded on the outside door. "What drunk is that?" John Jacob said crossly when Rosie stepped into Rachel's bedroom.

"It's a young mountain girl," Rosie answered, a frown on her face. "She's asking to speak to you."

"Do I know her?" John Jacob asked, carefully releasing Rachel's hand and laying it across her waist.

"I don't think so. I've never seen her around here before. She appears to be around fourteen years old. Do you suppose she's looking for work?"

"I doubt that," John Jacob said. "Her parents would never let a girl child work in a rough place like mine."

When John Jacob stepped into the kitchen, one look at the young girl with the curly black hair told him he was staring at a relative of Granny

Hawkins. The girl was the spitting image of his sweet Ida.

He walked over to the teenager and, giving her one of his warmest smiles, took her hands in his and said gently, "Are you related to Granny Hawkins?"

Although obviously nervous, the girl returned his smile. "Yes," she answered. "I'm her great-granddaughter, Jassy."

John Jacob pulled a chair away from the table. "Come sit down, Jassy, and tell me what brings you out alone tonight."

Jassy sat down on the chair he offered her, but only on the seat's edge, and John Jacob sat down across from her.

"Now, Jassy," he began, still smiling, "what can I do for you?"

Jassy gazed up at him a moment, swallowed a couple times, then said in a very low voice, "The womenfolk, Miz Ida's friends and neighbors, they come to lay her out, but she doesn't have any clothes fittin' to be buried in. That Jen—someone said that maybe Cousin Rachel could spare one of her dresses."

"Jassy, if you know Rachel, you know that she would give all her clothes to her mother for any reason." He turned to Rosie, who lingered nearby. "Rosie, will you go to Rachel's room and pick out a dress that you think is proper for Ida Sutter to be buried in. Maybe the blue one with the lace collar."

When Rosie left the room, he turned back to Jassy. "How would you like a cup of coffee and a slice of apple pie the cook made this evening?"

When it looked like Jassy might refuse, he urged, "My cook bakes the pies fresh every day."

Jassy smiled, ducked her head and said, "I guess I'll have to taste a piece to see whether or not you're tellin' me a brasser."

"You sit right there and I'll get you a slice. You're gonna have to admit it's so good it melts in your mouth."

John Jacob cut a generous slice of pie. Jassy had that hungry look all mountain children had. He placed the pie before Jassy, then poured her a cup of coffee.

He hid his smile so that the girl wouldn't know he had noticed how she was wolfing the pie down. Either the pie was uncommonly good or the girl was half starved.

When the pie plate was wiped clean of every crumb, and Jassy had started on her coffee, John asked, "Will Mrs. Sutter be buried tomorrow? Rachel's so beat up she won't be able to attend the funeral, but I intend to."

Jassy squirmed uncomfortably a moment, refusing to meet his eyes. Then she said in a voice so low he could hardly hear her, "Granny Hawkins said it would be best if you didn't come. She said it might start old gossip again. She said that you would understand."

John Jacob silently nodded his head. He did understand. He experienced a spasm of sharp pain. How his Ida must have suffered all these years.

"Tell Granny to rest easy. I won't be there. But I'm hopeful of seeing Granny again. We were good friends once."

Rosie walked into the room before Jassy could answer, if indeed she had planned to.

Rosie laid a paper-wrapped package on the table and said, "I believe I've thought of everything the women will need."

"I'm sure you did, Rosie." John Jacob smiled at her as he picked up the thick bundle. "Come, Jassy. I'll walk you to your horse."

"I ain't got a horse, Mr. Andrews."

"I'll walk you to your mule, then," he said, grinning at her.

"Ain't got no mule either." Jassy grinned back.

"Good Lord, girl," John Jacob burst out. "Are you telling me that you walked here, barefoot and in the dark?"

"It ain't nothin'. I do it all the time. All us women do. We save our shoes for the winter time when it frosts and snows."

John Jacob remembered teasing Ida about her little bare feet, never realizing she went barefoot out of necessity. "Jassy," he said a few minutes later as they were making their way to his stable of horses, "if you had a horse, could you keep it just for your own use? Or would your pa take it from you?"

"Ain't got no pa, Mr. Andrews. I live with

Granny Hawkins. She's the one who raised me. It I had a horse, it would belong only to me."

"Well, I'm going to give you your own horse." He stopped in front of a stall that held a pretty little brown mare.

"Mr. Andrews, you couldn't do that," Jassy protested.

"Do you have any way of making your own spending money?" John Jacob asked.

Jassy said eagerly, "I have some chickens, and Granny lets me keep a nickel every time we sell a dozen eggs."

"Alright, I'll sell you little Polly here for a dozen eggs. How does that sound?"

The moon picked up the excited gleam in Jassy's eyes. "It sounds like I'm having a dream. Are you sure you're charging enough for her?"

"Yes, I am. You see, Polly is a nervous little horse, easily spooked around rough men. I've been worrying about what to do with her. I think you two are ideal for each other."

John Jacob knew he was right when he saw how the two gentle creatures took to each other. Jassy would treat the little mare more like a pet than a beast of burden. He rummaged around in his tack room until he found a worn but still serviceable saddle and the rest of the gear needed.

He had just cinched the saddle on when Rosie came running out of the post. She carried a small, flat package. "I thought Jassy deserved something for making the trip down the mountain in the dark. I picked out one of Rachel's dresses that I thought might fit her. I hope it's alright that I took it upon myself to do that."

"You did fine, Rosie. I wish I had thought of it myself." He took the package and tied it on Polly's saddle.

John Jacob had just finished saddling his sorrel when Jassy asked, "Are you coming with me?"

He lifted her into the saddle and handed her the reins.

"I'll come partway up the mountain with you to make sure you're safe. Have you ever ridden in a saddle before?" he asked gently.

"No, sir, I never have. I've never ridden a horse before either. I've only ridden bareback . . . on a mule."

"Don't be nervous," John Jacob said as he shortened the stirrups to her size. "Polly is a gentle little mare, and by the time you arrive at the Sutter place you'll be riding as well as anyone."

When the coal-oil lamps in the windows of the shack came in sight, Jassy reined in. She looked at John Jacob and said with much embarrassment, "I guess you'd better not go any farther, Mr. Andrews. I'm sorry."

"That's alright, child." John Jacob reached over and patted the little hand that reminded him so of Ida's. "It's no fault of yours that I'm not welcome in the Sutter home. It's all my fault and nobody else's."

Jassy gave him a shy smile that said she didn't

understand, then urged the little mare up to where she was greeted by the baying of the hounds.

John Jacob decided that tomorrow when everyone was at the funeral, he was going to go up there and bring those poor starving dogs home with him. He doubted that anyone else would feed them.

He remembered the look of pure pleasure on Jassy's hungry face as she'd wolfed down the pie. If only he could have brought similar pleasure to poor Ida, instead of the life of pain she'd known. He paused once in the shade of a pine when he heard the refrains of "The Old Rugged Cross" being sung by the mountain women as they kept their vigil in the lonely shack by the wild woods. When their voices died away, he nudged the sorrel on.

Chapter Thirteen

The air was stifling among the trees. All day around the branding fire, it was dust, sweat and bawling cattle. The men were dirty and unshaven, having rolled out of their blankets before there was light in the sky.

Dylan stood up in his stirrups and gazed around. There was nothing to see but wide, unsettled country . . . and cattle. He pulled the makings of a cigarette from his vest pocket and rolled a smoke, drawing on it as he rode. He hoped that soon he would come upon the chuck wagon so he could get a cup of coffee, wash some of the dust out of his throat.

His hope was realized a short time later when he spotted a big vehicle lumbering across the plain. A broad grin lit up his face when he saw Shadow trotting beneath the wagon. The dog was smart enough to know that there he would escape the hot sun and the trampling hooves. His tongue lolled from the side of his mouth and he was panting heavily. The old fellow had worked hard in the early part of the morning, chasing wild cattle out of the brush. Dylan touched spurs to the stallion, and when he rode alongside the chuck wagon, he leaned down and scooped up the big black dog.

"Let him ride awhile, Charlie," he said to the driver. "He's heated, and he could stand a drink of water if you have some to spare."

"There's always water for this old galoot." The driver reached under his seat and pulled out a battered basin and a canteen of water.

Dylan rode on, squinting against the sun's glare and the salty sweat in his eyes. The big stallion plodded along, dazed with weariness. Dylan found the sound of the squeaking saddle somehow comforting.

Finally Charlie pulled the cumbersome wagon into a stand of aspen. He jumped to the ground just as Dylan pulled up. "You look beat, man." He grinned, wiping a sleeve across his sweating face. "How does a cup of coffee sound to you?"

"It sounds right good." Dylan slapped his hat against his leg, knocking off some of the dust.

"It'll be ready in just a few minutes. In the meantime, why don't you go down to that creek over there and wash up?"

When Dylan returned to the campfire, his long hair dripping water, Charlie handed him a cup of coffee. As he squatted on his heels, drinking it, the men began to drift into camp.

"The cattle are uneasy, Dylan," Monty reported

as he swung off his dusty cow pony. "Something is spooking them. Maybe a wolf, maybe a bear. I feel it in my bones that we're in for a stampede tonight."

"Don't say that, Monty," Dylan said, half jokingly. "I'm too tired to chase cattle tonight."

"I hope I'm wrong." Monty headed for the creek. "I'd better get cleaned up before supper."

While Charlie worked to prepare the evening meal, Dylan leaned his head back against a tree trunk and nodded off to sleep.

He slept but a short time, awakened by the creaking of wagon wheels and high, shrill laughter. He opened his eyes and swore angrily. The vehicle approaching him held three saloon girls from the trading post. He had given the men strict orders that there were to be no women in camp. Charlie, busy placing stones around the fire pit he had built, spat a stream of tobacco juice into the fire and snorted, "What are them bitches doin' out here? The men will be fightin' over them all night."

"No, by God, there will be no fighting." Dylan's eyes blazed angrily. "Those girls are going to turn right around and get back to the trading post."

Charlie shook his head in doubt. "You can try gettin' rid of them, but it ain't gonna be easy."

The rickety wagon was pulled to a halt. Giggling and laughing, the three scantily clad women jumped to the ground. "Surprise, Dylan!" they cried. "We've come to keep you and your men company tonight."

"Who invited you?" Dylan asked coldly as he stood up.

"Why, your men, of course." Gracie gave him a wide smile. "Ain't you happy to see us?"

"I'm as happy as if I'd been invaded by a bunch of lepers," Dylan replied, grabbing her arm to turn her around. "Now get back in that wagon and head back to the post. If you hurry, you can make it back before dark."

Gracie's face turned an angry red. Jerking her arm out of Dylan's grip, she snapped. "You don't own this whole valley, Dylan Quade. We'll just ride on a little distance and set up our own camp."

"Go ahead," Dylan answered smoothly. "Just be sure you shoot straight when wolves and grizzlies come around your camp."

At the startled looks that came over the women's faces, it was easy to see they hadn't thought of that.

But Gracie tried to brazen it out. With her chin in the air, she said smugly, "We won't be alone. Your men will be with us."

Dylan turned away from the women so they wouldn't see the startled look he was sure came over his features. He hadn't thought of the men visiting the women. He couldn't very well prevent his men from having a good time tonight, but he'd be damned if he'd participate.

"Who was that?" Monty asked as he returned to

camp just as the wagon was disappearing in a cloud of dust.

"Some of the girls from The Grizzly Bear," Dylan said, sounding as bad-tempered as a grizzly himself.

"Why'd you send them off?" Monty demanded.

"That's the last thing I need," Dylan shot back, "for Rachel to hear that I had a bunch of whores staying in camp. She'd throw me out on my ear next time I go down to the post to see her.

"Gracie won't take the girls far," he went on when Monty frowned his disappointment. "You and the men can still pay them a visit. I'll keep watch over the cattle till you get back."

"Sure thing," Monty agreed, but under his breath he added, "You've got it bad, old friend."

Rachel walked outside and leaned against the supporting post of the overhang. It was hot and the air was still. Heat waves shimmered in the distance. Sweat beaded on her forehead and she tasted salt on her lips.

During the weeks since her mother's death, Rachel's bruises and cuts had healed. Her physical injuries had disappeared, but the hurt inside had not faded. Her mother was gone forever, and some days she didn't think she could bear the pain of that loss.

She recalled Dylan's gentleness as he broke the news to her, the tenderness of his touch as he stroked her hair. She had seen another side of Dylan Quade that day. Beneath his rough exterior he was a caring man. Was it too much to hope that he cared for her? He had certainly seemed to as he'd held her in his arms while she sobbed her heart out.

But Dylan hadn't been down to the post since that day. Monty Hale, who was a frequent visitor there, said Dylan was working like a man possessed. He spent all day, from sunup to sundown, out on the range rounding up his cattle. He never took time for fun anymore.

Rachel had to admit to herself she was disappointed not to have seen him. At the very least she wanted to thank him for saving her life that night Taig Sutter had beaten her half to death.

Well, she decided suddenly, if Dylan wouldn't come to her, maybe it was time she went to him. She was pretty sure she could find her way to the Bar X, and there was still an hour of daylight left. Her mind made up, she hurried to the barn to saddle Goldie.

As she set out down the river road, a cool breeze soon dried the sweat on her brow. There was birdsong everywhere, and she felt a shiver of anticipation go through her at the thought that she would soon see Dylan again.

The sun was setting behind the mountains as she spotted the trail that branched off from the river road toward Dylan's ranch. At least she hoped it was the trail to the Bar X. The last time she'd traveled it, she'd been delirious with fever.

It seemed, however, that the farther she went, the wilder the country became. She began to fear she had never traveled this way before.

Twilight was almost settling in when from the corner of her eye she saw movement in the brush alongside the dim deer path she was following. But when she stopped and stared at the spot where she had seen movement, nothing seemed to be there. Still, every time Goldie started walking again, she felt sure that something or somebody was following her. And it seemed as if her pursuer was getting closer and closer.

It was dark now, the moon was up and full. Dismounting to lead the mare through the tangled brush, Rachel asked herself if she was maybe imagining demons and spirits, due to the stories the old people liked to tell.

She had just reached the edge of a wide valley where a little stream flowed through a stand of aspens, when in the moonlight she saw a grizzly. Her blood froze as Goldie reared up and took off back up the trail. The grizzly was on his hind legs, and he appeared to be about ten feet tall. She knew that when bears stood up it was a sign they were about to charge their prey. And she was this one's prey, she had no doubt. He had been stalking her for at least an hour. She let out an involuntary scream. Death was looking her in the face.

Dylan was keeping night watch over his cattle when he heard the scream. Unmistakably a woman's scream. A moment later he heard the deep roar of a bear. It had come from the underbrush at the edge of the valley.

"Dear Lord," Dylan prayed as he sank his heels into Devil's flanks, "let me get to her in time."

Urging the horse at a dead run toward the sounds, he practically flew across the valley. He brought the black to a rearing halt when he came to a copse of trees. To his horror, it was Rachel standing there in the moonlight, paralyzed, her eyes staring at a large grizzly. As Dylan snatched his rifle from its boot, the bear turned around and stared at him out of beady black eyes. Thank God, Dylan thought. His motion had distracted the grizzly's attention from Rachel.

Holding his breath, Dylan ordered his hands to stop trembling as he brought the rifle butt to his shoulder. He had only one chance to bring the big animal down. He must get it between the eyes. He waited until the bear started toward him, then took careful aim. It was only feet away when he slowly squeezed the trigger.

He thought for a horrifying moment that he had missed, for the beast continued to come toward him. But as his shaking hands brought the rifle to his shoulder again, the big grizzly dropped to the ground and lay there, not stirring a muscle.

Dylan rushed to catch Rachel in his arms as she started falling. He sat down in the same spot, cradling her against his chest. Her arms came up to clasp around his neck while her trembling body pressed itself as close as possible to his. He stroked her hair and crooned soft words to her, but her shivering only seemed to increase, and she still clung to him desperately.

The night air was cool and she was probably in shock from the bear's attack. He needed to get the blankets from the bedroll on his saddle. He started to ease away from her, but she protested plaintively and clung to him more tightly.

"I'm just going to get some blankets for you, honey," he murmured, then whistled Devil nearer.

Quickly he freed the tarp tied behind his cantle, then unrolled it onto the ground along with the blankets. Dylan lay down on it and took Rachel back into his arms.

It took several minutes to arrange the blankets around them. "Now, isn't that better, honey?" he asked as he became conscious of the slim, warm body in his arms.

"Y-yes," she said, her teeth still chattering a bit. "That's the second t-time you've saved my life."

"Shh," he crooned. "Thank God I was nearby."

Her lower body was pressed tightly against his lean hips. He felt himself growing hard and tried to draw back, but when her arms came up around his neck, he found it impossible to think straight.

Dylan bent his head and captured her lips with his in a kiss that went on and on. Finally, raising his head to catch his breath, he asked in a ragged whisper, "Are you sure this is what you want?"

When she nodded her head, he unbuttoned her

blouse and laid bare her breasts. He gazed at them a moment in the moonlight, then lowered his head and opening his mouth, drew most of one into his mouth. As he swirled his tongue around the hardened nipple, Rachel moaned and slid her hand down the inside front of his denims. He caught his breath when her fingers touched the tip of his hardness. He ripped the top button off the waistband in his hurry to free himself for the full feel of Rachel's fingers.

He gave a low groan of pleasure when her fingers immediately curled around him. His lips moved faster on her breasts as her hand began to stroke him. He wondered fleetingly if she was uncomfortable lying on the ground. She should be on top, he thought, and rolled over so that her soft mound pressed against his hardness, bringing him a thrill of pleasure despite the remaining barrier of her thin silk bloomers.

Dylan's eyes opened wide when she rolled her hips, moaning softly as she spread her legs around his waist to bring herself into fuller contact with him. Where had she learned a move like that? he wondered.

Carefully and slowly Dylan began a rhythmic movement of his hips as his hands gripped her small rear, holding her steady as he rubbed his throbbing manhood where she wanted it most.

When he heard the quickening of her breathing, her excited little cries, he knew she was ready to find release, so he suckled harder on one nipple while his fingers stroked the other one.

She exploded all at once, her cries of overpowering ecstasy lifting to the treetops.

Rachel lay on top of him, breathing heavily. Dylan's breathing was equally heavy, his manhood still full and stiff, throbbing against her feminine softness. He gritted his teeth. How he wanted to take her fully, to feel his shaft slide into her tight sheath and take her to ecstasy again.

He reminded himself that she was probably still in shock after her near brush with death. Even if it killed him, he would not take advantage of the situation more than he already had.

A couple owls in the trees hooted to each other and Devil stamped his hoofs restlessly. Dylan looked around to spot the source of the horse's restlessness.

Not fifteen feet away stood Monty Hale, the grin on his face clearly visible in the moonlight. "No wonder you weren't interested in what the saloon girls had to offer tonight, Dylan," he said with a chuckle. "If that's Rachel Sutter you've got with you, I suggest you two make yourselves decent pronto. John Jacob's got half the customers from the post scouring the countryside for her."

Dylan knew he had a serious problem. Here he lay, with his pants unbuttoned and a half-naked young lady astride his crotch.

"The men are about half a mile from here,"

Monty said urgently. "I met up with them as I was riding back to camp. They've been out searching ever since Andrews noticed Rachel was missing from the post. When they found Goldie, they knew they were on the right track."

"Thanks, Monty," Dylan said as he struggled to rebutton his denims and Rachel scrambled off him and hurried into the trees to refasten her blouse. "You probably saved me from getting some buckshot in my rear."

"You'd do the same for me," Monty said, then narrowed his eyes at Dylan. "Straighten the buttons on your pants. You're buttoned up crooked."

While Dylan corrected his fastenings with a red face, Monty hurriedly made a fire. When he saw Dylan looking at him questioningly, he explained. "Everything will look better if we're sitting here drinking coffee when they come upon us." Dylan grinned his thanks, then walked into the thicket where Rachel was still hiding.

"I can never show my face around Monty Hale again," she burst out. "I'd be too ashamed."

"Don't worry, honey," Dylan said gently, wiping a tear from her cheek. "Monty will never say a word about this."

"Can I really trust him?" she wondered out loud.

"I'd stake my life on it," Dylan said. "Now come sit by the fire and pull yourself together."

They were drinking their second cup of coffee when the search party came upon them.

"Rachel," one of the men called jubilantly when she was spotted, "we've been all over this valley looking for you. What happened?"

"I was attacked by a grizzly bear," Rachel answered shakily. "Dylan shot it just over there." She pointed to the spot where the bear's body lay.

"We just finished making some coffee to warm her up and calm her nerves," Monty put in. "Will you fellows have a cup with us?"

"Why not?" the leader said, sliding off his horse. "It won't hurt nothing if we're a little later, now that we know Rachel's okay. A cup of coffee sounds real good."

Fifteen minutes passed before Dylan helped Rachel back up onto Goldie. "Don't worry, honey," he whispered. "I'll follow you back to the post and explain everything to John Jacob." With that, he slapped Goldie's rump and she took off with the rest of the search party.

"I don't envy you that job," Monty chuckled. It was obvious he'd overhead Dylan.

"I'm not afraid of Andrews," Dylan shot back.

"No? A lot of men would be. He's pretty protective about Rachel, I've noticed, and he'll probably ask you a lot of questions."

"Well, he'd damned well better not. I saved her life. Besides, he's trusted her with me before."

"Has he, now?" Monty looked surprised. He grinned then. "Maybe he don't know you very well. The taking ways you have with women."

"That's all behind me now," Dylan insisted. "I'm

not the one who spent the night with a bunch of saloon girls."

Monty just chuckled. "Don't you think you should be going now? The others are halfway to the post by now."

Without answering, Dylan swung up on Devil, gathered the reins and headed down the mountain.

Chapter Fourteen

The moon was up and the whole country was bathed in beauty. John Jacob had been sitting on the porch, looking into the night since early twilight, watching for the men he'd sent out to come riding home with Rachel.

I should have gone with them, he thought for the dozenth time. *I could have locked the damn doors for one night.*

John Jacob stood up and paced back and forth. The search party hadn't found her or they'd be back by now. For the third time that night a wolf howled from up the mountain. For the third time John Jacob's blood ran cold. What if the animal was tracking Rachel? "Oh, God," he whispered, "don't let me lose her after just finding her. I don't think I could bear it."

Just then he heard the sound of horses' hooves coming up the river road. The search party had returned with Rachel, and to his surprise, Dylan Quade was with them.

"Is she alright?" John Jacob jumped off the porch and ran to the horses.

"She's fine," Dylan said. "She's just exhausted."

"Come here, honey." John Jacob lifted his arms up to help her off Goldie. "We'll get you something to eat and drink, then get you to bed." He cradled her in his arms a moment, then, smoothing her hair back, he kissed her gently on the forehead. She smiled up at him, then leaned her head on his shoulder and closed her eyes.

Jealousy, hot and thick, spread through Dylan. Andrews was old enough to be Rachel's father and here he was acting like he was her lover. Was he the one who had taught Rachel to take her pleasure by straddling a man?

He sat in the saddle watching John carry Rachel into the post. He decided suddenly that he was going to have it out with the man tonight. He wanted to marry Rachel, and he was going to find out just what she meant to John Jacob Andrews.

When Dylan had turned Devil over to the teenager who took care of the customers' horses, and warned him that the stallion bit when he had the chance, he went inside the post.

The big room was empty so he walked on into the kitchen where Rachel was probably eating something after her ordeal.

There was no one there but Rosie. "Where is everyone?" Dylan asked.

"John Jacob took Rachel to her room. She was falling asleep on her feet. He'll be back in a minute. Have a cup of coffee while you're waiting," Rosie offered.

Dylan was ready to slam out of the post without even answering, but John Jacob came into the kitchen at that moment. "She fell asleep as soon as her head hit the pillow." He grinned, pulling a chair away from the table. "Tell me what happened."

The last thing Dylan wanted to do was have a friendly talk with John Jacob. He would have much sooner hit him in the mouth with his fist. But the man would think him crazy if he did that, so he said crisply, "Goldie spooked when a grizzly bear came up on them. Fortunately, I heard Rachel's scream and got to her in time."

There was a silence as Rosie poured coffee for them. After Dylan had taken a long swallow of the strong brew, he looked at John Jacob and said, "I expect Rachel is a big help to you in the post, cooking and waiting on the customers. I'm sure she's grateful that you took her in and provided a home for her."

"I don't want her to be grateful." John Jacob said, his voice rough. "The girl is long overdue for some nice things in life." He went on to say, "I've been making plans for her future. Come September, I'm sending her to a school back East where she can get an education. I was once a teacher myself, you see, and it's important to me."

"Will she come back here to the wilderness when she's finished with her schooling?" There was a hint of desperation in Dylan's tone.

If John Jacob noticed this, he never let on, only continued to talk of his plans for Rachel. "While she's gone I'll have a little house built for her, close by the post where I can keep an eye on her. I know she can't go on living here with me. People are starting to talk."

The more John Jacob talked, the angrier Dylan became. He wanted to ask, *Who is going to protect her from you?* Instead he asked coolly, "How long do you think she'll be satisfied living alone? She's a beautiful young lady. Every man who comes in here has his eye on her. You won't be able to keep her long."

"Ha!" John snorted. "There's no man around here who will ever marry her. She's too good for any of them." He stood up and stomped out the door.

It was obvious that as far as he was concerned, the conversation was over.

Dylan struck a match and held it to the cigarette he had rolled while John Jacob spoke of his plans for Rachel. Its yellow flame cast shadows on his lean face and brought glints to his light-colored eyes as he watched Rosie move about the kitchen. He dropped the match when its flame reached his fingertips. He shook his head, bringing himself back to the present.

Why had he been foolish enough to think that he could ever marry Rachel Sutter? He should have known from the first time he saw John Jacob Andrews with her that the wealthy man had marked her for his own.

He took his Stetson off the table and slapped it on his head. As he headed for the door, Rosie asked, "Ain't you going to visit the saloon? John Jacob ordered free drinks for everyone in the search party."

Dylan shook his head and reached for the door latch. "I'd better get back to camp. We're branding cattle tomorrow." He stepped outside and closed the door behind him.

The stable boy was asleep on a pile of hay. Dylan looked at him a minute and didn't have the heart to waken him. He saddled Devil and headed down the river road. The stallion was rested and wanted to run. Dylan loosened the reins and Devil struck out at a full gallop. But no matter how fast they raced, Dylan couldn't outrun the crushing sense of disappointment that filled his chest.

The dust rose, stifling and irritating, as Dylan stood with some of his men around the branding fire the following day. For the past week they had worked from can see to can't see. He was going to have the biggest herd he'd ever driven to Abilene this fall. But what was he working so hard for? he asked himself. He had worked like a slave because of Rachel. He had hoped he'd have a chance with her if he could show he had something worthwhile to offer her. But John Jacob had shot down all his dreams.

He'd made it clear that he meant to keep Rachel to himself. Still, Andrews was not her father, had no real say over her life. Perhaps Rachel would decide she preferred Dylan to the older man. She'd certainly seemed attracted to him last night.

Dylan smiled in recollection as he leaned his back against a tree. He must continue to build up his herd and spruce up his house. It was a well-built house of four bedrooms. It had tightly constructed shutters that kept the cold out in the winter as well as the heat in the summer. The fireplace in the main room took up one outside wall. It had a wide hearth about a foot off the floor, and the mantel was wide enough to hold anything a person might want to put on it. At the moment it held only a big clock that had belonged to his grandfather. His collection of three different kinds of guns and rifles hung on the wall above it.

Two years ago when he'd attended a rendezvous, he had bought several bright-colored rugs from the Indian women who had attended the two-week gathering of trappers. Those women couldn't be beat when it came to working their looms. He'd purchased one large rug with the idea of spreading it out in front of the fireplace. But he had never had the heart to put its beauty on the floor. He had rolled it up and laid it with the other rugs he had bought. It was time he brought them out and placed them in the rooms.

To keep some of the winter snow and mud off

the floors, he'd had a special mat made for the entrance. Old Granny Hawkins, who lived high up in the mountains with only her great-granddaughter for company, wove him a fair-sized mat out of thin strips of rawhide. He kept it swept clean of snow and mud in the winter, and in the summer took it to the nearby creek, where with a flat stone he pounded the floor mat clean.

His place had no touches of female finery. There were no pictures on the walls, no bowls of flowers or greenery on the kitchen table. There was a coal-oil lamp in its center, also one on the table next to a rocking chair in the main room.

Everything was neat and clean, he prided himself on that, but the ranch house was plainly the home of a bachelor. What would Rachel think of it? he asked himself. Maybe he should ask Granny Hawkins to share some of her flower seeds with him. And it wouldn't hurt to dig a small vegetable plot.

With a deep sigh Dylan flipped a burned-out cigarette into the branding fire that had burned down to a few glowing coals. He straightened up and started back to work. A grown man day-dreaming. Well, it couldn't hurt to try to get Rachel Sutter for his own.

The afternoon was warm and sultry as Rachel sat on the post's porch, fanning her face with a folded-up newspaper. An occasional breeze moved the long grass in green ripples like waves before the wind. Frogs were peeping along the riverbank, and several yards down the slowly moving water, four Indian women were doing the wash by beating the clothes with rocks.

She thought how pretty and graceful the young maids were now, but how after marriage and two or three children they tended to get quite plump.

What kind of shape would she have after marriage and some children? she mused, watching an eagle sweep slowly across the sky. Her poor mother had always been thin, but that was from the hard work she'd done all her life. Folks said that hard work never hurt anyone, but in her opinion there were all kinds of hard work in this world, and some of it could kill a woman, or at least shorten her life.

She had been noticing that the men living in the valley worked harder than the mountain men. Ranchers had to watch over hundreds of cows, cut hay to feed them over the winter, not to mention the long days they spent branding the animals and then driving them to market.

As for the mountain men, they mostly trapped in the winter and hunted in the summer. It was their wives who scraped a meager living out of the rocky mountain soil. She thought of Dylan Quade. Was he a hard worker? She knew that he ran cattle in the summer months, then went up to the mountains to trap in the winter. His friend Monty had told her he was a hard worker. How else could he have accomplished so much?

As happened every day, Rachel fell to thinking of Dylan. For the first few days after he'd rescued her from the grizzly, she had daydreamed about him constantly. She had thought that he would ask John Jacob about marrying her and then they would talk, make plans for their future. But he hadn't even come inside the post that night or been near the place since.

She clenched her fist, hating herself. She had given her heart to him, done things with him she wouldn't have permitted with any other man, and he hadn't put any importance on it.

The next day she had told John Jacob she did not wish to go East, get an education. She couldn't bear the idea of being so far from Dylan. But now it was plain that Dylan had no interest in her, and she wondered what was to become of her. It didn't seem right to go on living with John Jacob indefinitely, no matter how kind he was to her.

Rachel saw the dust John Jacob's horse was stirring up before she saw the big sorrel. She stood up and and walked to the edge of the porch, waiting with a welcoming smile for him to ride up.

He returned her smile and stepped down from the saddle. He was covered with dust from the crown of his Stetson to the soles of his boots. As he climbed the porch steps, he took off his hat and slapped it against his legs. As dust and sand flew, Rachel clapped her hand over her mouth and nose. "Are you trying to choke me to death?" she joked. "What have you been doing to get so dusty?"

"I went out to where Dylan has been branding his young cattle. He has some fine-looking stock."

"I'm surprised he let you watch. He's such a grouch."

"You think he's grouchy?" John Jacob raised an eyebrow at Rachel. "He always seems friendly enough to me. Anyway, he wasn't there. He was busy chasing wild cattle out of the brush." John Jacob gave her a wide smile and switched the subject. "I heard something that might interest you."

When Rachel gave him a questioning look, he said, "There's going to be a picnic at the church in Jackson Hole this Sunday."

"A church picnic?" Rachel asked.

"Yep. There will be music and dancing in the evening, and the ladies will bring different eats. Dylan has donated a steer to be roasted. The single women will bring baskets with cakes and pies. The bachelors will bid on them."

John Jacob paused to give a short laugh. "The baskets won't have names on them, so the men won't know whose basket they're getting." He paused to laugh again. "A lot of them will be mighty disappointed at the ones they choose to bet on. Some of those women are long in the tooth, and a few are ugly as sin. However, each man is obligated to sit with the woman who made up the basket he chose and eat its contents."

John Jacob looked at Rachel and teased with a grin, "Can you bake a cake or pie?"

"I can indeed, Mr. Smarty." Rachel gave him a playful slap on the arm. "I will bake a peach pie. I noticed that you have several tins of peaches in your storeroom. My ma taught me how to bake. She was noted for her pies."

A sadness flickered in John Jacob's eyes. He knew what delicious pies Ida Sutter could make. They had shared many of them eighteen years ago. Every Sunday that summer, he and Ida would meet at their secret place along the river. The place where Rachel had been conceived.

John Jacob shook that memory from his mind and talked again about the picnic. "During the afternoon there will be shooting matches," he said, "and the winner will get a Colt revolver. Then the last event will be a horse race. The winner will receive a handsome hand-tooled saddle."

Her eyes sparkling, Rachel exclaimed, "I'd better wear that split skirt you bought me the other day."

"Now, why would you want to do that?" John Jacob questioned with a frown. "You're not planning on entering the race, are you?" he teased. "The men will ride over you with their big stallions."

"They'd have to catch me first," Rachel retorted. "I've raced big mountain horses ever since I can remember. That sorrel of yours looks like he's got a lot of speed in his long legs. I could ride him."

"He has. But I guess you also noticed how big he is. A little slip of a girl like you could never control him."

Rachel looked at John Jacob with twinkling eyes. "Don't worry about that. I've already ridden him several times."

"You have?" John Jacob gave her a thunder-struck look. "That big devil could have killed you."

"I don't know why you think that. He's gentle as a lamb."

"Hah! Prince is gentle? What put that in your head? He has bitten and kicked every stable hand that has ever come around him."

Rachel shrugged and quipped, "Maybe he just likes women."

Knowing that he wouldn't deny her, John Jacob said helplessly, "I wish you wouldn't enter him in the race. Why don't you enter the shooting match instead? You can shoot, can't you?"

"If I hadn't been able to shoot a rifle since I was nine or ten, there would have been many times when Mama and we children wouldn't have had anything to eat." She grinned at John Jacob and bragged, "I can shoot the eyes out of a squirrel fifty yards away. I'm going to win that Colt."

"For what?" John Jacob asked as they went through the post door. "You don't need a gun."

"I'll give it to you." Rachel gave him a sharp pinch in the side as they walked into the kitchen.

"Fine," John Jacob said, fighting to keep

amusement out of his voice. She would be competing against some of the best shots in the country. As he poured a cup of coffee, he said casually, "Therc will be some mountain men at the shooting match—I'm told that they are crack shots."

"They don't scare me," Rachel said with a lift of her chin. "I've probably shot against every one of them."

They sat down at the table and the subject was dropped as Andy, the cook, placed their supper before them.

Chapter Fifteen

When John Jacob and Rachel had finished eating, they took their coffee out onto the porch. "It's clouding up." John Jacob frowned up at the sky. "I hope we're not in for a rainy spell. The folks at the church have put a lot of work into the big to-do Sunday. And that steer Dylan donated is too good to waste if they don't get a good turnout."

"Well, at least your donation of spirits won't be wasted." Rachel gave John Jacob a teasing grin.

"I've been thinking about that," he said, a frown appearing on his handsome face. "I hope we don't end up with a bunch of drunks on our hands."

"I've thought of that, too," Rachel said. "Most mountain men like to drink and brawl, and pick fights."

"If any fights break out, you and I are going to head for home." John Jacob didn't say so, but he was thinking there would be fights over Rachel. Suddenly he wasn't looking forward to the festivities. He began to think that he and Rachel should go early to the picnic party, then leave before the men got quarrelsome. Before he could say anything, Rosie stepped out on the porch and said, "Iva wants to speak to you, John."

"Iva? What could she want?"

John Jacob looked puzzled.

"I don't know, but she's mighty upset. You'd better see what's troubling her. She's been sick in her room for the past few days. Doc Johnson was here today to see her."

John Jacob stood up and went to Iva's room. He was startled to see how wasted the woman looked. Her body was rail thin, her shoulder-length hair a mass of tangles. He had not seen her for a week or so, he realized, and now it was obvious she'd been seriously ill.

It was clear that Iva was nervous, so John Jacob gave her one of his warm smiles and asked gently, "What can I do for you, Iva?"

When the woman cast an uneasy look at Rachel and began coughing, John Jacob said to Rachel, "Maybe you can bring us some of that cold spring water Andy just brought in."

Rachel frowned. What was plaguing poor Iva? she wondered. She hurried off to the kitchen to give the woman the privacy she sought for her talk with John Jacob.

When Rachel returned with the spring water a minute later, Iva was nowhere in sight. Instead, her two little boys were sitting on chairs before John Jacob, their small fingers thrust into the pockets of much-patched homespuns.

John Jacob motioned Rachel closer and said, "You know Colby and Benny, don't you, honey?"

"Why, sure," Rachel answered, wondering what this was all about. "These two scamps are always pestering me to get one of Andy's cookies for them."

The boys ducked their shaggy heads in embarrassment.

"Well, boys," John Jacob said, "do you know why I wanted to see you tonight?"

"No, sir." The shaggy heads ducked again.

John Jacob stared out the window a moment. "Your mother has asked me to be your guardian. Do you know what a guardian is?"

"No, sir," answered Colby, the older of the two. "We don't know much of anything."

John Jacob reached over and patted the child's grimy fingers, which were now clutched together. "I doubt that," he said. "You just haven't had any schooling."

"That is true. Our ma has learned us a few things, but she is so sick now, she can't do it no more."

"I'll explain to you what a guardian is," John Jacob said and smiled at the boys. "He or she is a very important person. When a child has lost all his relatives, someone becomes his guardian.

Your mother has asked me to be your guardian if anything should happen to her."

Colby and Benny lifted their heads and stared at him with wide eyes. "Are you going to?" Benny asked anxiously.

"I'll be happy to. From now on you can call me Uncle John."

Two pairs of brown eyes glowed brightly. It was plain to see the boys were relieved to know they had a protector.

The brightness dimmed then and Colby's voice quivered when he asked, "Nothin's going to happen to our ma, though, right?"

"I don't know, child. Only the Lord knows that. You know that she's been very sick."

"Yeah," Benny put in. "I heard the doc say she's got lung fever. Is that real bad?"

"It can be, but I'm hoping she'll get better," John Jacob said gently. He stood up and pulled the two boys to him. Squeezing their narrow shoulders, he said, "But no matter what happens, Uncle John is going to take care of both of you." He directed their steps toward the back rooms. "Tell you mother I'll be in to talk everything over with her. I'd like to get you into school as soon as possible."

An uneasiness slid into Colby's dark brown eyes. "We wouldn't know how to act, Uncle John. We ain't got no clothes . . . or shoes."

"Don't you go worrying about that." John Jacob

ruffled the boy's hair, then wished he could take his handkerchief and wipe the grease off his fingers. "More than half the other kids are in the same shape as you. But we're going to buy you some new duds."

John Jacob was grabbed and hugged on both sides. He grinned at Rachel as the two boys scampered away.

"What a softy you are," she said, smiling. "I guess you just can't turn away a youngun in need."

"Guess not," John Jacob answered gruffly. "Poor Iva—she's in sad shape. I just couldn't say no to her."

"I'll help you with the boys," Rachel promised. "I know all about little ones. I practically raised my younger brothers."

The following morning Rachel and John Jacob took a ride up to her old home place. It was the first time she had been back to the shack since her mother's death. She wanted to cry aloud her grief but held it back until she saw the yellow rose bush in the chimney corner of the old log cabin. It was in full bloom. That sight brought a torrent of tears. "Mama loved that bush so," she sobbed as John Jacob took her in his arms. "It was the one bright spot in her drab world. Taig threatened to chop it down if he ever caught her wasting water on it. But Mama would not let it die, and every time Taig was gone off somewhere, she would carry water from the stream and lovingly give it a drink."

"Would you like me to dig up the rose bush for you, honey?" John Jacob asked gently. "You know I want to build you your own little cabin near the post. We could plant it there, in a chimney facing the mountain where your mother was laid to rest."

"That would give me something to remember her by," Rachel said, smiling through her tears. "I'll go fetch you a spade."

As John Jacob waited for Rachel to return, he recalled Ida's deep love of all plants. He imagined that at an early age Rachel had gone with her mother to the woods to gather certain barks, roots and plants. Even as a girl, Ida had been what they called an herbalist. A very honorable occupation for a female.

He remembered that Ida always carried a notebook when she met him in the woods and was always jotting down notes about some plant or other. He had teased her about it, but she had only laughed and said that he'd be surprised how many lives had been saved by what he called weeds.

His musings had given him an idea. When Rachel came back with a rusty spade in her hand, he said, "I seem to recall someone mentioning that your ma was an herbalist. Was she?"

Rachel gave him a blank look. "I don't know if she was or not. What is an herbalist?"

"An herbalist is a man or woman who goes into the woods and strips bark off certain trees, digs up special plants and roots. Life-saving medicine is made from those things of nature."

"Oh, that." Rachel smiled. "I guess you could call Mama that. Granny Hawkins taught her what to pick and what to use the plants for."

"I guess you used to go with her to gather roots and such."

"Yes." Rachel's eyes sparkled as she remembered those times. They dimmed a bit when she continued, "Since my earliest memory, unless it was raining or too cold, we went out every day, scoring the woods for Mama's medicine plants. I think we covered every mile on the mountain, looking for special plants and roots. I remember Mama was always looking for ginseng. She was paid well for those roots."

She paused a moment, then said, "Of course we never got to keep any of the money we made. Taig always took it and bought whiskey, even though we needed shoes or coats, or even food sometimes."

John Jacob was silent for some time, giving Rachel a minute to forget those times. He asked quietly then, "Did your mama keep any notes about the plants she gathered?"

Rachel's eyes sparkled again. "She kept every word she ever wrote about them. There are lots of them. They are all packed in a box in the cabin. Would you like to see them?"

John Jacob laughed softly. "Honey, I wouldn't know one from the other. But I think it is important that you bring them down to the post. I have a feeling they are going to be very important to you. There's a danger of someone coming here to your cabin to see what they can steal. And maybe out of meanness, someone will destroy all your mother's work."

"Oh, John," Rachel said, settling down on a rock to watch him put the spade to work. Her eyes were wide with alarm. "I couldn't bear that. Her notes and this yellow rose bush are all I have left of her."

As John Jacob began carefully digging around the roots, Rachel said, "Rosie told me my cousin Jassy came down to the post to get a decent dress for Mama to be buried in. I'm glad about that."

"Yeah, that poor little gal came all the way down the mountain barefoot and in the dark."

"I'm surprised Granny Hawkins let her come alone. She's always afraid something will happen to Jassy."

"Do you mean other children will tease her, maybe hit her?" John Jacob asked.

"No, I don't think that's her worry. The young'uns know better than to tease or hit Jassy. Number one, she's an awfully sweet girl, and number two, both the children and their parents are afraid of old Granny. Some think she's a witch because she knows all the old remedies," Rachel explained.

"You don't believe such nonsense, do you?" John Jacob asked, puffing a bit from his digging. The soil was hard and rocky.

"Of course not. Granny is the sweetest old soul you could ever meet. She always says she's glad the mountain people fear her, for that means they respect her too. I don't know what Mama and I would have done without her."

"Who does Jassy belong to?" John Jacob asked.

Rachel shrugged. "Granny Hawkins, I guess. She always says she found her under a tree that had been hit by lightning during a storm. Jassy was only a few hours old.

"I guess there's some mystery about who her real parents are, but Granny's the one who raised her. They sure love each other."

John Jacob paused in his digging. "But why is Granny afraid to let Jassy go about by herself? She's old enough not to get lost."

"It's the mountain men she's afraid of," Rachel said. "She always warned Jassy and me to keep our distance from them."

"She's a wise one, that Granny Hawkins," John Jacob said. "I've been told the mountain people have their own rules about courtship. Sometimes if a man wants a girl for his wife, he rapes her. Then the girl has to marry him or be an outcast in the mountains the rest of her life. I've heard that all too many mountain wives were forced into marrying a man they didn't love."

Rachel was silent for several seconds. Had her mother been raped by Taig? Surely gentle Ida couldn't have loved such a man. She looked down at her clasped hands and said quietly, "That's what Homer tried to do to me, but I hit him over the head with a tree branch. And he wasn't the only one."

"You're quite a scrapper, aren't you, honey?" John Jacob said.

"I had to be, growing up with seven brothers and sisters. I've bloodied a few noses." Rachel gave a tickled laugh. "Those mountain boys run away when they see me coming. I've watched them fight, and I can fight as mean as they can now. I know the best place to kick them, to stamp down hard on the arch of their feet, how to press my elbow into their Adam's apple and keep it there until their faces turn red."

She held up her slender fingers. "See these nails? I grow them long just so I can scratch the skin off their faces."

"Goodness, honey, that's not very ladylike," John Jacob said, half joking, half serious.

"Yes, I know, but Mama said it was necessary if I was to protect myself and make sure I wouldn't be forced into marrying some man I didn't like."

John Jacob nodded solemnly. "I expect she was right. If you couldn't hold your own in a fight, there's no telling who you might be married to now."

Rachel shivered. "But in the end Homer got me anyhow. He threatened Mama, you know. That's why I had to marry him."

John Jacob swore and kicked a rock. "I wish that bastard Homer were still alive so that I could shoot him dead. At least he can't hurt you anymore," he said, wrapping an old piece of sacking around the roots of the rose bush. "Come on," he said, "let's go get your mother's notes."

When Rachel stepped up on the porch of the old cabin where she had been born and raised, the familiar odor of pork belly and greens of all kinds hit her in the face.

"I'll be right out, John," she said, stepping inside the shack and hurriedly shutting the door. She was too embarrassed for him to see how she had lived.

She hurried across the room to the rudely built bunkbed that she had shared with three young sisters the first seventeen years of her life. As she knelt and lifted a loose plank in the floor, she wondered about those siblings. Were they well?

She decided that they would be treated well enough living with Taig's parents. Her sisters and brothers all had black hair. They wouldn't be referred to as white-haired little bastards.

Rachel held her breath as she untied the string that held the old cracked leather box together. Her hands paused a minute on the thin strip of rawhide. What if her mother's notes weren't there? She prayed that the secret place she and her mother had used for years hadn't been found by someone who had maliciously destroyed them. Jenny Quade would do that in a minute.

Rachel took a deep breath and slowly lifted the lid. A breath of relief whooshed through her lips.

Everything was there, just as her mother had left it. She lifted the box to her chest and hugged it tightly, a tear slipping down her cheek.

Rachel swiped a hand across her wet cheek and stepped out onto the rotting porch. She handed the chest to John Jacob when he straightened up from his lounging position against the porch post.

"Honey," John Jacob said, taking one of her fine-boned hands, so much like her mother's, "it is my firm belief that you can pick up where your mother left off. Since you don't want to go East to attend school, I'd like to see you become an herbalist. You will have your mother's notes to go by, and I'm sure Granny Hawkins will help you all she can. She will be happy to turn some of the doctoring over to you. She is getting old and can't walk all over the mountains like she used to."

Rachel sighed deeply as she looked at the leather box. "For you, Mama, I will do the very best I can."

"That's all I ask, Rachel. I know you're going to be the best medicine woman in all the territory."

When they turned toward the horses, John Jacob paused in surprise. As if she'd appeared out of thin air, Jenny Quade was standing in front of them.

Her hands on her hips, she demanded of Rachel, "What business do you have going into Taig Sutter's house? What's in that box you just handed to John Jacob?"

Rachel looked at her and, lifting her lips in a

taunting sneer, said, "You'll never know, will you Jenny."

"That's what you think, Miss High-and-Mighty," Jenny snarled, and with that she lunged for the box.

While John Jacob was debating how best to handle the situation, Rachel was suddenly all over Jenny.

At first John Jacob could only stand and stare at the infuriated Rachel. It was one thing to hear her claim to be a good fighter, quite another to witness just how well she could defend herself. He had had no idea how strong she was. Aware now that she could take care of herself, he leaned back against the cabin post and enjoyed the thrashing Jenny was getting.

He stepped in, however, when Rachel knocked Jenny to the ground and began laying into the woman with her small, hard fists.

John Jacob bent over the two women and laughingly said, "You don't want to kill her, Rachel. Let somebody else have the pleasure."

Jenny scrambled to her feet. She was panting for breath, and her nose was bleeding. It was plain that by nightfall she would have a black eye.

"I wonder how she'll explain her battered face," John Jacob laughed as he and Rachel started down the mountain with the leather box tied behind Goldie's saddle and the rose bush on Prince's.

"She'll probably say that a bear took a swipe at her," Rachel suggested.

"I'd say that a wildcat attacked her. But I don't think anybody will believe that she was attacked by a bear or a wildcat."

"Whatever they think, all I know is that she deserved everything she got." She looked up at John Jacob and gave him a shy smile. "I'm not Taig Sutter's white-haired bastard anymore. Since I came to live with you, I don't have to be afraid of anyone."

"That you don't, honey." John Jacob gave her shoulders a hug. "If you can't take care of yourself, I'm here to do it for you."

Rachel was still smiling when they came in sight of the post. "Why don't you go inside and look through your ma's notes," John Jacob said to her. "I'm gonna go over to the carpenter and see how long it will take to have that little cabin built for you."

John Jacob's lips twitched in amusement when Rachel made no response to his remark. She was deep in thoughts of the notes lying inside that leather box.

Chapter Sixteen

Rachel felt as though her mother sat beside her as she riffled through the thick stack of papers. Some small, some large, some just scraps of any kind of paper Ida could find. So many times Rachel and her mother had sat just this way, always with one eye on the window, watching for Taig.

Rachel had to brush away a tear at the thought of everything her mother had endured. She knew Ida would be thrilled at the changes that had come into her daughter's life. Already the foundation for the little cabin had been laid, and the yellow rose bush planted in the chimney corner.

Rachel had taken to studying her mother's notes every day, and she'd learned quite a bit this week. This morning she was reading about the sourwood tree. Her mother had written in her neat handwriting:

Sourwood tree . . . tart, sour taste; Teas made from the leaves make dropsy medicine, and also yield a black dye.

The sourwood is also called sorrel-tree. It has a lovely fragrance. Sourwood honey is very good for rheumatism and arthritis. It's also a good stomach medicine.

When John Jacob came in, his arms full of chopped wood for the fireplace, she held up a thick stack of paper and exclaimed, "Look, John, look how much I have researched already."

He took the papers, read a few pages carefully, then, smiling proudly, said, "I knew you could do it. You've seemed so happy the last few days. I guess you know now where your life is going to take you. You are going to take care of the ill. No man or woman can do anything more important.

"Now," John Jacob continued, "we must get ready for the church picnic."

"To tell you the truth, John, I'd rather stay home and do some more research."

"You've got a lot of time to do that. The mountains will always have roots and barks and plants," John Jacob said laughing. "Right now I want you to put on one of the pretty new dresses I bought you and go have some fun at the picnic. There hasn't been enough of that in your life."

"I'm not sure I'll know how to mix with all those folks, John. I always felt like an outsider at family gatherings up on Tulane Ridge."

"A pretty girl like you?" John Jacob exclaimed. "Why, you'll be the belle of the party." He glanced at her slyly. "And Dylan Quade will be there."

"Dylan?" she said sourly. "Why should I care if that polecat is there or not?"

"What's wrong, honey? I thought you were sweet on him after he rescued you from that grizzly bear."

"Well, if I was, he sure isn't sweet on me," she said angrily. "He hasn't come around here once since then."

"They say he's working like a dog up at his place, branding all day, then making repairs to the ranch house evenings. Sounds to me like he's fixin' to settle down with a woman," John Jacob said knowingly.

"You really think so?" Rachel asked, a hopeful gleam in her eye.

"I sure do," he answered, then said in a more serious tone, "Honey, there's one man I want you to steer clear of at the picnic. You know Preacher Robison, don't you?"

"Yes, he was the preacher who married Homer and me. The one who took in those two orphan girls. Why should I steer clear of him?" Rachel asked.

"Iva tells me he's a rough customer. I've told him not to come round the Grizzly Bear anymore, but he might be at the dance tonight. I don't want him causing any trouble, trying to catch your eye. He dresses in the latest fashion . . . and he's darn good-looking."

Rachel let loose a pealing laugh. "You can't hold his good looks against him. You're a handsome man, too."

"I don't look like that peacock in any way. He's a mite too fond of the ladies. I've been watching him. He eyes every pretty woman in the post and ignores the plain ones. That's why I'm afraid he might make a play for you."

"I doubt he'll even notice me," Rachel replied.

"I don't care what you say, Rachel, I'm going to keep an eye on that fancy preacher."

Rachel shrugged indifferently. "Do whatever you think best, John. Right now I'm going to put on the prettiest dress you bought me and go have some fun. I can't wait to see the looks on the faces of those mountain men when I win the shooting contest!"

There was a faint rustling of cottonwood leaves as the cattle stirred restlessly, rising, then lying back down. Dylan sat before his fire in the early twilight listening to the faint sounds of the cows, their soft mooing, the click of horn against horn.

He swore softly when he looked up at the lowering sky. Thunder rumbled sullenly and lightning flashed across the black sky. There was going to be a bad storm, and the cattle sensed it. At least the picnic had not been rained out. He'd better get started down the mountain, he thought, or he'd never make it to the dance.

He was kicking dirt over the fire when a big steer lifted his head and looked around him. It was but a moment before the longhorn spotted him. The big animal took a step forward, his nostrils flaring. He was full of fight, and now the herd was even more uneasy. The inside of Dylan's mouth grew dry as bone. This old mossyhorn was too big for him to wrestle.

As Dylan stood there, sweat running down his shirt, the cattle lunged to their feet and stampeded out across the prairie. "Run, you bastards!" he yelled in relief. "If you think I'm going to chase you, you're damn well mistaken."

He stopped kicking dirt on the fire when great sheets of rain blew in, almost knocking him off his feet. "I wish to hell Monty would ride in," he muttered, throwing the saddle across the stallion's back. He had seen his friend about a half hour ago up by a dry wash. It would soon fill with water at the rate the rain was coming down.

Dylan was about to ride up that way to look for Monty, to warn him of the storm that was on its way, when he saw his friend racing his horse toward camp. "Hurry up, you idiot!" Dylan yelled. "We've got to get back to the ranch house before the full force of the storm hits."

Together they raced their horses over the rough terrain, the hard-driven rain cold as ice against their faces. They reached the barn at a dead run. As they dismounted and led the animals inside the big, dry stable, Monty looked at Dylan and said with a grin, "At least we won't have to take a bath. I think the rain sluiced all the dirt off us."

Dylan smiled back. "I think it took some hide off me too."

As Monty headed out to the bunkhouse, he called, "I'll meet you back here in half an hour."

In his bedroom Dylan opened the double doors to his wardrobe and pulled out a pair of black trousers and a white shirt. Folding the clothes over the foot of the bed, he peeled off his soaking clothes and dried himself with a rough cotton towel.

Dan was right, he thought. He did feel clean and rejuvenated. When he had tucked in the shirt tail and done up the buttons, he knotted a dark blue kerchief around his sun-browned throat.

He tried to tame his dark curls, but gave up after about ten minutes. His hair was determined to curl and he might as well let it. What would Rachel think when she saw him all cleaned up?

"Good Lord, Monty," he snorted as he entered the barn, "you smell stronger than John Jacob's whores. Where did you get that God-awful-smelling stuff?"

"I got it from Charlie, your cook."

"What did you do, pour the stuff all over your head?"

"I did not. I just used a little bit. Just enough to make the ladies notice me."

"Well, I hope they like the odor of polecat."

"You're very funny tonight," Monty grumbled, leading his horse out of the barn.

Only a slow drizzle remained after the storm. The two men grinned at each other and urged their horses into a gallop. It wasn't an out-and-out race, but each man wanted to get to the dance first.

They arrived at the barn where it was being held at the same time. Monty, however, entered first because Dylan had to tie his black some distance from the other animals. There was another stallion tied on the picket line and he had started raising a ruckus as soon as he spotted Devil.

Dylan entered the barn ten minutes behind Monty. He stood a moment, looking for Rachel. He found her, looking more beautiful than ever in a cornflower-blue gown, and his face tightened with anger. Every single man there had gathered round her, hanging on her every word. And a lot of words and laughter were tumbling out of her mouth, too. He'd never seen shy little Rachel so animated. She certainly had never laughed that way with him. A wry smile twisted his lips. Most likely she had laughed *at* him a lot of times.

Well, he thought, *I'm not going to be one of those little dogs fawning on her, wagging my tail to get her attention.* "Let's go get ourselves a drink and watch them kick up their heels for a while. I've never before seen a bunch of men act like jackasses. Look, even Preacher Robison is making a fool of himself."

"Yeah, he's the worst of the bunch, can't take his eyes off her," Monty said, following Dylan to the makeshift bar made of two long wooden planks placed across three barrels.

The two men had each ordered a whiskey when John Jacob joined them.

"We missed you two this afternoon at the picnic," he said after they had talked for a bit. "You should have seen my Rachel at the shooting match."

My Rachel, Dylan thought scornfully. *We'll see about that, old man.*

"No one could believe it when Rachel outshot everyone," John Jacob went on. "That didn't set too well with the old-timers who are used to taking turns at winning. But she walked away with that brand-new Colt revolver just the same. Said she was going to give her prize to me since she has no need of it," he added proudly.

Dylan frowned but said nothing.

"She sure is having a fine time here tonight." Monty noted. "I never seen her looking so pretty. Or with so many admirers, even that preacher man."

At least, Dylan thought with a pleased grin, she hadn't given the preacher her prize. Robinson had not moved from her side all evening.

Dylan's thoughts turned to the baskets that were to be bid on shortly. Had Rachel prepared one? Maybe he could worm the information out of Andrews.

John Jacob was also thinking about Rachel's basket as the auctioneer prepared to open the bidding. The last thing John Jacob wanted was for Robinson to win Rachel's basket. Then she'd be forced to sit with him and share the pie she'd baked. Just as he'd feared, the handsome preacher had been sniffing after her all evening.

"I don't guess Rachel baked a pie for the auction," Dylan said with a sly look.

"Matter of fact, she did," John Jacob replied, welcoming the chance to tip Dylan off. "A peach pie tied up in a pink ribbon."

The bidding began then, and when the willow basket with the pink ribbon was held up, several men made offers for it. But Dylan Quade won it handily with an outrageously high bid of ten dollars. As he went up to claim his prize, he grinned meaningfully at Rachel, who lowered her eyes and blushed as pink as the ribbon on her basket.

Before Dylan could make his way through the crowd to her, a fiddle and banjo struck up a favorite mountain tune. Both men and women jumped to their feet and started hopping and jumping to the tune.

Rachel loved its rhythm and couldn't keep her toes from tapping. Dylan was wading toward her through the crowd, and she'd be in heaven if he asked her to dance. Just then a large figure loomed up before her, and before she could object, the shaggy-haired mountain man had swept her into his arms. "I seed you wanted to dance, little girl, and them other gents wasn't gonna ask you, so I said to myself, 'By God, I'll do the honors.' "

To her horror, Rachel realized she recognized the man. He was the same one who had tried to force himself on her at the post.

Dylan had lost sight of Rachel momentarily when everyone stood up to begin dancing. The next time he spotted her, she was struggling with the mountain man. He couldn't believe that all those men who had been acting like sick calves over her a few minutes ago were now letting that tobbaco-chewing galoot force her to dance with him. But he recognized the man's fat shape, even if he hadn't seen his face before, and Dylan knew he was up to no good.

Hardly knowing what he was doing in his rage, he sped across the floor, grabbed the man by the collar and jerked him away from Rachel. The fat man went flying across the room, coming to rest against a wall. The man shook his head as if to clear it, then sprang to his feet. Dylan put up his clenched fists and waited for him to come charging toward him.

But the man didn't plan to fight with fists. Instead, he had a hunting knife clenched in his hand. Dylan's mouth went dry. The blade looked at least ten inches long, and he had never fought with a knife. He had no idea how to handle himself. Even if he did, he didn't have a knife on him. The only time he carried one was when he was up in the mountains running his traps.

I guess I'm a dead one, he thought, when a familiar voice rang out. "Here, Dylan, use mine."

Dylan caught the handle of the knife Monty tossed to him. A little hope grew inside him, especially when Monty called out, "You've seen me fight many times with knives. Try to remember the things I taught you."

"Thanks, Monty," Dylan said, wishing he was wearing his moccasins instead of his nearly new boots. He would be sliding all over the place on the slick leather soles.

He looked at Monty for reassurance. "Can you keep the rest of that rabble from joining this no-good jackass?"

Monty gave a short laugh. "If I can't, these townspeople can. He's on his own. Go get him, Boss."

Dylan wished he had the same confidence his foreman had. He knew this ugly, tobbaco-chewing mountain man was out to kill him.

The crowd drew back to give them room, and they began circling each other. The lights from the lanterns hanging on the wall flashed on the thin blade that was trying to end Dylan's life.

Dylan lunged desperately at his opponent, but the mountain man had a longer reach and was able to fend him off. Then, just as he'd feared, Dylan's foot slid on his slippery sole. He hit the ground hard, the breath knocked out of him. His adversary was straddling him then, his arm raised to bring the blade into Dylan's heart.

I'm a goner, Dillion was thinking just as

Rachel's voice cried out, "No, no! Stop him, somebody!"

The anguished cry had barely faded away when there came the sharp crack of a revolver. The mountain man continued to straddle Dylan a moment, then leaped up, howling. A round bullet hole gaped in his right forearm.

Dylan rolled up to his feet. Who had saved his life? he asked himself as the mountain man disappeared through the barn door. If Monty wasn't standing beside him, he'd think his friend had fired the revolver.

"Who saved my life?" he asked unsteadily as Monty followed him outside while the dancing began again in the barn. They could hear the sound of fading hoofbeats as the fat man galloped off.

"I wish I could say that I did, old friend, but there was so many people crowding around, I was afraid I would hit some innocent person. I can tell you one thing—whoever fired that bullet was a crack shot. Maybe you have a friend that you don't know about."

Just then he spotted Rachel coming through the outside door. The preacher was with her, holding her elbow in a proprietary manner. Dylan wanted to walk up to them and smash the preacher in the mouth.

He contained himself, though. He had been involved in enough violence for one night.

"They're coming here toward us," Monty said. "I wonder what they want with two ole cowboys."

Dylan gave him a devilish grin. "Maybe Rachel wants a stronger sniff of that scent you splashed all over yourself."

Before Monty could make a sharp retort, Rachel and the preacher had joined them. "It's too bad you tangled with that Web Spencer," Preacher Robinson said, the concern in his voice sounding a little forced. "I know the family. Any one of them would kill a man without concern. The women are almost as bad."

"Jenny Quade must be related to them," Rachel laughed.

"Actually, she is," Robinson said on a serious note. "She's a sister to Web."

Monty looked at Dylan and said, half seriously and half in jest, "I guess you'd better stay away from the mountains for a while."

"I expect so," Dylan agreed, "but I'm not going to hide from that bunch. My Colt is just as deadly as their knives are."

"But keep in mind that they won't hesitate to back-shoot you," Monty warned.

"I'm aware of that," Dylan said. "I'll keep an eye on my back trail."

"Lucky for you Rachel was watching your back tonight," Robinson said.

"Rachel?" Dylan asked, surprise in his tone.

"Who did you think shot Web Spencer?" she said with a twinkle in her eye. "I couldn't let you always be saving my life without returning the favor."

"She whipped out that Colt she won this afternoon, took aim and shot him cool as you please," Robinson explained.

"My God, Rachel," Monty exclaimed. "Now you'll have to be careful up in the mountains, too. Spencer will never forgive a woman for getting the better of him."

Dylan looked at her a long time. When he finally spoke, his voice was deadly serious. "John Jacob told us you're going to take up your mama's work as an herbalist. When you go up the mountain to dig your roots and plants, don't go alone. Why don't you let me come with you? It's because of me that you might be in danger. The least I can do is make sure you're safe up there."

Rachel shuddered, remembering her helplessness as she'd tried to fight off the fat man. "Maybe you're right, at least till Spencer finds someone else to be mad at. I was planning to visit Granny Hawkins tomorrow. There are so many questions I want to ask her about the reading I've been doing."

"Well, that's fine then. I'll ride along with you. I've been wanting to go see Granny myself. I'm hoping she can give me seeds to start a garden at the ranch." Dylan smiled at Rachel, then looked at Monty and said, "I'm ready to go home, what about you?"

"But the dancing's just started," Monty objected.

"And you haven't had a chance to turn some poor girl's head with that scent you're wearing," Dylan laughed.

"What about you, Rachel?" Preacher Robison asked with a hopeful gleam in his eye. "Would you like to dance? With a gentleman this time?"

Rachel shook her head. "I've had enough excitement for one evening. I think I'm ready to call it a night too. Would you mind escorting me home, Dylan? I don't want to bother John Jacob. He and Rosie looked like they were having so much fun dancing together."

Rachel's matter-of-fact statement took Dylan's breath away for a moment. Had he heard her right? But she was looking straight at him. She had actually said that Andrews was dancing with another woman and she seemed completely unconcerned. And she'd asked him, Dylan, to take her home.

As Monty and the preacher returned to the barn, one looking eager, the other sullen, Dylan thought that this evening couldn't have turned out better if he'd planned it. When he had mounted the black and helped Rachel up in front of him, he asked as he gathered up the reins, "Did you ride Goldie to the picnic?"

"No," Rachel answered. "John Jacob drove us all down in the wagon. Monty will tell him I've gone home with you, so he won't worry."

She shivered as he tightened his arms around her, not from cold but from the proximity of Dylan's hard, warm body. Perhaps John Jacob was right. Perhaps Dylan was serious about her. His actions tonight certainly seemed to say so.

As they started up the river road, Rachel leaned back in Dylan's arms. She looked up at him, smiled and started to speak. At that moment there came the report of a rifle and a bullet ricocheted off a rock and whined past them. Devil shied, and Dylan tightened the reins and guided the stallion into a nearby stand of spruce. He swung down, putting his hand over the black's muzzle to keep him quiet.

"It must be Spencer," he said, pulling Rachel from the saddle and drawing her behind two large trees that grew close together. After a moment there came the sound of galloping hooves.

When the sound faded into the distance, Dylan helped Rachel back in the saddle, then remounted himself. "He must have been waiting for us," he said, lifting the reins. "I thought he'd head straight up the mountain for home since he's wounded."

"I guess the chance to take a potshot at us was too good to pass up," Rachel said as Dylan kicked Devil into action.

"We've got an enemy, all right," Dylan said. "The sooner I get you home, the safer you'll be." With that, he set the stallion at a pace that made further conversation impossible.

As Dylan drew up in front of the trading post, he was furious with himself for putting Rachel in danger. If only he'd killed Spencer when he'd had the chance, none of this would be happening.

"You be careful from now on," he cautioned. "Don't go riding alone. Don't even step outside after dark. There's a lot of places a sniper can hide back in the timberline."

Dylan's voice was short and sharp. Rachel looked at him and saw that his right hand rested on his thigh, only inches from the heavy Colt stuck in his belt. She knew he wouldn't hesitate to use it if he had to. She remembered the way he'd beaten Spencer at the post. Dylan was a man who knew how to handle himself in a fight. She felt safe in his company.

"I'll come for you tomorrow around noon," Dylan said as he helped her to dismount. "You'd better hurry inside now. No telling who's lurking about." He started to turn away, then hung back a little. "One more thing. I don't know if that preacher man is all that God-fearing. Be careful of his smooth talk."

Rachel looked up at Dylan with sparkling eyes. "I wonder if he could be like a certain other man who is not so God-fearing," she said.

Dylan felt his face flushing, but before he could get his tongue in gear, Rachel was running up the gravel path to the post. She hopped up on the porch, her laughter ringing out.

A wide smile curved Dylan's lips as he stared after Rachel. She had a lot of sass, teasing him about that night when neither one of them had been very decorous.

Rachel was preoccupied with thoughts of Dylan as she washed her face and changed into a nightgown. When she climbed into bed, she lay on her back a long time, listening to the hooting of an owl outside, recalling every word she and Dylan had exchanged.

When the big clock in the post room struck the midnight hour, Rachel turned over on her side. If only they hadn't been shot at on the ride home, she thought. It had been so romantic riding beside the river in the darkness, just the two of them. Surely Dylan would have spoken of his feelings for her. Instead, he'd issued nothing but warnings, even cautioning her about Preacher Robinson. She wondered if he and John Jacob were right about the handsome preacher. He certainly acted like a gentleman, and it was a fine thing he was doing, taking over the welfare of those orphan children. The two girls, around thirteen and fourteen, she thought, were so well-behaved. She didn't think they had moved once from the seat where the preacher had told them to sit.

All the same, Iva had called him a bastard, and there was something she didn't quite trust when she looked into the preacher's eyes.

As she fell asleep she was thinking about Dylan's devilish gaze, and how wonderful it had been that night he brought her indescribable pleasure.

Chapter Seventeen

Dylan was sitting atop a small hill watching the wild herd they had gathered. He and Monty had worked hard this morning driving them out of the brush and thickets. They hadn't taken just any horse that came along. Dylan was particular about the ones he would drive to his ranch. In time he wanted to raise only Morgans. They were the best of horseflesh, in his opinion. But until he could afford to buy some breeding stock, these wild mustangs would have to do. Once they were saddle broken, they made good cow ponies.

His mind drifted back to the night before and Rachel's surprising comment about John Jacob. Whatever Andrews's feelings for her might be, it seemed Rachel had no romantic interest in him. *Good*, Dylan thought, *that leaves a clear field for me*. He would have spoken of his feelings last night if Spencer hadn't bushwhacked them. Well, maybe he'd get a chance today.

He glanced up at the sun, which was almost directly overhead. Just about noon. He'd better get a move on. Swinging onto the stallion's back, he yelled to Monty, "I'm calling it quits for the day. I'm riding down to the post to meet Rachel."

"You're gonna take her up to see Granny Hawkins, right?" Monty said. "I'll come along, too, just to be sure Spencer doesn't cause any trouble."

When Dylan and Monty walked into the post, Rachel invited them to have some lunch while she saddled Goldie. In the kitchen, the cook had a big steak and fried potatoes waiting for them. When they had settled themselves at the table, Dylan looked at Andy and asked, "Is John Jacob around this morning?"

"No," Andy answered. "He's getting supplies in Jackson Hole."

"Do you have a paper and pencil, then?"

Without answering, Andy pulled a tattered tablet of paper from a kitchen drawer.

"Thanks," Dylan muttered as he picked up the stub of pencil accompanying the paper, whose corners were curled from age. When he had finished writing and folded the paper, he handed it to Andy.

"I want you to give this note to John Jacob and no one else. Do you understand? It's important he get it."

When Andy saw the seriousness on Dylan's face, he nodded. "Trust me, Dylan," he said gravely. "No one but he will lay eyes on it." He gave a short laugh. "As you know, I'm not much of a reader."

When Andy's face looked as if it might split from curiosity, Dylan explained, "Monty and I are taking Rachel up the mountain to see Granny Hawkins. Last night someone took a potshot at the two of us. We're pretty sure it was that mountain man Web Spencer. I want John Jacob to know it's important that there's a man around here to protect Rachel in case Spencer comes around the post looking for her."

"I guess I could protect her if the occasion arose," Andy said, a hurt tone in his voice.

"I know you would try your best, Andy," Dylan placated, "but this man I'm concerned about is a sneaky devil. I hope if the time comes, I can shoot him dead."

"You can do it, Dylan. You're the best gun-hand in these parts."

"Thank you, Andy." Dylan smiled at the grave-faced cook. "But this man doesn't face his adversaries. He's the type to hide behind a tree and shoot a fellow in the back."

Andy shivered. "Do you think he wants to shoot Rachel? It would kill John Jacob if anything happened to her."

"That's why Monty and I are going up the mountain with her. I think the man has worse things in mind for her."

A string of oaths escaped Andy's mouth when he realized what Dylan was hinting at. "If you know who he is, Dylan, let's go get the bastard. Shoot him in the back if necessary."

"No. Then we'd be no better than he is. We've got to catch him in the act to get proof. Then he'll stand trial and hang for his crime."

As Andy nodded his head in satisfaction, Dylan and Monty rose from the table. "Looks like Rachel's got Goldie ready. You can tell John Jacob we'll be back before dark."

A couple of old coon hounds announced the small party's arrival. When Jassy threatened to kick them off the mountain, the dogs quieted down and approached the three riders, their ropy tails swishing back and forth.

Granny sat in the shadows of the porch, rocking in an old bent wood chair. She stood and walked to the edge of the porch. "Rachel, honey, I'm glad to see you. What are you doing up here with these two handsome devils?"

"Oh, Granny," Rachel laughed. "They just came along for the ride. There was a speck of trouble at the church picnic yesterday, and now Dylan insists that it's not safe for me to ride up here alone."

Rachel went on to tell Granny about her plan to become an herbalist, and the old woman invited them all in to her homey little cabin. When Granny had finished answering Rachel's questions, she turned to Dylan.

"If you're not worn out from workin' cattle all day, I'd like for you to take a little walk with me."

"Now, Granny, you know I'm never too tired to take a walk with a pretty woman." He smiled down at her and took her thin arm to help her over the ruts and rocks as they went outside.

"I didn't ask you that, you smooth-talkin' galoot," she said, giving Dylan a toothless smile.

Dylan patted the thin, work-worn hand that lay on his arm. "What is your problem, Granny?" he asked soberly.

The old woman sighed. "It's about Jassy," she said in a low voice.

"Jassy?" He gave Granny a sharp look. "I can't imagine that child giving you trouble."

"Oh, no, Dylan. The girl has never given me a speck of trouble." Granny said no more for a while, and Dylan waited patiently for her to explain.

"It's the mountain men, Dylan. Now that she's turned sixteen, they're all sniffing after her, and that innocent child doesn't even know it. But I know what they're up to. I know their kind. I never let Jassy go huntin' ginseng alone anymore. A couple times I saw a man sneakin' along behind her in the woods. I've been walkin' her to school in the morning and bringin' her home in the afternoon. But now that school is out for the summer, I can't keep an eye on her every minute of the day and I just can't keep her locked up in that cabin with me all the time."

"No, that's not fair to a young girl like her."

"I know that, Dylan, but I can't stand to see one of those no-account men get her. Most of the mountain men have no ambition, and their wives live in constant drudgery. They and their children live in gnawing poverty all their lives."

They turned around and started back toward the old cabin. When it came in sight, Dylan said, "Why don't you send her down to spend a few weeks with Rachel? It'll do Jassy good to see how folks in the valley live, and I'm sure John Jacob wouldn't object. By the time school starts again, maybe her cousin will have showed her a thing or two about how to keep an unwanted man at a distance. Rachel sure knows how to do that," he said ruefully.

Granny was silent for a second, then said, "I think it's a fine idea. I can't do much to help Jassy in that regard."

Dylan looked at Granny and teased, "I bet there is still plenty of strength in those skinny arms."

"You'd be right if I had to protect my Jassy. I've always regretted that I left Ruthie alone in the house when I went into the woods to dig roots."

A ragged sigh escaped Granny as she thought of her younger daughter. "That's when that no-account Rafe Robins came along and raped my little Ruthie. I never wanted her to marry a mountain man, but it's the law up here. Once a girl has been used by a man, she has to marry him, or be considered a fallen woman the rest of her life.

"Ruthie tried her best to be a good wife, keeping his shack clean and cooking him good meals, but it was no use. That Rafe, may he rot in hell, didn't appreciate it. He beat her every day."

"She was Jassy's mother?" Dylan asked.

"Her grandma," the old lady sighed. "Her ma was Pansy, the only one of Ruthie's younguns to survive."

"I'm so sorry, Granny," Dylan said, hugging her narrow shoulders. "We'll make sure Jassy has a very different life. I'm going to be keeping a close eye on Rachel anyway. I promise I won't let anything happen to either of the girls."

There were tears of gratitude in the old woman's eyes. "Thank you, Dylan. You've put this old heart at ease. How can I ever repay you?"

"Well, I know one thing you can do," he said with a grin. "Give me some seeds so I can get a little garden started down at the Bar X."

"A garden?" Granny asked. "What does a bachelor like you need a garden for, and when would you ever have time to tend it?"

"Well, I'm hoping to have a woman around the place before too much longer," Dylan admitted sheepishly.

"So that's the way of it," Granny cackled. "You've got your work cut out for you if you've got in mind the girl I think you do."

"Jassy might as well go back to the post with us now," Dylan said, hoping to change the subject. "That way we won't have to make an extra trip. Also," he added, "there's going to be a dance at the schoolhouse next Saturday. Jassy will enjoy that, I think."

"That's a great thought," Granny said, "but the

child has no fancy clothes for something like that. Besides, she don't know how to dance."

Dylan laughed good humoredly. "There's nothing to dancing, Granny. It's just hopping and jumping to music. As for clothes, Rachel has enough to dress both of them for a year."

"Jassy will be so proud, wearing a fancy dress," Granny said. "It will be the first one she ever wore."

When Dylan and the old lady returned from their walk, they found Monty, Rachel and Jassy sitting on the porch, sipping tea.

"You were gone a long time," Jassy complained. "You must have had a lot to talk about."

"Well, Miss Smarty, we did," Granny said.

"Do I get to know what you gabbed about?"

"Maybe. If you bring us a glass of that sassafras tea you made for the others."

Jassy was on her little bare feet and almost out of sight before Granny Hawkins got the words out of her mouth.

"That girl does love her 'sas tea," the old lady laughed.

It was but a moment before the screen door slammed, announcing Jassy's return. She shoved a cool glass of tea in Dylan's hand, then sat down on the porch step beside him. She barely waited for him to take a swallow of the tasty herbal tea before asking eagerly, "What do you think? Is it worth telling me what you and Granny was talkin' about?"

Dylan smacked his lips a couple of times, then, looking at Rachel, said, "I'm not sure. What do you think, Rachel? Maybe it could use a little more sugar."

Jassy knew he was teasing by the twinkle in his eyes. She grabbed his hand and threatened, "I'll break your thumb if you don't tell me."

"Go ahead and tell her, Dylan," Monty said from his seat on the porch. "Tell her it's not fit to drink."

"It is too, you dunderhead," Jassy screeched, and her slender little feet were off the porch as she flung herself at Monty.

"Ouch!" he yelled when she filled her fingers with his hair. "I take it back!" he yelled. "It's the best damn tea I ever drank.

"You're sure?" She gripped his hair a little harder.

"I swear it's the truth."

Dylan was laughing so hard he could hardly catch his breath. Jassy had Monty on his belly, her skinny legs straddling him. She looked like a little tree frog clinging to him.

She crawled off him, demanding, "Well, am I going to be privy to your secret, Dylan?"

"Tell her, Dylan, before she kills me."

Dylan was tempted to laugh at his friend, but Monty's face wore a strange look, a cross between fascination and bewilderment. And he was uncharacteristically quiet the rest of the day.

Jassy was over the moon when Granny told her

she would be spending a few weeks with her cousin. In no time she had gathered together her meager belongings and saddled her little mare Polly for the ride down the mountain.

As they were nearing the post, Rachel turned to Dylan. "Would you like to see the cabin John Jacob is building for me?" she asked shyly. "The men have only been working on it a week or so, but you'd be surprised how fast its coming along."

"I'd like that," Dylan said as Monty led Jassy off to the post stable.

"I'm glad you're gonna have your own place," he added. "Tongues like to wag here on the river. The women will stop debating over whether you're sleeping with John Jacob now."

"Interfering busybodies," Rachel said sharply. "My relationship with John Jacob is nobody's business but my own."

"Not even mine?" Dylan asked quietly. "Would you say yes if he asked you to marry him?"

"John Jacob?" she laughed. "No, I certainly would not. I was forced to marry once, and I'm going to take my time before I marry again and have a houseful of children. I don't want to die young from childbearing and hard work."

"If you marry a man who loves you, none of that would happen," Dylan said, wishing he had the nerve to speak to her more directly. What was it about this girl that always tied his tongue in a knot?

"Hah!" Rachel snorted. "I'm sure half the women on the mountain were told a pretty tale of how wonderfully they would be treated. They received their first beating on their wedding night."

"I know that's true of many mountain men, but if you marry a rancher, you'll find they are more civilized," Dylan said, trying to smooth the way for his declaration.

"I'm not taking a chance for a long time," Rachel said stubbornly as they dismounted. "John Jacob is supplying me a home and I can dig roots and such, so I'll do fine making a living for myself." *And you're the only man I want for a husband*, she added silently.

"Yes." Dylan nodded. "You're luckier than most. But I wonder if you'll really be safe living here all alone, especially with Web Spencer on the loose."

Rachel whipped the Colt out of her pocket so fast Dylan stopped in his tracks. "I never go anywhere without this now," she said. "John Jacob told me to keep it after last night. He said not to hesitate a minute to use it if Spencer threatens me."

"He told you right. That is, if you have time to pull it out of your pocket. Just don't ever leave the house without it. In fact, sleep with it under your pillow at night. Then even if I'm not with you, honey"—he grinned—"I'll know you're safe."

Rachel took Dylan through the shell of the cabin, pointing out which space would be the kitchen, where the fireplace would be and the location of the two bedrooms.

"It's a good-sized place for one little ole female," Dylan joked when they left the half-finished building. "You're going to be lost in it."

"I'm sure she'll have plenty of company there," came Jenny Quade's voice from behind them.

Rachel's face grew tight with anger. "Every time I turn around, I find you behind me. Why are you following me?"

"I ain't followin' you. I just happen to be in the same place as you are sometimes."

"It never happened before, and I want it stopped. I don't trust you. I know you're up to something."

"Yo're tetched in the head," Jenny muttered and took off up the mountain.

"Do you believe what you said?" Dylan asked as they resumed walking toward the post, leading Devil and Goldie behind them.

"Yes, I meant every word of it. Ever since Jenny learned to walk and talk she has been a troublemaker. It took the mountain people a while to realize that half of what she says are lies intended to cause somebody grief. A lot of women have been badly beaten by their husbands because of the lies Jenny told them.

"I know that she's hatching up some kind of trouble for me. I gave her a beating last week that she won't ever forget or forgive."

Dylan agreed. "She strikes me as the type who

would carry a grudge to the grave. Honey, for a pretty little thing you sure have made a passel of enemies around here. When your cabin is finished and you move into it, I want you to take my dog Shadow with you. He'd let you know in a minute if someone was sneaking around the place."

"I appreciate that, Dylan," Rachel said, blushing, "but won't he miss you?"

Dylan grinned. "We'll just have to make sure I'm around too much for that to happen."

They had reached the post, and Rachel turned to look up at him as she stood before the porch rail where she'd tied Goldie. "I want to go out hunting ginseng tomorrow. Jassy says she knows where a big patch is growing. Will you have time to come along?"

"I will if you wait for the afternoon. Why don't we meet where the trail to the Bar X turns off the river road?" he suggested.

"We'll be there at three." She was about to step up on the porch when he turned her into his arms and lowered his mouth to hers. One hard kiss and he was swinging himself up on Devil and galloping off down the trail.

Rachel felt a warm glow as she stepped into the post. Andy had started a fire in the fireplace and lit the six wall lamps in the big room. Jassy and Rosie and the girls were sitting at a table with little Benny and Colby, at a table eating their supper. Even Iva was there, and it was rare to see her out of bed these days. The middle-aged piano player sat at the badly out-of-tune keyboard, managing to coax a soft melody from it.

A happy sigh escaped Rachel. There had never been enough light in the old shack where she grew up. There was only one coal-oil lamp affixed to the wall in the kitchen, and its wick was always turned down so low it was hardly worth lighting it. There was no lamp in the bedroom and none in the main room. Only candles and the light from the fireplace.

And there were never delicious aromas coming from the kitchen like there always were from John Jacob's kitchen. Andy, the cook, mixed up dishes the likes of which she had never tasted before.

In her bedroom she found that someone had lit the lamp there, too. Her gaze went to the feather bed in the corner and lingered a minute, admiring the colorful quilt spread over it. Her mother would have loved it so. For one who had appreciated beauty so, her poor little mother hadn't seen a great deal of it.

Rachel walked to the sturdy dresser opposite the bed and pulled out the middle drawer. She rubbed her hands over the neatly folded underclothing and nightgowns lying there. When she had removed what she would put on the next morning, she closed the drawer and opened the one over it. She lifted from it a pretty blouse and a pair of denims. Heavy socks joined the other clothes. She put everything on a chair, a satisfied smile curving her lips. She could hardly wait to go hunting ginseng tomorrow.

Chapter Eighteen

"Hey, Dylan," Monty called. "We've found a good patch of ginseng. It's about five yards to your right."

Monty and Dylan had met the girls half an hour earlier and the four had set out through the woods to the spot Jassy had told Rachel about. Rachel was walking hand in hand with Dylan, leaving the younger girl to search with Monty.

As the four bent down to examine the plants Jassy had found, Monty turned to the girl. "Do you want to be my partner? I bet we can find more ginseng than those two can. They wouldn't even know where to look."

"Oh you think so, do you?" Dylan smiled widely at Rachel. "Do you want to make a bet with them?" he asked.

"You bet I do," the smile Rachel gave him was so sweet he could hardly keep from sweeping her into his arms right in front of the other two.

"What will the wager be?" Monty asked.

"Something tells me you two are going to be paying more attention to each other than to any old ginseng."

"The loser has to bring a bottle of whiskey to the dance Saturday," Dylan said and hurried to lift a large pine branch for Rachel to walk under. Jassy frowned when Monty left her to lift the branch herself. She knew he saw her as nothing more than a little ragamuffin.

About three yards away from the big pine, the two pairs split up, Monty and Jassy going south and Rachel tugging Dylan to go west.

"Why do you want to go in that direction?" Dylan complained. "There's hardly any ginseng plants there."

"There's plenty of 'seng there, you'll see." Rachel grinned, seeing in her mind's eye her mother's patch of ginseng, hidden in a little hollow halfway up the mountain. Unless she was mistaken, it was only a few minutes' walk away.

"I love it up here in the summer," she said wistfully as they made their way up the mountain. "It's cool and shady, and the waterfalls and wildflowers are so pretty."

Dylan looked at her. Rachel seemed a part of the forest, as wild and free as the mountain itself. Yet she was making a home for herself in the valley, too. Like him, she was drawn to both worlds.

They had come to a little hollow where there was a natural clearing in the trees. Rachel paused and began searching the ground.

"I think we've found your 'seng patch." Dylan said with a smile. "I can really smell it."

"What would you know about what 'seng smells like?" Rachel teased.

"I know a lot about such stuff." Dylan reached over and tweaked her nose. "I spent my early years running in the woods hunting roots and barks. When spring came and it was time to go down to the lowlands, I always had quite a cache to sell at the post."

"Well, if you know so much about wild herbs, tell me about some of them," Rachel teased.

"Well," Dylan began after thinking a while, "I'll start with 'seng. Ginseng is its real name of course. It is one of the best of all wild medicines. It also brings the highest price. If you can find several four-prongers, you'll get a lot of money for them. When I was about fifteen, I had a 'seng patch. You probably know that the plants have to be at least five years old before they bring any big money.

"Well, my patch was just ready to be harvested when some sneak, I think it was a Sutter, came in the night and dug them all up.

"I don't mind telling you that I cried. For five years I'd waited for those plants to mature. I didn't know it, but somebody else was waiting, too."

Rachel placed her hand on Dylan's and gently squeezed. "I'm so sorry," she said softly. "Did you start another patch?"

"No." Dylan turned his hand over until their palms met. "I knew there was no use. Whoever stole the first bunch would be waiting and watching for the second growth to come along. I wasn't going to work for that thief again."

"I can't blame you, and you were probably right in thinking the thief was one of the Sutters. I never did feel like I was part of that family."

"You're as different from them as day is from night." Dylan smiled. "After that I did what the rest of the mountain people did. I hunted the woods. I best like to find young sourwood saplings. They have a lovely fragrance, and sourwood honey is very good for rheumatism and arthritis. Tea made from its bark is also a good stomach medicine. Then, of course, there is the dandelion, the first to come up in the spring. It's followed by Indian cucumber, wild ginger and wintergreen.

"Then come sheep sorrel and wood sorrel. Those two are rich in vitamin C. Then there's rhubarb. Use only the stems, though. The leaves are pure poison.

"Now," Dylan teased, "Let's hear what you know of mountain medicine."

"Well," Rachel said, grinning at him, "It's only fair that I tell you I've been reading my mother's notes. She was also a fair illustrator of wild plants, so I know how to recognize all the different herbs."

Dylan looked at her with amusement. "I think you're just talking to kill time."

"I am not!" Rachel shot back. "I know just as

much, if not more, than you do about plants, barks and roots. My mother taught me from the time I was little."

"Alright, let's hear some of the things your mama taught you." Dylan's eyes twinkled at her.

"Alright, Mr. Smarty. We'll start with salad plants. There are the plants that you mentioned, but let's add mustard greens, lamb's-quarter and cress. Then there are the spring tonics: sassafras tea, spicewood tea and sweet birch. Make sure to avoid the plants of the parsnip family.

"Then there are berries you didn't mention: blackberries and huckleberries, mulberries and—"

"Alright, that's enough," Dillion exclaimed with a laugh. "I admit that you know more than I do."

He put his arm around her and, gazing down at her as he played with a white-blond curl at the nape of her neck, he said huskily, "You are so beautiful, Rachel."

"Do you really think so, Dylan?" She reached out a hand to stroke his cheek.

"You know you are," he murmured as he captured her mouth with his own.

Jassy had wandered off a little distance from Monty as they hurried to gather as many ginseng roots as possible. He might annoy her mightily with his teasing and taunting, but she still wanted to help him win the wager. It would be Dylan Quade who had to bring the bottle of whiskey to the dance.

She smiled softly. She couldn't wait for Saturday. She wanted to think of her first party dress; how she would arrange her hair. She had no idea how to do that. She felt sure that Rachel would help her do it if she asked her to, but she hated to let her pretty cousin know just how ignorant she was.

Jassy never dressed her hair fancy. She most always wore the dark curls loose, hardly even bothered to brush them.

Jassy yanked a big healthy root out of the black loam just as Jenny Quade's voice whined behind her, "That's a right good root of 'seng. I hope you intend to share the money it brings you with your Quade relatives."

Jassy made no answer for a minute as she rubbed the dirt off the root, which resembled a little man. Then she looked up and said clearly, "Hope ahead, Jenny. Ain't no Quade gonna get a dime from this root. I don't count any of your family as kin of mine. I only have Granny Hawkins. She's the only one who would take me in when my ma died."

"Well," Jenny said, her hands on her hips, "act the big lady while you can. You think you're special, staying at the post with Miss Uppity Rachel? I know what'll bring you down a peg or two. My brother Web has his eye on you. He'll teach you to sass me."

"You think so, do you?" Jassy glared at her. "I'll just tell Monty and Dylan what your brother is plannin' to do. He'll put a stop to that real fast."

"Hah! those cowboys couldn't stand up to a mountain man for two minutes."

"I'll tell you one thing," Jassy said, scowling at Jenny, "they would never hide behind a tree and shoot a man in the dark."

Jenny's voice tightened. "Our mountain men don't do that kind of thing," she squeaked.

"Your brother did, and you know it," Jassy retorted. "Rachel told me all about it."

Jenny had opened her mouth to argue further when a light rain began to fall. Relief was plain on her face. She had a good excuse to walk away, now. Jassy hid a look of amusement.

"Just remember what I told you," Jenny threatened as she turned away.

"Oh, I will, never fear," Jassy said as she bent over and formed a big ball of mud. Her skinny arm wound up and sent the mud ball right at the back of Jenny's head. It looked for a minute as if Jenny would retaliate, but then she struck off through the trees.

Dusk had been hastened by the rain, and the forest was suddenly gloomy and somehow frightening to Jassy. Where had Monty disappeared to? The trees became figures of men who stalked her, and Jassy shivered.

"You just put such thoughts out of your head," she muttered to herself as she walked cautiously and quietly. Ever since she could remember she had walked these trails. They were lonely, wild paths, ones a wise man trod with caution.

She had just rounded a curve in the trail when she came up against a hard male figure. The breath was knocked out of her and she staggered backwards.

"You!" she gasped, terrified to recognize the burly form of Web Spencer. His shaggy hair was filthy, and around his right arm was wrapped a bloody bandage.

"Well, now, ain't you turned into a purty little thing." He gripped both her upper arms, holding her fast.

Jassy knew she was in trouble. Twice this man had tried to accost her cousin. He wouldn't think twice about forcing himself on a young girl alone in the woods.

Jassy began to tremble. She would be helpless against this big brute of a man. She had no weapon with her, nothing to stop him from raping her.

Out of the corner of her eye she saw Jenny dart behind a tree. *The bitch*, she thought; *she put him up to this.*

She tensed her muscles and gathered her strength, ready to do battle with this huge mountain of a man. She kicked and scratched, at the same time screaming at the top of her voice. He might have his way with her, but it wouldn't be easy.

Gradually she realized she was losing the battle. She could feel her arms and legs weakening; even her voice was growing fainter. As she felt herself being slowly pushed to the ground, into the mud, with the rain peppering her face, she was only gasping her cry for help.

Jassy couldn't believe it when suddenly Web Spencer's fat body was lifted off her as if it weighed only a few pounds. Panting for air, she gazed up at her liberator.

"Vamoose," the man said, pointing a rifle at Web Spencer, and the fat man scrambled away into the forest.

However, when she got a close look at the bushy, bearded face gazing down at her, Jassy wasn't so sure she was out of danger. The man was a wild lobo who ran the hills alone. She had seen him many times over the years, slipping through the trees. And though he always peered at her, she never felt any fear of him. Even stranger, Granny never got upset when Jassy told how she had seen the raggedy wild man. She had asked her great-grandmother why she didn't fear the strange fellow who ran through the mountains like some wild animal. "Aren't you afraid he will do me harm some day?"

"Jasper Dunn will never harm you, child," the old woman had answered, but she would say no more.

"Are you alright, girl?" Jasper asked roughly but kindly. "That varmint didn't hurt you, did he? I got here in plenty of time, didn't I?"

Jassy didn't know exactly what Jasper meant by his getting there in time, but she had a pretty good idea. She gave him a wobbly smile and said, "Yes, sir, you got here in plenty of time."

The way the older man blushed, she had an idea that it was the first time anyone had ever smiled at him.

He was helping her to her feet when Monty came crashing through the rain. "Was that you yelling for help, Jassy?" he demanded as he came to a puffing halt. "Jasper," he said before Jassy could answer. "Did you do any harm to this little girl?" He pulled Jassy to his side.

"Dammit, young feller, if you'd keep your yap shut a minute, I'll tell you what you already know. I didn't touch this little girl in any harmful way. I'd cut my hand off first."

Monty gave a small, sheepish laugh. "I know that, Jasper. I was just so upset, I spoke without thinking."

He turned his attention to Jassy. "I've been searching for you for the last half hour, Jassy. What happened?"

"I got lost," Jassy answered in a voice that still shook a little. "And then Web Spencer found me. He tried . . . he tried . . . thank God Mr. Dunn came along when he did."

"I'll echo that," Monty said, then grinned at Jasper. "Let's go down to the post and I'll buy you a drink."

"Thanks, but I best be gettin' up the mountain and take care of my livestock. My old mule will be braying that he's hungry and the cow will want to be milked."

"Well, next time I see you in the Grizzly Bear, I'll buy you that drink," Monty said as they began to walk in different directions.

"Thank you for saving me from that awful Web Spencer," Jassy said just before Jasper disappeared around a curve in the path.

When the two of them met Rachel and Dylan returning to the post on the river road, Monty told them everything that had happened. "That Jasper looked as happy as if someone had given him a hundred dollars," he concluded.

Rachel nodded and said that she didn't imagine the reclusive fellow had received many thanks in his lifetime.

Chapter Nineteen

Dylan stood beside the corral at the Bar X, watching the mustangs. He'd begun the arduous process of taming the wild horses, but he wanted to round up still more. He knew the army would pay well for as many saddle-broken mounts as he could provide. He and Monty were planning to ride out the following day to go after a small herd he'd located several miles away.

But first they'd kick up their heels at the schoolhouse tonight. It had fallen to Dylan to bring the bottle of whiskey to the dance. He and Rachel had spent more time kissing than gathering ginseng that afternoon, and Monty had won the wager. Dylan couldn't say he regretted the way he'd spent his time, though. He grinned. He was looking forward to more of the same tonight.

Those thoughts were driven from his mind by the sound of galloping hooves approaching. Monty drew up beside him in a cloud of dust.

"What's your hurry?" Dylan asked, shading his

eyes from the setting sun as he looked up at his friend.

"I've just come from the post," Monty said, swinging down from his horse. "Poor Iva's real bad off. Doc Johnson says there's nothin' more he can do for her, but there's a specialist in Denver who might be able to help her. John Jacob's gonna take her there."

"What about Rachel and Jassy?" Dylan demanded. "Who's going to protect the girls from all those rough men at the post?"

"That's just it," Monty said. "John Jacob is afraid Web Spencer might come round while he's gone. He wants you to stay down at the post till he gets back."

"Damn!" Dylan swore angrily. "What am I to do for all that time down at the post? And what about that herd of wild horses we want to go after? They won't wait till Andrews gets back," he fumed. "We can't leave Rachel at the post with only the protection of the cook either. You know Andy gets drunk every evening after he finishes serving supper."

"He'd be no use at all," Monty agreed.

"Well, we can talk about that later. I'd better pack up a few things and ride down there," Dylan said, striding toward the ranch house.

"Yeah, John Jacob already took off with Iva. Rachel's trying to comfort them two little tykes, now their ma's gone."

It was almost dusk as the two men tied their

horses up at the hitching rail in front of the post. Rachel poked her head out the door in answer to their knocking.

"I'll be out in a minute, fellows," she said, her voice hushed. "I'm just trying to get Benny and Colby settled down for the night. Rosie says she'll sit with them while we go to the dance. The poor little mites are all broken up about their ma."

When the door closed behind her, Dylan turned to Monty. "I've been thinking on what to do about Rachel and Jassy."

"Have you come up with any ideas?" Monty asked as they settled into chairs on the porch.

"Well," Dylan said after a stretch, "I've come up with one conclusion. I have to keep after my wild horses. The money I make from their sale will buy feed for my cattle through the winter and leave some cash left over to begin buying breeding stock. This is the only chance I'll have to go after that herd of mustangs before we start the trail drive to Abilene."

"So what's your idea? Come on, tell me." Monty grinned at Dylan. "It couldn't be any wilder than some other things that have jumped up in that empty head of yours over the years."

Dylan said gruffly, "We could take the girls with us on the mustanging."

A wide smile split Monty's face. "That's a fine idea, but I doubt Rachel would want to go with us. She's taking her responsibility to Colby and Benny very seriously."

"But those boys aren't in any danger here, and Rachel is. Rosie could look after the kids. We'd only be gone a night or two." Dylan pointed out.

"I think it's a great idea," Jassy burst out, letting the door slam behind her as she breezed onto the porch.

"Have you been eavesdropping on us?" Monty demanded.

"Of course not," Jassy replied indignantly. "I just happened to overhear what you were saying."

"I think that's a big blazer," Monty said, laughter in his eyes when he looked at her.

"It's not a lie!" Jassy said angrily. "Anyway, I bet Rachel would be happy to go with you. She loves horses, you know."

"That's true, she does," Dylan mused, "but she wouldn't care to sleep out at night, listen to the wolves howl."

"That is a poser," Monty said thoughtfully. "But she'd be safer out there in the wilderness with us than back here with the two-legged wolves that hang around this place."

Just then Dylan whispered, "Shh, I hear Rachel coming. Let me do all the talking," he cautioned Monty.

"Here you are, Jassy." Rachel smiled at her cousin as she sat down in a chair on the porch. "It's almost time for us to get ready." She looked over at Dylan and Monty and asked with a smile, "What are you two gabbing about?"

"We're just discussing a band of wild horses we

want to go after. We were planning to ride out tomorrow, but now we're stumped. You know John Jacob wants me to stay here at the post while he's gone," Dylan began.

Jassy shot him a sly look, then heaved a deep sigh. "I wish I could go with you men. I've always wanted to go mustanging. Sleep out under the stars, eat food cooked over an open fire."

"I don't suppose Granny would let you go with us," Monty said, playing along.

"She might if Dylan asked her," Jassy answered promptly. "She thinks the only reason the sun comes up is to shine on him."

"Hah!" Monty snorted. "Your granny doesn't know him like I do. Why, if I had a daughter, I wouldn't let him get within a mile of her. What does Granny Hawkins think of me, Jassy?"

"You're another story. Monty Hale." Jassy gave him a playful punch on the arm. "Granny says that you're a dickens, but that at heart you're an honorable man who wouldn't take advantage of a nice girl."

Monty looked at her teasingly and asked slyly, "Are you a nice girl, Jassy?"

"It's none of your business," Jassy flared out, "but I'll tell you anyhow."

Her eyes flashing dangerously, she opened her mouth to tell her tormentor that she was indeed a nice girl, but Monty spoke first.

"You don't have to tell me." He gave her a crooked grin. "I can see what you are. You're a scrawny-looking little girl who never brushes her hair or washes her face."

Monty regretted his words as soon as they left his mouth. Jassy's dirty little face had turned bright red with embarrassment. She jumped up and darted away.

"You went too far, this time, friend," Dylan said disapprovingly.

Monty snorted a laugh that didn't ring true. "I'm sure she's heard worse from other men. She will have forgotten about what I said by the time she gets to the schoolhouse."

"I somehow doubt that," Dylan said, then, cupping his hands around his mouth, he called, "Jassy, come on back here."

Jassy's only response was to dart behind the building toward the kitchen door.

"I hope she's not crying," Rachel said.

"You know something, Monty," Dylan said, "those hateful words you said to Jassy are going to come back some day and slap you in the face. Beneath the dirt and rags she wears is a lot of beauty."

Monty's only answer was a snort of disbelief. "She'd be an old woman by the time she scraped the dirt off her face, never mind combed the snarls out of her hair. I'm surprised Granny lets her go around looking like that."

Dylan made no response to his friend's disparaging words. He had his own thoughts about the girl. He had a hunch that the old woman deliberately encouraged Jassy to run around looking like a ragamuffin. The men wouldn't be interested in her if she looked like a dirty little ten-year-old.

But he'd bet his last dollar that more than one man had seen beneath the dirt and ragged clothes and seen the beauty that lay there.

When they heard the back door bang as Jassy took refuge inside the post, Rachel looked at Dylan and said wistfully, "I wish I could go mustanging with you, too."

"Do you think John Jacob would mind? It would be a dusty, hard trip."

"I'm not a softy, Dylan. I wouldn't cause a lot of work for you, and I'm good with horses. Besides I don't look forward to being alone here with old Andy."

"I know, honey," Dylan said. "Andy means well, but he wouldn't be much protection for you."

"No, he's not. He goes to bed right after supper every night, and you don't see him until the next morning."

Which is just as well, Dylan thought to himself. She wouldn't think so highly of the old man if she saw him stumbling around, talking to himself.

"Well, Dylan, what do you think? Can I go with you?"

Dylan wanted to shout his pleased laughter. Rachel had played right into his hands. He avoided Monty's amused eyes as he said, "I'll take a chance that John Jacob won't shoot me for taking you along."

"That's settled, then." Rachel jumped to her feet. "I'm going to go to my room now and help Jassy get ready for the dance." She turned to Monty with a mischievous grin on her face. "Just wait till you see her in my pink silk dress with a pretty ribbon in her hair. You're going to eat your words."

Chapter Twenty

The dance at the schoolhouse proved to be a boisterous, merry affair, with both townspeople and mountain folk in attendance. The fiddle player had them all kicking up their heels, but Monty found he had little desire to dance with the girls he usually pursued.

Ever since Jassy had walked out on the porch enveloped in a filmy gown of pale pink, he'd felt as if a mule had kicked him in the gut. In Rachel's borrowed dress, she no longer looked scrawny, but delicate and feminine. To his complete frustration, Monty found himself at a loss for words.

While the others had laughed and talked, Monty had hurried to get the wagon. Once they'd reached the schoolhouse, it had been even worse. Dylan immediately had swung Rachel into his arms, leaving Monty to stand awkwardly beside Jassy while all around them people danced and laughed.

Monty couldn't take his eyes off the trim little

figure who crossed the room now toward the punch bowl. Could this be the same Jassy he had teased so mercilessly just hours ago? he asked himself, his eyes raking over her glowing pink complexion, her long, wavy hair, black as a raven's wing.

Monty noticed then that he wasn't the only man in the room staring at her. He was wondering if he dared ask her to dance when their eyes met across the room. Jassy's bold gaze challenged him to treat her as anything less than a lady. With a grin, he headed toward the punch bowl to prove just how much of a gentleman he could be.

Dylan enjoyed the dance more than any other he could remember. For the first time in his life, he felt no desire to flirt with the girls who approached him or to sneak off behind the schoolhouse with one of them. He wanted only Rachel, couldn't get enough of holding her in his arms.

As he went to get a glass of punch for Rachel, he spotted Monty dancing with Jassy. "I think it's time we called it a night," he shouted in order to be heard over the music. "We want to get an early start tomorrow."

"Where you all going?" Preacher Robison asked from behind him. "You going to be gone long?"

Dylan turned and gave the preacher a cold look. "We're riding out to round up some mustangs. We'll be gone a couple days."

A quick discerning interest leapt onto the preacher's handsome face. "I hear John Jacob is on a trip, too. I believe I'll stop by the post to make sure Rachel is alright."

"That won't be necessary." Dylan looked at the dandy with faint disdain in his eyes. "Rachel is going with us. Jassy is coming along, too. She'll be company for Rachel."

Dylan saw disapproval growing on the smoothly handsome face and warned, "Don't speak aloud what you are thinking."

"How do you know what I'm thinking?"

"It's as easy as reading a book. You think it's not proper for the girls to go out alone with Monty and me."

"It surely is not," the preacher intoned with righteous indignation. "Purity and chastity are virtues to be guarded."

"You damned hypocrite," Dylan said in a hard tone. "I know how you visit the girls at the post when you think no one's looking."

"John Jacob would never—" Robison sputtered.

"John Jacob is the one who asked me to watch out for Rachel to make sure none of you men got near her. And no matter your holy words, preacher, you're a man just like the rest. Matter of fact, I have a hunch you've got a dirtier mind than some of the others." Dylan gave him a long, meaningful look.

The handsome man's face grew dark with anger. "How dare you speak that way to a man of the cloth?"

Dylan looked at the other man scornfully. "I dare plenty. And if you don't leave Rachel alone, I'll dare to smash your face in."

It looked at first as though Robison would hold his ground as he stood staring at Dylan, a sullen look in his eyes. But when Dylan took a step toward him, he spun around and hurried toward the door. Something told Dylan that he had made himself a bad enemy.

Jassy shivered and wrapped her arms around her silk-clad shoulders. The wind that blew down from the mountains was raw and cut right to the bone at night, unlike the days, which were warm and lazy.

She rubbed her tired feet as she waited for Monty to join her outside the schoolhouse. Dylan and Rachel were still inside making their farewells while Monty was fetching the wagon. He'd cautioned her to stay near the door while she waited, to avoid any men who might be lurking outside in the dark.

She grinned, remembering how every time a man started toward either her or Rachel with the intention of asking them to dance, Monty or Dylan stepped in front of him. Everyone in the schoolhouse knew what was happening and they all wore wide smiles. Some of the thwarted men were livid, but they knew if they started anything, they'd have a fight on their hands. Apparently, no one wanted to tangle with Dylan or Monty.

Still, Jassy was nervous and she started at every unusual sound. She would give a big sigh of relief when Monty returned with the horse and wagon. She still couldn't believe how nice he had been all night. She wondered if he would kiss her good night. Would she let him if he tried?

She was just wondering what could be taking so long when she glimpsed a movement at the corner of the schoolhouse. She made a motion toward the door, but a whispered caution advised her to stay still. She didn't know if she should heed the advice or not, but found she was frozen to the spot in fear.

As she watched the corner of the building with round eyes, there slowly emerged the shape of a large man. As he slowly and quietly advanced toward the door, just steps away from where Jassy stood in the shadows, her heart pounded frantically.

"Don't move, honey," that soft voice said again.

Two things happened then simultaneously. Jassy could see clearly now that the fat man was Web Spencer. She narrowed her eyes and peered at the male figure coming from the opposite corner of the building. Her heart gave a happy lurch. It was her new friend, Jasper Dunn.

"Oh, Jasper," she cried and took a step toward him.

"Stay where you are, honey," Jasper said quietly. "Me and this skunk has some business to settle."

"Are you sure you want to tangle with me,

lobo?" Spencer sneered. "What if I should go to the sheriff with what I know?"

Jasper dropped his hand on his Colt and said coldly, "If you've got a gun, use it."

The fat man's reaction was fast, but Jasper's was faster. His gun was a blur as it left the holster. Spencer went over backwards, landing in an awkward sprawl that said he was dead or near death.

Jasper shoved his Colt back in its holster and hurried to kneel beside Web Spencer. He lifted the fat man's wrist and felt no pulse. "You low-down polecat," he said in low tones that Jassy couldn't hear. "Take your secret to hell with you."

Jasper stood up. "Jassy, honey," he said quietly. "I think you'll find his horse tied up back in the pines. Bring it to me, will you?"

The horse was tied to a pine just a few yards behind the schoolhouse. "You poor old thing," she murmured, running a hand over his back and down his bony flank. "I don't know how you ever carried that big tub of lard around.

"What are you gonna do with the body?" Jassy asked as Jasper tugged Spencer onto the old nag's back.

"I'm going to send him to hell without anyone around here being the wiser," Jasper said in a matter-of-fact voice. "This is the second time he went after you, honey. I had to make sure there would never be a third." Once he had the body secured on the bony old horse, he said, "You go on back to the post with your friends now, honey, and forget anything you saw or heard tonight. If anyone ever asks you any questions about this skunk, you just say you don't know anything about him. That's why I'm not telling you anything. You won't be lying when you say you don't know nuthin' about Web Spencer."

Jasper waited until the schoolhouse door closed behind Jassy. There was such a ruckus going on inside, no one had noticed the sound of his gunshot. Grinning, he got on his mule and took off up the mountain. He had quite a ways to go, but he knew every step of the trail.

When he reached his destination, he slid out of the saddle, then tugged Spencer's body off his old horse. He dragged him to the edge of the bluff where Taig Sutter had met his end. "Seems fittin' you should meet the same end as that low-down bastard. May you rot in hell together." Jasper muttered as he heaved the corpse over the bluff. He did not wait to hear the body hit bottom.

"What to do with this old bag of bones?" he wondered out loud as he stood stroking Spencer's thin old horse. He might as well take this poor horse up to his place, a land that was lost and unvisited. No one ever came to call on Jasper Dunn . . . there would be no one to ask awkward questions.

He turned his horse's head up the mountain, and the bony gray plodded wearily behind him.

Chapter Twenty-one

When the morning sun rose above the horizon the next day, Dylan and Monty had three miles behind them and the horses were eager to travel. That wasn't true of the girls, though, when the men arrived at the post house to pick them up. Their huge yawns said they could sleep another four hours.

Andy had fixed them a big breakfast of bacon and sausage gravy, which they'd consumed in about fifteen minutes. Jassy said, "Don't tell Granny, but that was the best sausage gravy I ever had."

"I'll be sure to let Granny Hawkins know that the next time I see her," Monty said with a wicked grin.

"You'd better not," Jassy snapped, and their old squabbling was on once more.

"They don't care much for each other, do they?" Andy commented with a grin.

"Don't let their bickering fool you," Dylan said

as he rolled a smoke. "That bitchin' back and forth is just a smoke screen to hide their true feelings for each other."

And it become more evident as the day passed that Dylan was right. Now that Jassy was acting like a tomboy again, Monty never missed an opportunity to torment her. She, of course, came right back at him, calling him a tobacco-chewing cowpoke. Yet Rachel noticed that Monty couldn't seem to take his eyes off her cousin.

She'd become a good little rider, her movements were so graceful, she and her mare seemed to be as one. As they rode across the valley in search of the wild herd, Monty's gaze seldom strayed from Jassy.

As usual, Dylan had little to say. With his rope gathered into a coil and hung on the pommel of his saddle, he was ready to lasso any stray mustang they might come across. Rachel's eyes followed him as he led them north, his mind completely focused on the task at hand. She had decided some time ago that he was a hard man with a taste for wild horses and women. Would he ever give up the wild women and settle down with just one? Last night at the dance she'd begun to hope so. He hadn't danced with anyone except her. But was that just because John Jacob had asked him to keep an eye on her? When they'd returned to the post, she'd overheard Gracie and the girls talking about Dylan's staying power in bed. She agonized over every word when she went to bed last night. How could a man of such lusty appetites be satisfied with one woman?

At noon they stopped briefly, and the aroma of coffee and frying bacon filled the air. The meal was soon eaten and they mounted up again. The coolness of the morning vanished and the sun became hot. Sweat streaked the horses' hides and ran down the men and women's faces. Up ahead, heat waves danced about. In a short time everyone felt stupid with heat and weariness.

"Where do you think the wild herd is?" Jassy asked as she rode up alongside Dylan.

"Last time I saw them, they were grazing in a little valley on the other side of that stream."

"Do you think they'll still be there?"

Dylan nodded his head. "Wild horses tend to stay put till an area is grazed out."

"I never knew that," Jassy said just as thunder rumbled down from the mountain.

"I hope we come across a deserted house before the rain hits," Monty grumbled. "Them clouds are pure black and are gonna dump a lot of rain on us if we get caught in the storm. And the horses are feeling the heat. They are walking slower."

Nevertheless, when they neared a gulch, Dylan's black gathered himself and soared effortlessly across, running as he landed.

"That's some horse you've got there, Dylan. How did you come by him?" Rachel asked.

Dylan grinned. "I got him in a poker game . . . in a dead man's hand."

"What do you mean, a dead man's hand?" Jassy asked.

"You don't know much, do you, Jassy?" Monty teased. "Two black aces over a pair of eights is a dead man's hand."

When Jassy would have flared out at Monty, Dylan cautioned, "Stay sharp now. The mustangs are nearby. Look at the way Devil's ears are laid back. He smells the other stallion."

That quieted the two in short order. No one wanted to scare off the herd. There was complete silence as they circled around to position themselves downwind of the mustangs.

Suddenly it grew so dark it was like the dead of night. Then, without warning a veritable wall of rain hit them. Where would they go? Dylan asked himself, peering into the darkness. He could hardly see a foot ahead of him.

He could hear the mustangs' hooves as they began running ahead of him, and decided that they might know of some sheltered spot. He loosened the reins on the stallion's neck, hoping Devil would be able to follow the herd.

The big black gave a startled whinny and almost bucked Dylan off his back as he collided into something. Dylan grabbed up the reins just in time to keep from falling out of the saddle. Devil, blinded by the rain, had run into Monty's horse, almost knocking them both down.

"Are you alright?" they both called out in unison.

"I guess we'd best keep going on. I'm hoping

the mustangs are heading toward a sheltered spot," Dylan said. "Are you still in the saddle?"

"Yep. You girls alright?" Monty asked.

They answered that they were, except for being half drowned.

At that moment a streak of lightning cut into the darkness, lighting the area as if it were daylight. A glade of pines stood before them. The mustangs seemed to have disappeared.

"What do you think, Dylan?" Monty asked. "Should we take shelter in here? We're all drenched. And I've got a feeling this rain is going to continue a while."

"I think you're right," Dylan said as he dismounted. "About two yards to our right I saw a big ground-hugging pine. The next time lightning makes it possible to see, head for it."

"I always heard that a person shouldn't stand beneath a tree in a storm," Rachel said.

"It will be safe under this tree," Dylan said. "All the trees standing around it are taller. They would be hit first."

As if to prove Dylan's words, a moment later a tall tree lost its top to an ear-shattering blast of lightning. Both girls squealed and grabbed hold of the soaking-wet arm of the man next to them.

It took Dylan but a split second to reach out and wrap a protective arm around Rachel's waist, then guide her beneath the tree he'd spotted. To stop her shivering, he pulled her around to face him, holding her tight against his body.

She felt so good—soft, warm and wet. He almost wished that lightning would strike them dead so they would never have to be parted again.

When nature lit up the area again, Dylan looked for Monty and Jassy. They stood nearby, holding on to each other. Before everything would go black again, Dylan hurriedly looked around, wondering where the mustangs had gone.

He grinned. They hadn't gone far. It looked to him like they had all sought shelter in the pine grove. In fact, a big, mean-looking stallion was standing about two feet away from him. When the storm stopped, what would happen? Both the wild stallion and Devil were meaner than hell, and neither one would give an inch. He and Rachel could climb a tree if a fight errupted between the two animals, but that damn mustang might injure Devil with his hooves or teeth.

He put his hand on his Colt. If he had to, he'd shoot the other stallion.

He opened his mouth to call to Monty, to tell him there might be a fight between the two stallions, when suddenly the rain slackened.

"I'm going to boost you up in the tree in case the leader of the herd wants to fight Devil."

"What about you?" Rachel asked fearfully. "Are you planning on fending those two stallions off with your bare hands?"

Dylan gave a dry chuckle. "I'm not that dumb," he said, patting the holster strapped to his waist.

"If necessary, I'll put a bullet between the eyes of that mustang."

"That would be too bad," Rachel said. "He's just protecting his mares. Why don't you let Devil go? We can find our horses again after the storm. They won't wander far."

"Alright," Dylan agreed. "It would be a shame to shoot such a fine-looking animal." As they released Devil and Goldie, there came a crack of lightning and a roll of thunder so loud it made the two animals take off at once. Rachel squealed and threw her arms around Dylan's neck. When she lifted her face to him, his head dipped down, his mouth capturing hers.

Dylan was softly moaning his pleasure as he moved his lips on Rachel's when the sound of a loud slap reached them. Dylan lifted his lips from Rachel's, and while he was wondering what had happened, an outraged female voice split the air. "Get your hands off me, Monty Hale, before I claw your eyes out!"

Dylan didn't know whether to laugh or knock his friend on his rump. The big galoot should know better than to try anything with Jassy.

At first his intention was to go to Jassy's aid; then with a devilish grin, he changed his mind. Jassy could well take care of herself. And it would really be something to hear the stories Monty would make up, explaining how he got his face so clawed up. And from the swearing coming from

Monty, the little mountain girl was getting a lot of licks in on his face.

Dylan sobered up suddenly. What if Jassy told her grandmother that Monty had made a pass at her? Granny Hawkins had entrusted Jassy to his care. And though Monty would never hurt the girl, Granny might take after his friend with a pair of shears. And it wouldn't be to cut his hair, either. Dylan was thinking he'd better get over there and make some peace between them when, without any hint of a warning, it stopped raining.

The mustangs were beginning to stir, moving away from the humans whose presence they had tolerated during the midst of the storm. There would be time enough to round them up tomorrow, Dylan decided. Right now they must make some kind of camp, get a fire going, get themselves dried out.

As he told his companions what he thought they should do, Monty didn't look him in the face and Dylan knew why. He didn't want his scratched face to be seen. As for Jassy, she was still fighting mad and didn't care who knew it. Dylan knew that sooner or later he must talk to the girl, explain Monty's actions.

A recollection hit Dylan when he began to think about where to set up camp. There was an old abandoned shack somewhere around here if he could only remember where. He thought it was back by the stream they had crossed.

After catching up Devil and Goldie, Dylan led the others back to the stream. He followed the running water until he came to the abandoned cabin. The building was old, wind-harried, and had probably never been painted. As he stepped up on the slanting porch, he prayed that the roof didn't leak.

He gave a heartfelt thanks when they all went inside and found the room bone dry, with the exception of rainwater that had blown through the crack where the window hadn't been closed tightly. Thunder rumbled in the distance as he hurriedly checked the windows in the two bedrooms and a small kitchen. Monty struck a match and held its flame to the stub of a candle that sat on a wobbly table.

There wasn't a bed in any of the rooms, but that didn't matter much. At least they had their bedrolls and a roof over their heads to keep them dry.

They congregated in what they figured was the main room because it had a fireplace. Dylan could tell by the charred pieces of wood that many meals had been cooked here. Squatting down, he pulled the burned end pieces of wood together, then shook his head.

"We're going to need more wood," he announced. "Let's split up outside and gather up all the dry twigs we can find."

Nobody objected to the way Dylan paired them off. They were too wet and cold to fuss about anything. Dylan reminded them to tie up their horses before they took off and to give them some feed. Then he turned to Jassy. This would be as good a time as any to talk to her, he decided.

When they were out of earshot of Monty and Rachel, Dylan said rather than asked, "Old Monty got feisty with you. I didn't think he would, although I know he's quite smitten with you."

"He is?" The question was asked doubtfully.

"Oh, my, yes. I think it began that day up at Granny's cabin, but his fate was sealed last night when he saw you in that pink dress."

"But if he's smitten with me," she asked shyly, "why does he tease me so? Why wouldn't he stop kissing me when I told him to?"

"I think he's not quite sure how to behave," Dylan said seriously. "He's never been around an innocent girl like you. He forgets how young you are. Try to have a little patience with the big galoot." He grinned, thinking how odd it was that a hell-raiser like himself should be giving advice in matters of the heart.

When they returned to the shack, Dylan stepped up on the porch and looked out at the dripping trees. He frowned when he saw a flash of lightning and heard the renewed rumble of thunder far up in the mountains. Damn, he thought, where were Monty and Rachel? The storm wasn't over yet. He sent Jassy inside with the twigs they'd gathered, but hesitated on the threshold. Was

Rachel afraid of thunder and lightning? Should he go looking for them? On the heels of that thought, he heard the sound of running feet. She might not be afraid, he grinned, but she sure was in a hurry to get back to the cabin.

Once they got the fire going, the old shack became quite cozy, and they shared a simple meal of beans and bacon and coffee before the crackling flames. The two girls decided to sleep in one bedroom, with Monty in the other, while Dylan volunteered to keep the fire going in the main room. A chill had swept down from the mountain with the storm, and they would need its warmth.

By the time he bundled Rachel in her blankets, lightning was crackling and thunder drumming in the mountains. The night wind moaned in the passes, and he noted the anxious look on her face as he took the candle from the room, leaving her and Jassy in the pitch black.

Before long, Dylan could hear Monty snoring away in the other room. Apparently, his friend had decided to behave himself where Jassy was concerned. Dylan grinned. He hoped Monty would speak to Granny Hawkins about the girl. He was just the kind of man the old lady wanted for her great-granddaughter.

Dylan was trying to make himself comfortable when there came a crack of thunder louder than all the rest. It sounded as if the world had been split in two.

A moment later he heard the padding of bare

feet, and Rachel scrambled into his bedroll beside the fire. Her body was trembling as she clung to him.

"Are you alright, honey?" he asked, kissing her gently.

"I am now," she whispered. "I never could stand thunder," she admitted.

"You're safe with me," he half whispered, his hand trailing down to play with the top button of her nightgown.

I should make him stop, Rachel thought. But when his fingers undid the button and moved on down to the second one she felt herself weakening. When he slid his hand inside her nightgown and began to stroke her breast, her arms, as though they had a mind of their own, came up and slipped around his shoulders.

A warm surge of desire rushed through Dylan, and he undid the third button and spread the placket apart; the firelight shone on her alabaster breasts. Groaning his desire, he lowered his head and settled his mouth over one nipple. He sucked gently on the pale pink nub, all puckered and waiting for him.

When Rachel fumbled for the buttons of his denims, he couldn't believe it. In seconds he had the pants' fly open and his hand was holding a hardness like he had never held before. He took her hand and placed her fingers around the aching part of him. When she only held him, he realized that she didn't know what to do.

"Move your hand up and down on me," he whispered.

"Are you sure?" she whispered.

"I'm sure," he chuckled. Then he groaned as she did what he'd suggested.

"You are so big," she said, a little uneasy, wondering if he could possibly fit inside her.

As though reading her mind, Dylan said softly, "Don't worry, Rachel. I'll be gentle with you." And lowering his mouth to her breast again, he pulled up the hem of her nightgown, then slowly eased his hardness inside her.

She tensed a moment and gave a small cry when he came up against the thin barrier that protected her virginity. He immediately held his body still. "Shall I stop?" he asked anxiously. "I had no idea that you had never known a man before. Married to Homer and all."

"He was shot before he had a chance to do anything except beat me."

Dylan made as if to remove himself from her, but she clamped her legs tighter around his waist.

"Are you sure?" he asked.

When she nodded, he dropped a tender kiss on her forehead and began to slowly rock in the well of her soft, firm legs.

Before very long the pleasure became so intense he could no longer control himself. He had wanted this little white-haired beauty too long.

Rachel gave a low, objecting cry when he

pulled away from her. "What's wrong, honey?" he asked, smoothing the hair off her brow. "Did I hurt you? I tried to be as careful as I could."

"Oh, no, you didn't hurt me . . . at least not much. I . . . I just feel incomplete, like there's something more."

Dylan raised himself off her and lay alongside her. His eyes twinkled down at her. "Give me a minute," he said, "and I'll make you think I'm taking you to heaven."

"Silly—" Rachel smiled at him. "You couldn't do that."

Dylan gave her a knowing smile and, gathering her close, rolled his long length on top of her. She raised her arms to clasp them around his shoulders and he began a slow, rhythmic movement in and out of the well of her hips.

In just a few minutes Rachel's body stiffened and her hips began to buck against his. Dylan felt himself swelling, filling her completely. When her release came, he muffled her joyous cry in his kiss so as not to wake the others.

Dylan lifted his weight off Rachel and stretched out on his back beside her.

When his breathing returned to normal, he asked with a hint of humor in his voice, "Well, did I take you to heaven?"

"Let me think a minute." Rachel pretended to be musing his question over in her mind. "You sure did," she said finally. "Maybe we should try it again." She grinned at him mischievously. "The girls from the Grizzly Bear say you can go all night."

"Oh, they do, do they?" Dylan laughed. He pulled her back into his arms and proceeded to show her that Gracie hadn't been exaggerating one bit.

They were both exhausted when Monty's loud voice called out, "Hey, everyone, it's almost daylight. We've got a bunch of mustangs to round up."

Neither of the two had ever moved so fast in their lives as they scrambled to get into their own bedrolls.

Chapter Twenty-two

Jasper Dunn shaded his eyes against the light of the rising sun. He was still upset from his encounter with Web Spencer. Saturday night. It didn't bother him that he had caused the man's death; what made his blood race was the fact that little Jassy had to put up with such beasts as Spencer.

Well, he thought, his lips firmed grimly, that was going to come to an end. From now on, she was going to have the protection of her father. Everyone in the area was going to know that he, Jasper Dunn, was Jassy's father.

He stepped outside the sturdy cabin he had built seventeen years ago. Instead of setting about his chores, he sat down on a bench just outside the door. He had sat there many times over the years when he had troubles on his mind.

His thoughts went immediately to the night Jassy was born.

An icy rain pelted the windows of the cabin.

Off in the distance, over the mountains, lightning flashed and thunder rumbled. Inside, in their cozy bedroom, his young wife gripped his hands with each contraction. Between her legs knelt Granny Hawkins, an old woman even then.

One time when Pansy tried to rest between contractions, he took the old woman aside and asked in worried tones, "What's wrong, Granny? Is the baby stuck?"

Granny nodded solemnly. "The baby is comin' feet first, and it makes for a hard delivery. Plus," she continued, "her water broke an hour ago. I'm doin' my best son. Now go get a basin of water. You can bathe her face."

Hurrying into the kitchen, he grabbed the handle to the pump he had installed the year before. On his way back to the bedroom, a high-pitched scream pierced the air, then a heartbeat later came the wail of a newborn baby.

Hurrying to Pansy's side, he kissed her softly on the lips. "It's a little girl, Pansy, love," he said softly.

"Thank you, God," Pansy whispered, then fell into an exhausted sleep.

Granny Hawkins cleansed the baby, then wrapped her in a blanket. But as she turned to put the child in the wooden cradle he had made, Jasper saw the dark spread of blood on the bedsheet. His beautiful Pansy was bleeding. As the baby cried loudly in the cradle, Granny tried frantically to stop the flow of blood.

Within minutes Jasper's wife stopped breathing. Granny shook her head and sighed, dabbing at the tears that started running down her cheeks. "I'm sorry, son, but Pansy has passed."

Jasper ran to the bed and, gathering the limp body in his arms, covered Pansy's face with kisses. "My darlin'," he wept, "I am so sorry. I feel it is my fault that you are no more."

He didn't know how much time had passed before he noticed the baby was still crying. Granny Hawkins picked her up and began pacing the floor with her.

"She's hungry, Jasper, she needs food."

"What are we gonna do?" Jasper asked nervously. "Can she drink from one of our cows?"

"Heavens, no!" Granny was scandalized. "Go milk that nanny goat you've got out there in the shed."

When Jasper returned with a pint of milk, Granny strained a part of it into a coffee cup. When she had placed a spoon into the milk, she handed the cup to Jasper.

"See if she will sip it from the spoon."

The little one took readily to the spoon, and while her tiny lips sucked greedily of the milk, Jasper looked closely at his daughter. "She is beautiful," he whispered. Her brows were finely arched and what little hair she had was dark and curly. She looked just like his wife, and just like her great-grandmother. He would love and protect her all his life. Her mother had said once when she was still carrying the infant that if it was a boy, he would be named Jasper, after his father. And if they had a little girl, she would be Jassy.

"And Jassy it is." Jasper kissed her fat little cheek.

Jassy was two weeks old the night Jasper went hurrying through the woods to Granny Hawkins's cabin. "Granny," he called, pounding on the door. "I need your help. I can't bear the memories of poor Pansy anymore. And I'm not cut out to raise this little one by myself."

"I've been worrying about this happening ever since Pansy's death," Granny said. "What do you want me to do?"

"I don't know the first thing about raising a girl child," Jasper said. "But you do, Granny. Could you take her in, love her like she was your own? For poor Pansy's sake?"

Granny Hawkins wiped a tear from her eye. "I'll be happy to take care of this little one," she said softly. "My two granddaughters never had much chance in life—Pansy dying so young, and poor Ida saddled with that no-account Taig Sutter. I'll make sure your little Jassy finds more happiness."

Jasper had walked away in relief, He had found a home for Jassy; now he had to find a job. There was no real work up in the mountains. Instead, work on a ranch down in the valley. He learned he could make a living hiring out his gun to various ranchers around Jackson Hole. Over the years he built himself a reputation as a man to be feared, a fast gun, but between jobs he always returned to Tulane Ridge. He wanted to see his little Jassy, even if only from a distance.

A few years ago he'd made the mistake of taking a job on the wrong side of the law. Web Spencer had been in on that holdup with him, and afterward they'd both had to hide out up in the mountains. That was the secret Spencer had threatened to tell. But Jasper's identity as a wanted man had died with the fat man. He was now free to tell the world he was Jassy's father.

Chapter Twenty-three

Jenny Quade stood on a small hill a week later, watching as Dylan and his men started a large herd on the dusty trail to Abilene.

She'd heard that John Jacob had returned to the post, and that Rachel had moved into the cabin he'd built her. Why should that white-haired little bastard get all the luck? thought Jenny enviously. A house of her own and that good-looking Dylan Quade panting after her. What did all the menfolk see in the skinny little bitch?

It was a hot, sultry day, and after Jenny had haphazardly done her weekly laundry—two pairs of homespuns for her husband and a couple of faded dresses of hers—she decided to take a short walk to a shallow spot in the river, where she could splash around a bit to cool off.

She slipped through the willows with the stealth of a cat, a manner she had used almost as soon as she learned to walk. Thanks to her eavesdropping over the years, there were few people living on Tulane Ridge or in Jackson Hole who held any secrets from her. Consequently, she was disliked and distrusted by all.

When Jenny came to the shallow spot in the river where folks went to swim, she was surprised to see that the spot was already taken. She hadn't heard the sound of splashing water or laughing children. But when she saw who was there, she wasn't surprised that she hadn't heard the usual happy sounds of playing children.

Preacher Robison's two orphans were waist deep in the river, quietly wading around in the cool water. The preacher sat on the riverbank watching them. Jenny's eyes narrowed. She had suspected for some time that there was something strange about a young preacher taking care of girls. The younger one was probably ten years old, the elder fourteen. Why wasn't he taking care of young boys?

She sat down on a big rock hidden beneath a large willow branch. She had sat there about ten minutes when Robison called to the girls that it was time they got home and made lunch. The girls immediately did as they were told, leaving the river and climbing up the bank, water streaming from their dresses and petticoats. The older girl waded out last, and Jenny's eyes bugged at the sight of her.

The girl wore no petticoat and her dress was thin, clinging wetly to her body. But the thin dress and absence of a petticoat weren't what had stunned her. The young teenager was well along in a family way.

Jenny sat chewing on a dirty fingernail, her brain racing as the girls dried themselves off. How, she asked herself, did the girl manage to get away from the preacher to meet some man in the woods?

It came to her then. The girl didn't have to sneak out of the house to meet a man. She was living with one.

She sat on after Robison and the girls left the river and disappeared up the mountain. She must carefully ponder this new knowledge, decide how to get the most out of it.

She was ready to go home when the laughter of a child reached her. She peered through the branches and saw Colby, Benny and Rachel coming along. Rachel carred a basket on her arm, the tops of herbs she had dug up hanging over the edges of the wicker container. *Miss High-and-Mighty, you don't know it yet, but pretty soon you and that stuck-up Dylan are going to fall off your high horses.*

Jenny waited until she figured the preacher and the girls had changed into dry clothes and maybe started fixing lunch. She walked up the path to the preacher's house then and knocked on the door. The low murmur of voices inside the shack stopped immediately. A minute later the door creaked open about twelve inches. Robison stood there frowning down at her. He did not open the door wider as an invitation for her to enter. Jenny smiled knowingly. She knew the preacher had never thought much of her. Without being told to do so, the two girls faded into a back room. Impatience was in his voice when he demanded rudely, "What brings you here?"

His eyes were contemptuous as he looked over her bare legs and feet, which hadn't seen soap in a long time.

"I think someone should talk to you about that older girl you have livin' with you."

Robison's eyes were suddenly icy, and he stared at Jenny with hate blazing in his gaze. She took a step back, sure that he was going to strike her. "What about my Millie?" he demanded coldly.

"You know as well as I do that the girl is expectin'. The problem facin' you now is, what man bigged her?"

Robison's eyes were ugly when he demanded, "I suppose you know who the man is."

Jenny's eyes narrowed defensively as she said, "Know as well as you do name of the man who did it."

When alarm flickered in the preacher's eyes, she grew bolder and reclaimed the step she had lost a few moments ago. "The question is, do we want that man to be found guilty, or is there another one who would do better?"

"Do you have one in mind?" Robison narrowed his eyes at her.

"I do," Jenny answered immediately. "He would make your charge a fine husband. He has a lot of money and two properties."

A knowing gleam came into the preacher's eyes. "If you have in mind that arrogant Dylan Quade, forget about it. No one would believe he would stoop to lie with ugly little Millie, who doesn't even have a last name."

"That's where you are mistaken. Dylan Quade, with his high-falutin' ways, has many enemies. Most of the mountain men hate him and would love to see him jerked off his high horse. They would swear to anything we asked them to."

Her lips spread in a malicious, twisted smile. "They would grab him some night after he had gone to bed, take him high up the mountain where you could be waiting. In five minutes time Mr. Dylan Quade would be a husband."

Robison gazed at Jenny, reluctant admiration in his eyes. He would never want this one for an enemy.

"Will you be able to convince the girl to name Quade as the father?" Jenny asked, pushing her greasy hair off her forehead.

Robison looked at Jenny with arrogant confidence. "Millie will do as I tell her." An evil glint flashed in his eyes. He had his own way of making sure Millie would do as she was told.

"It's agreed, then," Jenny said, hardly able to contain her gleeful satisfaction. As she left the preacher's house, she was already planning her course of action. The first step would be a visit to the general store in Tulane Ridge.

Midway up the single street, Jenny spotted women who had come to town to do their weekly grocery shopping. They ignored her as she approached them. That didn't deter her from walking up to the group and saying, "Howdy, ladies. It's a fine day, ain't it?"

One of the women looked up at the blazing sun and, fanning her face, said, "It's a mite too hot for me."

She was ready to turn back to her friends when Jenny spoke again in her irritating nasal voice. "I was just talkin' to Preacher Robison. He's all broken up over one of them girls he's been takin' care of."

Jenny had their attention now and she rushed on to keep it. "It's clear you ladies haven't been payin' much attention to her. She's showing big."

"I'm surprised to hear that Preacher Robison chose you to confide in," one of the women said with a sniff.

"Well, he didn't confide in me exactly," Jenny said shyly. "I was fishin' at the river when the preacher and the two girls came along to take a dip in the water. They didn't know I was there. Robison sat on the bank watching them. The only thing they had on was their dresses. I didn't pay any attention to that. That's the way we mountain girls go swimmin'. Then the older girl, Millie, stood up, and the way the wet dress clung to her belly, it was plain as day that she was bigged."

"Does the preacher know who the father is?" one of the women asked. "Is it one of the boys from the ridge?"

"Not exactly." Jenny looked away from the women. "The preacher's pretty sure Dylan Quade is the pappy."

Chapter Twenty-four

It was a dark night with only glimpses of stars between slow-moving clouds.

"It's sure-enough gonna rain, maybe even storm," Jasper Dunn mumbled to himself as he scurried through the woods to Granny Hawkins's cabin. He shouldn't have left his own place tonight, he thought. But after spending all week thinking about Jassy, and how he wanted her to make her home with him, he knew he had to clean up that pigsty he was living in.

The condition of his home was the reason he was hurrying along to Granny's. She had raised his little Jassy. She would know what was lacking in his old cabin, things that would please his daughter.

Money was no problem. He had saved what he'd earned over the years. Except for buying some grub, the rest of his earnings had been placed in a copper boiler and buried in the cellar beneath his cabin. No one knew its whereabouts except Granny. She knew where it was to go at his death.

Jasper walked up the rocky, narrow path to Granny's cabin. He stepped up on the small porch and rapped twice on the door after wiping his feet on the rug that had been put there for that purpose.

"Come in, Jasper," Granny's voice called out.

"How did you know it was me?" he asked.

"I knew it was you because you are the only one who wipes his feet before entering my kitchen. Besides, I knew you'd show up here sooner or later."

"How did you know that?" Jasper watched Granny pour him a cup of coffee.

The old lady grinned as she poured herself a cup. "Gossip rides a fast horse," she said. "You saved little Jassy from a life of hell. How did she take to you? She probably thought you were a wolf man, with all that bushy hair and tangled beard on your face."

Jasper shook his head. "She wasn't a bit scared of me. She gave me the sweetest smile you'd ever want to see."

"Jassy says she don't know what actually happened to Spencer after you shot him," Granny said.

"I threw his body over the bluff," Jasper said. "Ain't nobody gonna find him down there or connect his death with me."

"Well, that's a blessing," Granny said. "Now if

I could scare off the other mountain men, I wouldn't think twice about bringing her back up here on the mountain. I sure have missed that little gal while she's been stayin' at the post. She's real good about comin' to visit, but it's just not the same."

"Granny, I want Jassy to live with me. She belongs with me."

"And about time, too," the old woman said. A resigned look came into her eyes. "I'm getting up in years. I've been worrying about Jassy. She has no one but you when I am gone. I asked Dylan Quade to keep an eye on her while she's visitin' Rachel, but he's off on a trail drive now."

An angry light jumped into Jasper's eyes. "I don't want him or anybody else taking care of my little girl," he said curtly, giving the table a rap of his fist. "I intend to take care of her now that Spencer can't link me to that holdup."

"Well, my old friend," Granny said, her eyes twinkling. "You've got to do some housecleaning, not to mention getting yourself in shape. You've got to trim your hair and beard first off."

"I was thinking about going down to the barber in Jackson Hole tomorrow," Jasper said with a shamefaced grin.

"I'm glad to hear that. What about your cabin? The last time I saw it, it didn't look fit to raise a young daughter in."

"I know it." Jasper looked down at the floor. "I was wonderin' if you'd help me purty' it up some after I clear out all the junk that has accumulated over the years."

The doubtful look that came into Granny's eyes said she doubted it was possible to purty the place up at all. But her voice was gentle when she said, "I'd be happy to, Jasper. I'll be up to your place tomorrow and see just what-all you need. I'm so glad Jassy will finally know her father."

"I don't know how to thank you for everything, Granny. Pansy would be so proud of the way our little girl turned out. When I saw Jassy at the schoolhouse, I couldn't believe my eyes," Jasper said, emotion roughening his voice. With that, he slipped out the door. He looked up at the sky. It was a sullen gray and would rain most anytime. In another hour it would be daylight. He'd better hurry on home. Anyway, he was eager to get started on cleaning out the cabin.

As he approached his sturdily built cabin, the wolf he had found as a cub and tamed came bounding off the porch to greet him. "You're hungry, I know." He roughed up the black hair on the big body and finely shaped head.

Jasper started to push open the door to walk inside as he had done for years. He paused when a thought hit him. There would be no more tracking mud into his home. He unlaced his boots and carried them inside the cabin. They would get a good cleaning after he had his breakfast.

Twenty minutes later he was eating a breakfast

of fried salt pork and fried potatoes, plus a chunk of sourdough, all cooked over the small fireplace. *I've got to buy a wood stove*, he thought. Jassy might burn herself cooking over an open fire.

When he finished his meal, he gathered up everything he had used and tossed it all into a wooden tub at the end of the table. As there came to him a crackle of chinaware, he frowned. That was something else he had to stop doing. In fact, he thought, he would most likely have to buy all new dishes and some glasses. It wouldn't hurt to buy some new frying pans and stew pots, too.

Jasper stood up from the table and looked around, wondering where he should begin shoveling out the dirt and trash.

He decided that the kitchen was the most logical place to start. The two bedrooms could be last. No one ever saw them.

With the first load of trash Jasper carried outside, it began to sprinkle a misty rain. He paid no attention to it as he lugged broken pieces of furniture, scraps of stiff, dried-out fur, and pieces of raggedy clothing. There were five pairs of boots, the laces missing, the soles broken and the toes with big holes in them.

And still waiting to be carried out to the scrap heap were broken snowshoes, sleds with broken runners and old harnesses from the mules he had owned over the years.

When he had carried all the useless things ouside and swept a small mountain of dirt into the fireplace so he could shovel it out, he couldn't believe how big the room looked.

Jasper was thinking how hungry he was when his old mule started braying in the corral behind the barn. "No wonder we're both hungry," he muttered. "It's way past time for our supper."

When he had led the mule into the barn and wiped him down with burlap bags, he fed him and Spencer's bony horse a bag of ground corn, then coaxed his ten chickens into their coop with a special chicken food he'd bought at the mercantile. He sloughed back through the mud puddles to the cabin. He stopped just in time not to tramp mud on the kitchen floor. He hadn't mopped it yet, but still he didn't want to clean up more dirt than necessary. He stood in the doorway and unlaced his boots, then kicked them off and set them outside the door. He would clean them tonight in front of the fire.

He grinned wryly. To stop tracking mud into the house was only one bad habit he had to correct. He couldn't wait for Granny to see how much he'd accomplished.

Chapter Twenty-five

"Hello, Granny, are you there?" Jassy called out as she came up the path to the cabin where she'd lived all her life.

"Yes, honey. I'm here. Come on in. You're just in time to help me fold the wash."

The pair greeted each other fondly and soon fell into the familiar routine of sorting and folding the fresh-smelling laundry. They had been at it a few minutes when Jassy suddenly began to giggle.

"What are you snickering about, little miss?" Granny frowned at her.

Jassy held up a pair of men's red long-legged underwear. "Boy, Granny," she teased, "these sure ain't from our house. Have you got a boyfriend that I don't know about since I've been gone?" Her eyes twinkled.

Embarrassed, Granny jerked the drawers out of Jassy's hands. "You mind your manners, young lady," she snapped. "It so happens those belong to

Jasper Dunn. I've been helpin' him clean up his place and do a little washing for him."

"Oh, Jasper," the girl said. "He's my friend too now."

"I know, child. When we finish foldin' these clothes, I want you to run them up to him."

"I will," Jassy agreed readily. "You know, Granny, most people think he's strange, maybe even scary, but he has always been nice to me. I'm happy to help him."

The two finished the chore in silence, then Granny laid Jasper's folded clothes into a basket. Handing the wicker to Jassy, she said, "Take your time. Jasper's looking forward to seeing you.

Arriving at the sturdy cabin, Jassy set the basket on the ground and knocked on the door. Almost immediately a face appeared at the window next to the door. It was a familiar face, yet different somehow.

The door opened and she let out a surprised squeal. "Mr. Jasper," she exclaimed, "I never saw your face shaved before. You look like a young man. Granny sent me to bring your clean clothes." She bent over to pick up the basket.

"Here, honey, let me do that." Jasper took the laundry from her. "And I thank you for your compliment. I figured it was time I trimmed up my shaggy hair and got rid of that old beard."

As he took the clean clothes into another room, Jassy looked around the kitchen and was amazed at how clean everything was. There were bright curtains at the window, a rag rug on the floor. She looked through the door to the main room and continued to be amazed. She couldn't see much, but there was a beautiful brightly colored crocheted afghan spread over an old sofa. She ventured into the room and saw a rocking chair with a small table next to it. There was a Bible on the fireplace mantel, and beside it an old framed picture. She reached up and took the picture down so she could see more clearly the young couple who had posed for it. It looked very much like a wedding picture. "My goodness," she said to herself, "I never knew Jasper had ever been married. I wonder if anybody else in the mountains knows it." Taking the picture to the window, she looked closely at the bride, then inspected the groom. Jasper stood ramrod straight and his bride stood beside him, her hand on his shoulder.

"She is very pretty," Jassy half whispered.

"Actually, she was beautiful in real life," Jasper said from behind Jassy.

Jassy blushed, her cheeks a rosy red. "I'm sorry. I didn't mean to be a snoop."

"Why don't we go into the kitchen and have some sassafras tea," Jasper said gently, "and I'll tell you about my young wife."

Jassy's face lit up. "I'd love that," she exclaimed.

Once they were seated at the kitchen table, a cup of tea in front of each of them, Jasper lovingly smoothed his palm over the glass covering the picture. "She was only a few years older than you are now when we met at a church social. I bid the highest on her dinner basket, and we talked on the church steps until the party was over. I fell in love with her that night. We were married just a week later."

Jasper sighed. "We were so happy that first year together. Our happiness was complete when Pansy got with child.

"But," he sighed again, "our happiness wasn't to last. My little wife died trying to give birth to our little girl."

"I'm so sorry, Mr. Jasper." Jassy laid her hand on his arm. "What happened to the little one?"

After a long pause and a deep breath, Jasper said, "I gave the baby to Granny Hawkins to raise."

"Granny Hawkins?" Jassy looked confused.

Jasper was silent so long it seemed as if he wasn't going to answer; then, almost in a whisper he said, "That baby was you, Jassy."

Stunned, Jassy pulled away from Jasper. "Are you saying that you're my father?" she finally managed to ask.

"I'm afraid I am, Jassy. I hope you're not too disappointed. You see, I just wasn't cut out to raise a little one all by myself, and I never wanted another woman after I lost your mother. So I took you to Granny. I knew that she would be good to you and that I could watch you grow up."

Jasper sat silent then, and so did Jassy. After a

while Jasper asked in a low voice, "Do you forgive me, Jassy? I wanted to tell you I was your father, but I couldn't until now."

Jassy shook her head and clasped Jasper's hand, which lay on the table. "I'm glad that you took me to Granny. No child could have had a better parent. I'm just sorry it has taken so long for us to get together."

"I am so glad you feel that way, child." Jasper leaned over and hugged his daughter. "I'd have told you sooner, but there was a secret hanging over me, one that can't hurt me no more now that Web Spencer is gone." He grinned at her. "It is my big wish that you come live with me now, that we let the mountain people know you're mine and that men had better let you alone."

"I'll be so glad to have you protecting me," Jassy exclaimed. "Though there is one fellow I wouldn't mind seeing some," she added shyly.

"That Monty Hale?" Jasper guessed shrewdly. "You've got plenty of time for courting, and if he's the right fellow, he won't mind waitin' till you've growed up a little more."

He drew away from Jassy. "Will you come and make your home with your father?" He asked the question half fearfully.

"Oh, I will, Jas . . . Papa," Jassy answered with shining eyes. "I will move in today. I will love being mistress of my own home."

Jasper, his face beaming, stood up. "Let's go tell Granny."

Chapter Twenty-six

The wind was cold and the river choppy as Rachel stood on the porch of her cabin gazing out over the water. The shadows deepened, and she hugged herself. Autumn had come to Jackson Hole.

Across the river she glimpsed the dim shape of a wolf or a coyote slipping along, and her skin tightened. Every night she lay awake listening to the distant howling of wolves while coyotes prowled around her new cabin. She was more conscious of the wild animals now that she was living away from the post. Web Spencer was no longer a threat to her, but there were plenty of other dangers.

Rachel thought of Colby and Benny. The tough little boys weren't so tough when the animals came close at night. Nor were they tough when it stormed and lightning streaked across the sky and thunder rumbled in the mountains. Quiet as mice, they would slip into her room and ease into bed beside her. There they would fall asleep, their skinny little bodies cuddled close to her. It wasn't unusual when she awakened in the mornings to find them snuggled up to her, their thin arms lying across her waist.

Poor little fellows, she thought. John Jacob had returned from Denver with the sad news that Iva hadn't made it. The two little boys, who had grown close to Rachel since their mother's departure, had begged to move into her little cabin with her. They spent all their time with her now and especially loved to sit beside her at night and listen to her read a story.

Would the boys be staying on with her? she wondered. She hoped they would. She had grown fond of the orphans. John Jacob had promised their mother that he would watch over them, and so far no relative had come forward to claim them. They were a big help when it came to searching for roots and barks and plants. Benny, especially, knew much about them and their medicinal uses. He had a quick intelligence and would make a fine doctor when he grew older if John Jacob could find some doctor to teach him.

And what kind of man would little Colby grow up to be? she wondered. She suspected he would be very much like Dylan. He adored the long-legged rancher. Dylan had been gone six weeks now, driving his herd of cattle to Abilene; he would probably be home in another week. "I don't care if he never comes back," she said through gritted teeth.

The older of the two girls Preacher Robison was taking care of, fourteen-year-old Millie, had come up expecting. She had named Dylan as the father. Due to Dylan's past wild ways, most everybody believed the girl. A few people, John Jacob among them, declared that although Dylan was a wild one, he was a decent man and would never get a young girl in a family way.

But Jenny Quade said otherwise, and when the gossip began to die down and it was decided that everything would be settled once Dylan came home, she began traipsing all over the mountain, keeping the womenfolk stirred up.

And what do I think? Rachel asked herself. There were days when she believed the girl was lying, but most nights when she lay awake and the wolves howled, she had serious doubts about Dylan's innocence.

Rachel smiled when she heard the brothers coming down the river road. As usual, Colby was rambling on about something, shooting questions to his brother. And as usual, Benny answered him in grunts or not at all.

The boys jumped up on the porch and dropped a good-sized cloth bag at her feet. "There's nothing in there but 'seng," he bragged.

"It's quite heavy," Rachel said, hefting the white sack.

"And there is much more where that came from," Benny said excitedly.

Rachel was reminded of the story Dylan had

told her about planting ginseng and tending the bed for five years, only to find that someone else had harvested the roots.

"Benny," she began in a serious voice, "you didn't get the 'seng from somebody's private patch, did you?"

"Oh, Rachel," Benny exclaimed, his eyes big and round, "I would never steal a man's hard work. I found these in a mayapple patch. They were way up in the wild woods. I don't think anyone has been up there for years. It's a real spooky place." He stopped to catch his breath. "I'll take you up there tomorrow and show you."

Rachel smoothed a hand over his rough hair. "That won't be necessary, Benny. I believe you." She turned to Colby. "And what do you have in your bag, Colby?"

Colby ducked his head and said in a voice so low Rachel could hardly hear him, "Not much. Just some bark and plants."

Benny laughed and dodged Colby's knobby little fist when he explained, "Colby spent all afternoon playing with the Indian younguns."

A tiny frown creased Rachel's forehead. "Are all the children your age, Colby?"

"Just about, excepting for Brown Feather and Little Buck. They are teenagers. Yellow Feather won't let the young ones go out alone."

"That's very wise of him," Rachel said.

"When Yellow Feather heard that Uncle John was our guardian, he asked if Uncle John had told you about his time as a teacher up on Tulane Ridge. What do you think he meant by that?"

"A teacher?" Rachel said wonderingly. "I have no idea, Benny. I never knew he'd been to this area before he won the post in that poker game. I'll have to ask him." She let the subject drop and said instead, "It's time you fellows wash up and get ready for bed."

They gave her no argument. Both had had busy days, one way or the other.

Rachel stood, gathered up the two sacks of roots and hurried inside the cabin. She fed the boys a quick supper, then settled them into bed.

It was completely dark when she returned to the porch to sit for a while before going to sleep herself. As was her wont, she fell to thinking about Dylan. During the first days after they had spent the night together, she had daydreamed about him constantly, making plans for their future. There had been little opportunity for private talk while they rounded up the mustangs with Monty and Jassy and drove them to the Bar X. She'd expected he would propose when they returned to the post. She knew there were matters they needed to discuss. For example, where would they live? She thought she would prefer living in Jackson Hole, but Dylan loved his ranch and his cabin up in the mountains.

She didn't care really, as long as they were together. But he hadn't proposed. She'd hoped he was just waiting for John Jacob to return, so he could ask for his blessing. But as soon as John Jacob came back, Dylan had set out for Abilene with his cattle.

She clenched her fists, hating herself. *How mistaken John Jacob is about Dylan*, she thought. He said a man like Dylan would treasure a woman who'd known no other before him. But she'd given him her virginity, and he'd gone off to Abilene as if it were of no importance to him. *Maybe those old wild ways of his are just to hard to break*, she thought sadly, brushing away a tear as a wolf howled in the distance.

Dylan listened to the howling of a wolf and shifted in his bedroll. He'd been riding hard all day, but he just couldn't seem to sleep tonight. He got up and went to sit by the campfire.

There was a pot of coffee resting in the coals. Taking up a tin cup, he filled it to the top, then went and sat down on his saddle pulled up close to the fire.

He stared into the fire, watching the leaping flames. As usual, his thoughts turned to Rachel. He had never missed anyone the way he had missed her ever since starting on the drive.

But a week from now he would be back home, sleeping in a bed again, and best of all being with Rachel again. He couldn't wait to ask her to marry him. He'd longed to speak to her after the night they first made love, to make plans for their wedding.

But on further reflection, he'd decided it would be best to wait till after the drive. "It's important that I go to her with money in my pocket," he'd told Monty. "I want to show her how different I am from those mountain men she's used to. I need to prove I'm nothing like my cousin Homer."

Had he been right to wait? What if Rachel had taken his silence for lack of interest? Hearing the wolf howl again, he prayed he hadn't made the worst mistake of his life.

Chapter Twenty-seven

On this Sunday morning it was close and airless inside the little church upon Tulane Ridge. There was a little breeze created from the many fans being waved back and forth by the ladies. They beamed at Preacher Robison, who had given them the pieces of white cardboard.

When the congregation had settled down, the reverend stood up behind the pulpit and motioned everyone to do the same. There was a rustling of clothing and a shuffling of feet for a moment; then Robison, after clearing his throat, began, "It gives me great joy to see you all here to listen to the word of God."

He had barely begun to talk when the church door slammed open with such force, it banged against the wall. Everyone turned around to stare at whoever had caused the commotion.

But their heads swiveled back toward the pulpit as the two young girls who lived with the preacher marched purposefully toward the suddenly white-faced Robison. When the two reached him, the older girl, Millie, swung around to face the wide-eyed congregation.

"I have come here to clear the name of a good man," she began. "This babe I carry"—she touched her stomach—"is not Dylan Quade's. I let Robison and Jenny Quade spread that rumor, but it isn't true. I spoke a lie because of this man"—she jerked her thumb over her shoulder toward Robison, who had started to step down from the pulpit—"who claims to be a man of God, but is actually a man of the devil."

"Don't listen to her," Robison begged, his eyes darting to the open church door. "She's mad at me because I make her work hard. I won't abide idle hands." He took the girl by the arm and started trying to drag her out the back door.

"Let the girl have her say!" Granny Hawkins shouted in her cracked voice.

Millie jerked loose from Robison's grip. She was near tears and her voice was trembling as she began. "You people are probably wondering why I didn't tell the truth before. I thought I had a good reason to keep quiet. This devil of a man said that if I didn't keep my mouth shut, he would start sleeping with my little ten-year-old sister.

"Well, last night I discovered that he had been been visiting her room for the past two years. I had kept his secret for nothing. He had been using my little sister all this time."

Knowing the jig was up, Robison darted out

the back door. Every man in the church rose to his feet. "Let's lynch the no-good," one man called out.

"I have a good stout rope," another said.

"You women and young'uns stay inside," someone else directed. "This ain't gonna be purty."

The instant Millie had burst into the room, Jenny Quade had turned white and her eyes filled with alarm. She knew that her troublemaking had finally caught up with her. She had no doubt that she would be hanged beside the preacher. While the women and children crowded to the window to see what they could of the proceedings outside, she began edging toward the back door. She had to get away.

She eased the door open, then stopped short. The tree the men had chosen to hang the preacher from was only about three feet away. He was blubbering incoherently.

"Tie a rag across the coward's mouth. I'm tired of listenin' to him," one of the men shouted. A dirty rag was pulled from someone's pocket and tied firmly across Robison's pleading mouth. As Jenny slipped away, she could hear the drumming of the preacher's heels against the tree trunk. She was well on her way down the mountain when suddenly everything grew quiet for a moment. Then there was a joyful shout. It was over.

Jenny hurried on. She'd better hide out down in Jackon Hole for a while, she decided. Once people's tempers had cooled, she could go back home.

Some time later, as she was passing the trail to

the Bar X, she noted smoke coming from the chimney. That arrogant Dylan Quade must be back from Abilene. A sudden idea came into her head and she smiled slyly. There was one more piece of mischief she could take care of before she had to lie low. Laughing to herself, she turned onto the trail to the Bar X.

Dylan had slept later than usual Sunday morning. They'd ridden in late the night before and he was exhausted. He'd pushed himself and Devil as hard as he could in his eagerness to see Rachel again.

It was almost noon when Dylan walked down to the bunkhouse. "Got any coffee made, Charlie?" he asked the cook.

"Yeah, just made a fresh pot. Help yourself."

Dylan filled a cup and carried it to the table. Sitting down, he leaned back and took a sip of the hot, strong coffee. He realized suddenly that Charlie, who usually talked a mile a minute, was very quiet this afternoon.

"Anybody pass by today?" Dylan broke the silence.

"Yeah. That trashy Jenny Quade," Charlie said after a pause.

"What kind of gossip did she have to pass on?" Dylan took a long swallow of coffee.

Charlie gave him a sideways look, then after a moment half growled, "Nothin' that you would be interested in hearin'."

"Why don't you let me be the judge of that?"

Dylan frowned at his cook. "What is that gossipmonger peddling now?"

"Alright." Charlie got real busy stirring a pot of stew. "But you ain't gonna like it."

"Oh, forget it," Dylan said and swallowed the last of his coffee.

"Alright, alright, I'll tell you." Charlie replaced the lid on the stewpot. "That girl Millie who's been livin' with the preacher has come up big-bellied. The preacher's been tellin' everyone you're the pappy."

"What!" Dylan jumped to his feet, slamming his empty cup down on the table. "Nobody believes it, do they?"

"Well, Jenny says they do. Worst of all, Rachel believes it. Jenny claims she's been spendin' all her time with that preacher man. Said she'd shoot you between the eyes if you ever dared to come around her again.

"Where are you goin'?" Charlie called after Dylan as his irate boss went stamping off toward the barn.

"Where in the hell do you think I'm going?" Dylan yelled back. "I'm going down to the post to get this straightened out."

"But . . . but . . ." Whatever Charlie wanted to say, it would be finished in the trail of dust Dylan was leaving behind him.

Rachel was enjoying a lazy Sunday afternoon, sitting on her porch, watching a hawk circle against the gray sky. She sighed. She should have gone to church today. Her mother would have been disappointed in her.

But in Granny Hawkins's words, she was too dismal these days to do anything but sit and ask herself how Dylan could have been sleeping with that Millie girl all the while he was courting her.

She stood up and called Shadow to her side. Dylan had seemed so concerned about her welfare when he'd given her the dog for protection. Had it been nothing more than an act? she wondered as she noticed two figures approaching from the post.

"What brings you down here?" she asked as Shadow bounded up to Granny Hawkins, who was being escorted by John Jacob.

"All hell's broken loose," John Jacob said as he helped Granny climb onto the porch where she sat down in one of the rockers.

"What do you mean, all hell's broken loose?" Rachel asked as she sat down beside Granny.

"Do you want to tell her or do you want me to?" John Jacob asked Granny.

"One of you had better tell me or I'll hit you both," Rachel snapped.

"It will be my pleasure to tell you," John Jacob said as he sat down on the edge of the porch and leaned against the post. "They hanged that preacher man this morning up on Tulane Ridge."

"What?" Rachel exclaimed, sitting forward, gripping both arms of her chair. "Why did they do that?"

"Do you want to tell her, Granny?" John Jacob grinned at the old lady. "I think you should be the one to tell her good news."

"I don't understand you, John," Rachel sniffed. "A man has been hanged—a man of the church, no less. What good news is there about that?"

"Well, you'll understand pretty soon," John Jacob said slowly. He paused a minute, his eyes studying Rachel. "You see, he was hanged for getting a girl in a family way. And the girl in question is Millie. She accused him this morning in church."

Two emotions ran through Rachel simultaneously: shock that a man of the cloth had committed such a sin and been hanged, and overwhelming joy that Dylan was innocent of the gossip that had gone around.

Another emotion gripped her. One of shame. Why hadn't she had more faith in Dylan? She looked at John Jacob, pink with embarrassment. He had tried to tell her Dylan was an honorable man. When he gave her a look that said *I told you so,* Granny gave him a sharp glance, then began to speak.

"There is another truth that is long overdue to be told."

"Now, Granny," John Jacob said nervously, "that's nothing to be bothering Rachel about."

"Hesh up, John Jacob," the old woman snapped. "This child has a right to know who her pappy is."

John Jacob stood up and leaned against the porch post, his back to them.

He shuffled uneasily, knowing what Granny was going to say. He flinched when she began speaking. "Rachel has a right to finally know who her father is," the old lady said.

"Alright, tell her!" John Jacob half shouted. "I've been meaning to tell her and never seemed to find the right time or words."

Rachel rose to her feet, her eyes wide with disbelief and incredible joy. "You are my father, John?" she asked, her voice shaking.

"Yes, I am, honey." He smiled at her and reached his arms toward her. "I hope you're not too disappointed."

"I couldn't be more pleased," Rachel exclaimed, jumping up to throw herself in his arms. Then suddenly she froze, her face going as cold as ice. She had remembered the hellish life this man had caused her mother. Granny caught her dress tail as she started to lunge at his face.

"No, Rachel," she said. "Calm yourself. Listen to what John Jacob has to say."

"But, Granny," Rachel protested. "You know the awful life my poor mother had to live because of him."

"I know that, child," Granny said gently, "and I'm sure there is no one who regrets that more than John Jacob. Go now, the two of you. Walk along the river and have that long talk that has been waiting all these years."

As John Jacob and Rachel walked along the river, he told his daughter that he had loved her mother dearly and explained the circumstances that had kept him from returning to her. He ended by saying, "I never loved any other woman and I often thought of your mother." He took Rachel's hand as they returned to her porch. "Can you forgive me?"

"Yes, I can, now that I know the whole story. I'm glad that she knew love and happiness at one time in her life."

Just at that moment Rachel caught sight of Dylan's stallion racing up the river road toward the post.

He drew up before her cabin in a cloud of dust, and his face when he swung down off Devil was a thundercloud.

"Welcome back," John Jacob called out. "Have you heard the news?"

"Don't keep him waitin'," Granny scolded.

"They hanged that preacher man this morning for getting little Millie in a family way," John Jacob said straight out. "I guess you've heard that some folks were saying you were the one responsible."

His face stone cold Dylan said, "I have. So they've found the real culprit and hanged him. How does that make you feel, Rachel? I also heard you've been keeping company with him while I was away."

"Keeping company with him?" Rachel repeated in astonishment. "I certainly have not!"

Dylan bounded up on the porch and with angry strides marched over to where Rachel and Granny sat. Wordlessly he jerked Rachel to her feet and, still silent, half dragged her inside the cabin. John Jacob and Granny Hawkins took one look at each other and started back toward the post.

"Dylan! What's wrong with you?" Rachel demanded, trying to pull away from him.

He dropped the bar across the door, then pushed her into a chair and said coldly, "I have a few words to say to you and I want to say them in private."

Her chin in the air, Rachel pulled away from him and stamped across the room to stare out the window, "Say your few words and get out of my home," she retorted.

"How could you have thought for one minute that I would have anything to do with that girl Millie? That I would get a child on her."

"Why shouldn't I believe it?" Rachel shot back. "Everyone else did."

"But I thought it was different between us," Dylan said. "I didn't think anything would ever come between us."

"Oh, really?" Rachel stepped away from the window. "I don't suppose you ever wondered how things were between John Jacob and me." She looked at Dylan with keen eyes.

He tried to hold her gaze, but after a moment he had to look away. His eyes flashed in defiance then. "Why shouldn't I have moments of doubt? The two of you were always together, talking and laughing. He was always buying you things, even built you your own cabin. There were times when I wanted to kill him."

Her hands on her hips, Rachel glared at him. "It's a good thing that you didn't."

"Really?" Dylan growled, half threatening. "Why do you say that? What would you have done? Shot me, I suppose."

"I might have," Rachel came back at him in the same tone. "You see, John Jacob is my father."

Dylan stopped in his tracks as though he had been kicked by a horse. After a long moment of stunned silence he said, "Your father? How long have you known that?"

"He just told me today."

"Oh, Rachel, what fools we've been," Dylan exclaimed, rushing across the room to swoop her into his arms. He started toward the bedroom, but just as he was about to lower her onto the bed, two pairs of young feet hit the porch. Dylan swore under his breath and hurried to the cabin door, where he lifted the bar that locked it.

Rachel smothered a giggle and called out, "Boys, Uncle John wants you two to spend the night with him."

After a strained pause, a young voice asked nervously, "When we come back tomorrow, will we be livin' with you as usual?"

"Of course, you silly boys. You're my young-'uns, aren't you?"

"You bet we are," Colby and Benny called out as they raced off toward the post.

Dylan smiled and shook his head, muttering, "Two more males to keep my eyes on," as Rachel lifted her arms to him.

They helped each other off with their clothes. After Dylan had laved his tongue over most of Rachel's body, had her shivering with her need of him, he slid his hands under her narrow hips and lifted her up to meet the slide of his eager need.

Rachel sighed her pleasure as he went deep inside her. He paused for a moment, just enjoying the feel of her. Then with a low groan he began to pump and slide rhythmically against her.

The western sky was ablaze with sunset when Dylan, exhausted, turned over on his side and stared down at Rachel. He stroked a hand over her pale blond head, treasuring her nearness. "Are you all right honey?"

"I've never been better," she sighed, grinning up at him. "Let's go tell John Jacob we've got a wedding to plan."

"I don't guess we'll have to tell Granny a thing," he added, kissing her quickly. "I think she's seen this coming for quite some time."

Turn the page
for a special sneak
preview of

by

PAMELA CLARE

On sale now!

Prologue

The Ohio Wilderness, July 15, 1757

"They're going to burn us, aren't they?"

Nicholas Kenleigh ignored the panic in Josiah's voice and Eben's frightened whimpering, strained in vain to free himself from the tight leather cords that held him to the tall wooden stake. His hands, bound fast above his head, had long since lost any feeling.

There would be no escape.

"I don't want to die!" Eben sobbed, his freckled face wet with tears.

Nicholas took a deep breath, sought for words to comfort the two younger men, found none. He had taken them under his wing shortly after he'd joined Washington's forces, tried to teach them to track and to shoot well.

None of that mattered now.

"I have no wish to die either." *Especially not*

like this. "But if death is all that is left to us, then we must face it with courage."

His words sounded meaningless, even to his own ears, but seemed to calm them. Josiah was nineteen, Eben only seventeen. They reminded him of his younger brothers—Alex, William and Matthew. They didn't deserve this.

No one deserved this.

Nicholas had known from the moment they were taken captive what the Wyandot would do to them. He'd warned Josiah and Eben, but they had not listened. Instead, they'd allowed themselves to be deceived by feasts, promises of adoption and the pleasures of sex with comely young Wyandot women. But those promises were false, food and sex merely part of the ritual of sacrifice.

Nicholas supposed that caring for the physical needs of their prisoners and bringing them pleasure took away some of the guilt the Wyandot must feel at torturing people to death—if, indeed, they felt guilt. But he had seen the deception for what it was, had eaten his food in silence, turned the woman away. Dark-eyed and pretty she had been, but he would not risk getting her with child and leaving a piece of himself behind to grow up here. Nor would he betray Penelope, his fiancée.

Fidelity when death was imminent might seem strange to most men, but Nicholas had been raised to keep his word and to put loyalty to family and friends above all else. He would try to die the way he had lived.

Washington's force had been encamped near the Ohio when the Wyandot had attacked under cover of night. Nicholas had been discussing the next day's march with George over a bottle of Madeira when they'd been interrupted by the sounds of war cries, shouts and gunfire. He'd fought his way across the camp toward Josiah's and Eben's tents and spied them in the distance, wild with bloodlust, pursuing a group of fleeing Wyandot into the forest.

He'd charged after them, shouted for them to stop, warned them it was a trap. But it was too late. They had been ambushed and overcome before his words reached them. And though Nicholas had managed to kill several warriors in an attempt to free them, there were simply too many. One blow to the temple with a war club, and Nicholas had found himself a prisoner, too. Now they would die together.

His mind flashed on his mother, and he felt a moment of deep anguish. His death would be hardest on her. She had opposed his decision to join Washington and serve as a tracker, had begged him to stay at home, take up his role as heir of the Kenleigh shipbuilding empire and produce an heir himself. But at twenty-six, Nicholas had felt certain there was still plenty of time for such things. Besides, Washington was a good friend and a fellow Virginian—and his need was dire. The outcome of this war would make or break British authority on this continent.

Jamie—Nicholas's elder by four years and his uncle—had served with Washington during his march north in 1754 and had fought beside George in the blood and mud of Fort Necessity. But Jamie now had a wife—lovely Bríghid—and two small sons. He would not leave them. Nicholas had reasoned he could do the job just as well as Jamie, as they had been taught together by Takotah, the old Tuscarora healer who had made her home with his family since long before he'd been born. It had seemed right that he fill Jamie's shoes.

And now?

Now he would need every ounce of strength, every bit of courage he possessed. He was not immune to fear.

Eleven fires had been lit in fire pits running down the center of the enormous longhouse. Old women busied themselves building up the fires, adding wood until the lodge was uncomfortably warm in the already stifling July heat.

As the fires crackled, Eben again began to weep, Josiah to curse the Wyandot.

"W-will it be quick?"

Nicholas had heard stories, accounts of the French priests who'd first encountered the Wyandot a hundred years before. He prayed the priests had lied. "I don't know."

"Bloody savages!" Josiah spat on the dirt floor. "It's good they like fire, because they're goin' to burn in hell!"

Wyandot villagers began to drift through the

low entrance—men, women, children. Soon the longhouse was packed from end to end. The Wyandot stared at their prisoners with solemn eyes, and Nicholas could sense an undercurrent of expectation.

Last to enter was the Wyandot war chief, Atsan, who had dressed in ceremonial garb, a great bearskin cape draped over his bare, aged shoulders, a single eagle feather in his scalplock. He held up his hand to silence the murmurs and whispers of his people, began to speak in Wyandot.

His words floated just beyond Nicholas's comprehension, strangely familiar and yet utterly foreign. He did not speak Wyandot, but it sounded somewhat like Tuscarora, which Nicholas knew well. Several times he thought he understood a word or phrase—Big Knives, fight, river—but the words were spoken so quickly that Nicholas couldn't quite catch them.

And then Nicholas recognized one: "*See-tah.*"

Fire.

A few feet away Eben wept like a frightened child. Josiah trembled but glared at the Wyandot with youthful bravado.

How vulnerable and alone men are at the hour of death.

The thought, detached from emotion, flickered through Nicholas's mind, left dark regret in its wake. Why hadn't he been able to get to the youths faster? Why hadn't he been able to stop this? Why hadn't he found a means to escape?

He closed his eyes, sent up what might have been a prayer. *Let it be fast. Let us be strong. Do not let them suffer!*

Even as the last thought faded, several women stepped forward from the crowd and walked toward the captives. Nicholas felt cool fingers brush against his skin as his shirt and breeches were cut from his body, leaving him entirely naked. A glance showed him Josiah and Eben had likewise been stripped. Both were red in the face, and Nicholas realized they felt shame at being unclothed before strangers.

As Atsan's last words drifted into silence, the women who'd undressed them moved to the fires and began to stir the flames.

Something twisted in Nicholas's gut. He tried to force down his fear.

A young woman appeared at his side, the same young woman he'd rejected the day before. She looked up at him, her brown eyes dark with an emotion that might have been anger—or lust. In her hand was a knife.

Nicholas just caught a glimpse of the blade before she slid the tip into the skin of his belly. His muscles tensed in surprise at the razor-sharp pain.

To his left, Eben shrieked.

Nicholas watched in odd detachment as the woman deftly carved a small pocket from his flesh and wondered for a moment if she intended to skin him. Hot blood poured down his belly, past his exposed groin to his bare thighs.

She looked up, met his gaze, a faint smile on her lips. Then she stepped aside to make room for an old woman who carried a small, glowing ember from the fire on a flint blade. Nicholas realized what they were going to do a moment before they did it, took a deep breath.

I will not cry out. I must not cry out.

The crone slipped the tip of her blade into the cut, pried the pocket of flesh open and dropped the ember inside.

A sizzling sound. Searing pain. The smell of burning flesh—his own flesh.

It hurt far beyond anything he had imagined.

He heard screams. Were they his screams?

No. It was Josiah and Eben.

A hiss of breath was all that escaped him. His gaze met the young woman's and held it.

They will not break me.

The women worked efficiently. Swiftly they cut him again and again, carved deep gashes in his belly, chest and back, tucked live embers inside each.

Pain consumed him—blistering, searing pain. His entire body seemed to burn. Sweat poured down his face, stung his eyes. He fought to control his breathing, to keep his thoughts focused, but felt himself growing dizzy, disoriented, almost delirious, as if his mind were seeking escape from the unbearable torment that had become his body.

They will not break him.

Several feet away, Josiah jerked and writhed like

a tortured puppet on a string, screaming in agony. Eben had fainted and hung limply in his bonds. Women worked to revive him, splashed water on his face and chest. It was not compassion, Nicholas knew, but a desire to prolong the boy's suffering.

Rage. It cut through Nicholas's pain, through his muddled thoughts, burned like a brand in his gut. He searched the crowd for Atsan, found the old man watching him, met his gaze. Drawing on his knowledge of Tuscarora and doing his best to imitate Wyandot inflection, Nicholas spoke, his voice rough with pain and hatred.

"E-hye-ha-honz, o-negh-e-ke-wishe-noo."

I am dying, but I will conquer my enemy.

Whether Atsan understood him, Nicholas could not tell. The old man did not react. And Nicholas wondered for a moment whether, in his pain, he had imagined speaking or whether his words had been meaningless babble.

Another cut, another ember.

Breath rushed from his lungs. Every muscle in his body screamed in protest. He closed his eyes, bit his tongue, fought desperately not to cry out. Dear God, how much more of this could he take?

Lyda stepped back from the prisoner, her hands slick with his blood, tried not to show her surprise at his words. Though awkwardly spoken, and sounding more like the speech of their enemies, the Tuscarora, than their own language, his message was clear.

He would die, but he would not give in to pain.

Something fluttered in her belly.

Here was a warrior.

He was a beautiful man—taller than most men in her village, with hair almost as black as a raven's wing. His face was proud and strong, its male strength softened by long, dark lashes. And his body . . . She let her gaze travel the length of him, seeing beneath the blood and burns, from his powerful shoulders to his broad chest, slim hips and muscular thighs. His breast was sprinkled with an intriguing mat of crisp, dark hair that tapered in a line between the ridges of his belly to his sex. She let her eyes rest there for a moment and felt renewed outrage at his rejection of her. Had he not turned her away, she would now know what it was like to have such a man pleasure her.

She had noticed him the moment the warriors had brought him and the other Big Knife prisoners into the village. The men claimed he had slain at least nine Wyandot warriors before one of them managed to strike him on the head with his club, leaving a gash on his left temple. Still, it had taken four men to subdue him and bind his wrists.

Lyda had known from the moment she saw him that she wanted him. When he looked her up and down and then turned her away as if she were worthless, the humiliation had been almost unbearable. She was considered a great beauty by the people of her nation. More than that, she was a woman of power, a holy woman, granddaughter to holy women dating back to the beginning of her people, and a daughter of Atsan, the great war chief. No man had ever turned her away. Until yesterday.

She had rejoiced then to know he would be sacrificed in flames and had vowed to play a role in his torment. But now?

Her grandmother slipped another ember beneath his skin. His body jerked, every muscle taut as he strained against the cords that held him. Breath hissed from between his clenched teeth. His brows grew furrowed with obvious agony. Sweat drenched his black hair, ran in rivulets down his face. But he did not cry out.

Lyda knew what she wanted. She'd had lots of men in her twenty-three years, had taken a few into her mother's lodge as husbands. Though she had grown tired of them all rather quickly and set them aside, she had rejoiced in the pain of birth and rush of waters that had brought her three daughters into the world. But with a man such as this—a man who looked at her with hatred in his strange blue eyes, who was bold enough to reject her and who endured suffering with the strength of the bravest Wyandot warrior—think of the children she might bear! They would be proud, handsome and strong, and their courage would bring her honor.

She would have his seed.

Of course, it wouldn't be easy. Her father had already committed the man to fire and death. And after witnessing his courage, the warriors would be eager to eat his flesh, particularly his heart, so that they might take in his strength. They would not wish to spare him.

But, of course, her father had never been able to deny her anything.

Chapter One

Fort Detroit, Northwestern Wilderness,
March 3, 1763

Nicholas leaned back in thc wooden tub, closed his eyes, let the hot water soak the chill from his bones. It had been months since he'd had a hot bath. It was a luxury he availed himself of only when he came into one of the forts to trade—three or four times a year at most. The rest of the time he bathed in icy rivers and lakes when he could. Survival took precedence over cleanliness in the wild.

The lingering scent of the woman's perfume—a cheap imitation of roses—mingled with the smell of lye soap as Nicholas allowed his mind to drift. From beyond the door came the rumble of men's voices, the thud of horses' hooves and the tread of boots on wooden walkways. Fort Detroit was crowded these days—too crowded for Nicholas's taste—and abuzz with rumors that some of the northwestern tribes were banding together for an organized attack against settlers and the English forts that protected them.

The rumors were true, of course. Nicholas had run into a small band of Shawnee not a month ago and had been warned by one of their warriors, a man Nicholas had traded with in the past, that Englishmen were no longer welcome west of the mountains—with very few exceptions.

The war with France was just ending, and already the frontier was about to collapse into new violence and redoubled bloodshed. Whether they were Indian or white, it seemed to be the nature of men to kill. Nicholas ought to know. He had more blood on his hands than most.

Footsteps approached the door.

He reached for his pistol, which sat primed and ready on the wooden floor beside the tub, wrapped his fingers around its polished handle. It was a reflex born of six years in the wilderness. He was no more aware of his action than he was of breathing.

The footsteps passed.

His grip relaxed, and he began to doze in the steamy water.

Doze only. He never slept, not deeply. He didn't want to dream.

The water was still warm when the sound of quick, light footfalls roused him.

She was back.

The door to the tiny room opened, bringing a rush of cold air and the rustle of skirts.

Nicholas opened his eyes, watched as she approached him. She was young, not yet twenty, he guessed, and pretty. Her dark hair and skin revealed her mixed ancestry—probably the daughter of a French trapper and his temporary Indian wife.

"Is monsieur finished with his bath?"

"Aye." Now it was time for pleasure of another sort.

Without ceremony, he stood, dried himself with the linen towel, walked over to the small bed. She had removed her gown and lay passively on her back in her chemise, a tattered bit of cloth that might once have been white. She parted her thighs, bared her small breasts, drew one rosy-brown nipple to a taut peak, smiled. It was a smile that didn't quite reach her eyes. Then her gaze came to rest on his scars. Her smile faded.

She had, of course, seen his scars when she'd helped him bathe. Then she had averted her gaze. Now she simply stared, clearly repulsed. "Was it terrible, monsieur?"

Nicholas ignored her question, allowed himself to feel only the pulsing need of his erection. How long had it been since he'd been inside a woman? Six months?

He stood at the foot of the bed, grasped her hips, pulled her toward him. Then he lifted her legs, rested her slender calves on his shoulders, filled her with one slow thrust.

It felt good, so good. And he found himself rushing headlong toward orgasm.

It was over in a few minutes, his seed spilled in a pool of pearly white on her belly. Nicholas lay staring at the timbered ceiling, while she washed all trace of him away in the cooling bathwater. Neither of them spoke.

A vague dissatisfied feeling gnawed at his gut. When had he become the sort of man who would take pleasure with a pretty woman, even a whore, without even knowing her name?

Normally, he tried to forget the past. But now he wondered when he'd last made love to a woman, when he'd last devoted himself to giving a woman pleasure heedless of his own? His mind stretched back through the emptiness of the past six years, back through the nightmare that was Lyda to Penelope.

Sweet Penelope. Fickle Penelope.

He tried to conjure up an image of her face, failed. They'd been engaged to marry when he'd ridden away to war with Washington, but when she'd learned he had been taken by the Wyandot and was believed dead, she'd waited all of two months before marrying someone else. When he had finally escaped and made the long journey home to Virginia, he had arrived to find her quickening with her husband's child.

"What was I supposed to do, Nicholas? Was I to wait for you? For how long? We all believed you dead!"

And, indeed, he *was* dead.

He had tried to go on as if nothing had

changed, to return to his old life. His parents, overjoyed at his unforeseen return, had done all in their power to help him. But nothing had been able to silence the screams that haunted his nightmares or restore the spirit that Lyda had so expertly wrenched from his body. Hatred for the Wyandot had consumed him, but no more than hatred for himself.

And when he'd awoken from one of his nightmares to find his hands fast around his little sister Elizabeth's throat—poor Elizabeth, only sixteen, had heard him cry out and come to comfort him—he'd known he was no longer fit to live among those he loved. He had packed a few belongings—a bedroll, his pistols, his rifle, a hunting knife, a change of clothes, powder and shot—and had saddled his horse and prepared to ride away, hoping the wilderness would finish what the Wyandot had not.

But his mother had awakened and, standing outside the stables in her nightgown, had begged him to stay, tears streaming down her face. "Please, Nicholas, don't go! You've just returned! Give us a chance to help you, son!"

Her words, the desperate tone of her voice, had almost been enough to stop him. He did not wish to cause her further pain. But then he had remembered Elizabeth's frightened face, his hands wrapped tightly around her throat. He might have killed her.

He had climbed into the saddle, steeled himself

against his mother's tears. "I regret to inform you, madam, that your son is dead."

Then he had urged his horse into a canter and ridden west, away from home, away from war, away from memories. He'd ridden over mountains, across rivers, through forest and grassland to the great mountains in the Far West that no other Englishman had seen—but never fast enough or far enough to escape himself.

He had not yet found death, but in the vastness of the wilderness and the rhythm of the seasons, he'd found some measure of . . . if not peace, then forgetfulness.

"*Excusez moi, monsieur.*"

The young prostitute. She wanted her fee.

"*Pardonnez moi, mademoiselle. Je crois que je vous dois votre paye.*" *I believe I owe you your fee.* He rose from the bed, still naked, and strode to the corner where his peltries lay in a bundle. Quickly he worked the knots and unrolled the bundle, his hands moving deftly over the soft furs, searching.

"*Vous parlez très bien le français.*" *You speak French well.*

He glanced up at the surprised tone in her voice, on the brink of saying that he had studied French at Oxford and had traveled extensively in France. But he was struck again by her youth and her beauty, felt a momentary stab of guilt at his thoughtless use of her young body. The words died on his lips.

He released the marten pelt he had been about

to give her, pulled free the white wolf instead. Much larger, much more rare, its value far surpassed that of the marten pelt. He stood, handed it to her.

She gaped at it, then at him, her brown eyes wide. "*M-merci, monsieur!*"

Nicholas felt an absurd momentary impulse to apologize or explain himself. There had been a time in his life when he would have asked her what had happened to make her sell her body, when he might even have tried to help her find a better life. But those days had long since passed. The truth was, he no longer cared. "*De rien.*" *It was nothing*.

And as she hurried out of the room, wolf pelt clutched to her breast, that was what Nicholas felt.

Nothing.

Elspeth Stewart woke with a start, heart racing.

The geese!

She rose as quickly as she could, grabbed the rifle, which sat, primed and ready, next to the bed.

If it was the same vixen that had harried them yesterday, she would shoot, and this time she wouldn't miss.

And if it were Indians or renegade soldiers?

Her mouth went dry.

Quickly, quietly, she crossed the wooden floor of the cabin that was her home, lifted the heavy bar from the door and slowly opened it, dread like ice in her veins. Outside it was still dark, the first light of dawn only a hint in the eastern sky. She peered past the door toward the poultry pens and saw a small honey-colored fox dart into the underbrush.

In a warm rush of relief, Elspeth stepped quickly onto the porch, raised the rifle, cocked it, fired. A yelp, followed by silence, told her she had hit her mark.

She stepped back inside long enough to put down the rifle, put on her cloak and slip into her boots—she had taken to sleeping fully clothed since Andrew's death, but that didn't include boots—before going outside to see what damage had been done.

The vixen lay dead in the bushes. Its teats were swollen with milk, and Elspeth felt an unexpected pang of empathy with the dead animal. It had only been trying to eat so that it could feed its new litter of cubs.

She pressed a hand protectively to her rounded belly. In a few weeks, a month at most, she would be doing the same. Which was why she needed to protect the geese and chickens, she thought, brushing aside her sentimental response.

She squatted down, picked the vixen up by its tail and carried it away. She didn't want the smell to attract bears or wolves.

When she returned, the geese were still honking and flapping angrily about, but there were no bloody wings, no broken feathers that she could see. Andrew's fence had held.

"Quit your flaffin'!" she scolded. She wasn't truly angry with them. Geese were better than dogs when it came to alerting their masters to danger. Her life—and that of her unborn baby—might well depend on them one day.

As it was so close to dawn and she'd be getting up soon anyway, Elspeth decided to start her morning chores. She fed the geese and chickens, gathered the few eggs that had been laid and set off to the cowshed for the morning milking. By the time the animals had been fed and Rona and Rosa, her two mares, had been led out into the paddock, the sun had risen behind a heavy blanket of clouds.

She drew water from the well and carried it inside to heat for washing and for her morning porridge. She had just stepped through the door when she saw that the fire had died down to embers and needed wood. But there was no firewood stacked in the corner. And then she remembered.

She hadn't had time to split more wood for the fire yesterday and had been so tired after supper that she had fallen asleep at the table, leaving the chore undone.

Her stomach growled.

"Well, Bethie, you cannae be expectin' the wood to chop itself." She lifted the heavy water bucket onto the table, took the ax from its resting place beside the fire, went back out into the chilly morning.

The woodpile stood on the west side of the

house, and it was dwindling. She hadn't worked out how she was going to fell trees by herself; that was a problem for another day. She awkwardly lifted a large piece of wood onto an old stump, hoisted the ax and swung. The ax cut halfway through the wood, stuck. She pried it loose, swung again. The wood flew into two pieces.

In the two months since Andrew's passing, she had gotten better at chopping firewood. She no longer missed the logs and sometimes even managed to split the wood with one blow as Andrew had done. Still, it was an exhausting chore, one she did not enjoy.

How long could she last out here alone? The question leapt, unbidden and unwelcome, into her mind. It was followed by another.

Where else could she go?

She lifted another piece of wood onto the stump, stepped back, swung and soon found herself in a rhythm.

Perhaps after the baby was born she could go to Fort Pitt or one of the other forts and find work there. At least she and the baby would be safe from Indians and wild animals. But would there be other women? Would they be safe from the soldiers?

Perhaps she could journey to Harrisburg or even to Philadelphia. But that meant traveling for weeks alone through wild country, across the mountains, over rivers and through farmsteads. The very idea of swimming across rivers with her baby or sleeping in a bedroll in the open without the protection of four sturdy walls terrified her.

One thing was certain: She could not go home.

Nor could she stay here forever. She'd managed well enough so far, but what would she do when it came time to plant crops? Could she manage the plow? And what of the harvest? Could she care for her baby, harvest the crops, slaughter the hogs, make cider and salt the meat all at the same time? Her days had been full and long when Andrew had yet lived. How could she manage to do both his chores and hers with a newborn?

And what would she do when her time came?

She'd never given birth before, never even seen a baby born. And though she'd helped cows to calve, she knew having babies was different for women. Would she know what to do? Would both she and her baby survive the travail?

And then there was the threat of Indians and others who prowled the frontier. Few families had escaped unscathed during this war. Men, women and children had been butchered like cattle—shot or burned alive and scalped by Indians fighting for the French. A family only a few miles to the north had been attacked at midday while working in their fields. The oldest sons had been killed and scalped, the daughters and younger boys kidnapped. The oldest daughter had been found several miles away a few days later. She'd been tied to a tree, her body consumed first by fire, then by wild animals.

Of course, Indians weren't the only two-legged

danger. Criminals flocked to the frontier, eager to escape the gallows. Deserters, too, hid in the forests, both French and English. Everyone knew of the family near Paxton that had welcomed two travelers to sleep before their hearth one evening, only to be murdered in their beds.

Andrew had done his best to protect her from these dangers. But he had died just after Christmas of a lingering fever. Although Bethie had tried everything she knew to save him—every poultice, every herb, every draught—he was not a young man and had died one night in his sleep while she sat beside him and held his hand. Already in her seventh month, she had barely managed to dig a shallow grave for him in the frozen earth.

She hadn't had a peaceful night's sleep since, waking to every sound with her heart in her throat.

There was one other possibility, of course, one she almost refused to consider. She could try to find another husband. After the baby was born, she could ride to the nearest settlement, visit the church or meetinghouse and tell the minister that she was widowed and needed to find a husband. But would any man want both her and her child? And if she did find a husband, would she regret it?

Her mother, widowed when Bethie's father was killed by a falling log, had found Malcolm Sorley in much the same way. A big man with a dour temperament and fists like hams, he'd moved with his bully of a son, Richard, into the cabin that had once been a happy home and had done his best to beat the fear of God into his new wife and step-daughter. Bethie had tried to avoid the rages of her new father, but Malcolm Sorley had left his share of welts and bruises on her. Then he had turned her mother against her.

Richard had done far worse.

And though a husband brought protection, marriage brought duties that pleased her not at all. She had no desire to lie beneath a man, to feel him touch her, to feel him inside her. If she could devise it, she would be content to live as a widow for the rest of her life.

And so Bethie arrived at the same stalemate she always came to whenever she allowed herself to think of the days ahead. There was no place for her to go and no way she could safely stay.

Coming to the frontier had been Andrew's idea, not hers. And though he had been kind to her and had taken her from a living hell, she found herself feeling angry with him for abandoning her and her baby to this life of fear and doubt.

She rested the ax on the ground, out of breath, her arms and lower back aching, glad to find a good stack of wood piled on the ground beside her. It was enough to last her the rest of the day and the night, but she would need to chop more this afternoon if she didn't want to be in the same fix tomorrow morning.

She rubbed a soothing hand over her belly, felt

her baby kick within her. Then she squatted down and picked up as many pieces as she could carry. She stepped around to the front of the cabin, her arms full, and froze, a scream trapped in her throat.

A man on horseback.

Chapter Two

He sat on a great chestnut stallion only a few feet away from the cabin's door, staring down at her through cold eyes, pistol in hand.

The firewood fell from her arms, forgotten. She glanced wildly about for the rifle, realized that she had left it inside the cabin. A deadly mistake?

She forced herself to meet his gaze, tried to hide her fear, the frantic thrum of her heartbeat was a deafening roar.

Where had he come from? Why hadn't she heard him? And the geese—why had they made no sound?

He was an Indian. He must be, to have crept up on her so quietly. Dressed in animal hides with long black hair and sun-browned skin, he certainly looked like an Indian. But his eyes were icy and blue as a mountain lake, and most of his face was covered with a thick black beard.

Heart pounding a sickening rhythm in her chest, she swallowed, pressed her hands protectively to her belly. "M-my husband will be back soon."

"Your husband?" His accent was distinctly English and cultured, his voice deep. He smiled, a mocking sort of smile. "Is he the poor fellow buried out back? Aye, I've already met him."

The man started to dismount.

"Nay!" Close to panic, Bethie wasn't sure where her words came from. "Stay on your horse and ride away from here! I am no' wantin' for means to protect myself!"

He climbed slowly from the saddle, his gaze dropping from her face to her swollen belly, a look of what could only be amusement in his eyes. "I'll keep that in mind."

It was then she saw the blood. His hands were stained with it.

Her heart beat like a hammer against her breast, and for one wrenching moment, she knew he was going to kill her. Or worse.

If only she had the rifle! If only she could get inside the cabin, bar the door. But he stood between her and refuge. She took several steps backwards, was about to run into the darkness of the forest, when he sagged against his horse.

Blood. It had soaked through the leather of his leggings on the right side, darkened the back of his right leg all the way to his moccasin. Was it *his* blood? Aye, it must be. He had tied a cloth around his upper thigh to stanch the flow.

He was injured, weak, perhaps nigh to collapsing. Some part of her realized this, saw it as the chance she needed.

She ran, a desperate dash toward the cabin door, toward safety, toward life. She had only a few steps to go when arms strong as steel shot out, imprisoned her.

"Oh, no, you don't!"

"Nay!" She screamed, kicked, hit, fought to free herself with a rising sense of terror.

"Ouch! Damn it, woman!"

The click of a pistol cocking. The cold press of its barrel against her temple.

She froze, a terrified whimper in her throat.

His breath was hot on her cheek. "I have no desire to harm you or the child you carry, but you *will* help me, whether you wish to or not! Do you understand?"

She nodded, her mind numb with fright.

Pistol still in hand, he forced her to hold the stallion's reins while he unsaddled it and carried its burdens inside the cabin. Then he watched as she led the animal to a stall in the barn, settled it with hay and fresh water from the well. And although she had hoped he might fall unconscious, he showed no further sign of pain or weakness apart from a bad limp.

"Get inside and boil water."

She crossed the distance from the barn to the cabin, her stomach knotted with fear, the heat of his gaze boring into her back. Then she saw the firewood scattered on the ground. She stopped, turned to him, half afraid to speak lest she provoke his ire. She had no doubt this man was capable of killing. "I-I'll need the wood."

Blue eyes, hard and cold as slate, met hers. He nodded—one stiff jerk of his head.

She stooped down slowly, began to fill her arms.

Nicholas watched the woman pick up firewood. She had no idea how close she had come to escaping him moments ago on her doorstep. Dizzy from blood loss, he had found it surprisingly difficult to subdue her, had been forced to wield the threat of his pistol. He could not risk getting close enough for her to knock it from his grasp. He was fast fading, and without the weapon he would not long be able to bend her to his will. He had no doubt that if given the choice she would leave him out here to die, or even kill him herself.

He didn't blame her. There was only one rule on the frontier—survival. A woman without male protection could not be too careful, particularly a young and pretty one. And even heavy with child, she was a beauty.

How old was she? Nicholas guessed eighteen. Her cheeks were pink from exertion, her skin flawless and kissed by the sun. A thick braid of sun-streaked honey-blond hair hung down her back to her waist. Her curves, enhanced by her pregnancy, were soft, womanly and easily apparent despite the plainness of her gray woolen gown. And although she was great with child, she had felt small in his arms. Her head just touched his shoulder.

He looked on as she struggled to stand. Though she was obviously very near her time, she was surprisingly graceful and was soon back on her feet and walking toward the cabin, arms full, her braid swaying against the gray wool of her cloak with each step.

Nicholas followed, but even this small effort left him breathless. His heart hammered in his chest, fought to pump blood no longer in his body. The Frenchman's blade had gone deep, and though it had failed to sever his tendons and drop him to the ground as the bastard had no doubt hoped, it had clearly cut into a major blood vessel.

He'd left Fort Detroit early in the morning almost a week ago, having earned more than enough from his pelts to replenish his supplies. He'd traveled south for most of four days before he got the feeling he was being followed. The signs were subtle—the twitching of Zeus's ears, the cry of a raven startled from its perch somewhere behind him, a prickling on the back of his neck. He'd urged Zeus to a faster pace, kept up his guard, hadn't stopped to rest or eat until well past nightfall.

They attacked just after midnight. The first sprang at him out of the darkness and might have succeeded in killing him had Nicholas not been awake and waiting. And while he'd grappled with the first, the second had leapt from hiding to deal a surprise blow. Nicholas had quickly dispatched the first attacker, but the second managed to slash his thigh before Nicholas buried his knife in the man's belly. He'd recognized them both from the fort—French trappers who weren't ready to relinquish the Ohio Valley to the English.

Nicholas had realized immediately he was badly hurt. He'd have treated the wound himself had he been able to see it and reach it with ease. Instead, he'd tied a tourniquet around his leg and had reluctantly ridden through the night, hoping to cross some farmstead where aid might be available.

As he'd grown weaker, he'd all but resigned himself to death. He was already dead inside. What did it matter if his body died, too? Wasn't that what he'd secretly been searching for all these years? But just before dawn, he'd heard a gunshot to the east and had followed it until he'd heard the sound of someone chopping wood. He hadn't expected it to be a woman, much less a woman alone.

He hadn't asked a soul for help in more than six years. It galled him to have to do so now. He followed the woman inside. "Build up the fire."

The cabin was small with a puncheon floor that looked as if it had been newly washed. The only light came from a small window covered with greased parchment. A rough-hewn table sat in the center of the room, a hand-carved bedstead against the far right wall. In the far left corner on the other side of the fireplace sat a cupboard and before it a loom, a spinning wheel and a rocking chair. Dried onions, herbs and flowers hung from the rafters, a feminine touch that for one startling moment reminded him of the cookhouse on his plantation. A rifle leaned against the wall beside the door.

Nicholas checked the rifle to make certain it was not primed and loaded. Next he removed his buffalo-hide coat and his jacket, tossed them over one of the wooden chairs.

Black spots danced before his eyes. He pulled out another chair, sat, watched as she stirred the fire to life and poured water into the kettle to boil. "You'll need thread and a strong needle."

She started at the sound of his voice. She was terrified of him, he knew. He could taste her fear, smell it, see it in the way she moved.

Smart woman.

Of course, he hadn't meant to frighten her, not until she'd left him no choice. Had his need not been so dire, he would have tried to win her cooperation in some more civilized fashion. Then again, if his need had not been dire, he wouldn't be here.

"If I wanted to kill you, you'd be dead already."

He heard her gasp, saw her eyes widen in alarm, realized his words had done nothing to calm her. But then, it had been a long time since he'd tried to comfort a woman.

He tried again. "I'm not going to hurt you."

She set needle and thread on the table, began to ladle hot water into an earthenware bowl, watched him through wide and frightened eyes. "P-please. Y-you'll need to . . . to remove your leggings and lie down on your belly if I'm to stitch you."

She had a faint accent—sweet and melodic. Scottish?

But what she'd suggested was easier said than done. To remove his leggings, he would need to remove the tourniquet. If he removed the tourniquet, the blood would flow freely again. He might lose consciousness, perhaps even die. But she wouldn't be able to treat him if he kept his leggings on.

There was only one solution. He pulled out his hunting knife, began to cut through the supple leather.

Bethie watched as he sliced the leather from his right leg with smooth, strong motions, noticed things she hadn't noticed before. A thin white scar ran down his left temple to his cheekbone, made him seem even more dangerous. But his face was ashen—what she could see of it above his beard—and his lips were pallid, bloodless.

Clearly, he had come close to dying. He might die still.

When his leg was cut free, he tossed the blood-soaked leather by the door. Pistol still in hand, he stood, a bit unsteady at first. Then he took up his great shaggy coat, strode to the bed, spread the skin on the homespun coverlet. In one fluid motion, he stretched out over the skin and lay down on his belly. He was trying to keep from getting blood on the coverlet, she realized—an oddly considerate thing to do.

The sight of him lying on her bed was more than a little disturbing. His dark hair spilled over his broad shoulders, fanned across the undyed linen of his shirt to his narrow hips. He was so much bigger than Andrew—leaner, more muscular, taller. His feet hung off the foot of the bed, and he seemed to fill it, just as his presence dominated the tiny cabin.

Then she saw his wound. Gaping and raw, it was at least six inches long, parting the skin of his upper thigh, digging deep into the muscle. If it festered, he would lose his entire leg, perhaps even die.

She must have gasped.

"That bad?"

"I'll need to wash the blood away first." She added a bit of cold water to the hot, tested the temperature with her fingers. Then she pulled a chair over to the bed, set the bowl of water on it, together with the needle, thread and several clean strips of linen.

She sat beside him, careful to keep her distance, tried to gather her thoughts, which had leapt in all directions like frightened deer at the first sight of him. He would not harm her now, she reasoned. Not yet. His hurt was grievous, and he needed her help. But what would he do later when he recovered his strength?

As Bethie knew only too well, there were many ways a man could hurt a woman. And this man was dangerous. Every instinct she had told her that. Hadn't he already threatened her with his pistol and used his strength against her?

She must not give him another chance to harm her. She must find a way to take his weapons from him, to render him helpless, to gain the upper hand. Christian charity might demand that she help him, but that didn't mean she had to leave herself defenseless against him.

She dipped a linen cloth into the water, squeezed it out, began gingerly to wipe the blood from his leg. It was unsettling to touch the stranger in such an intimate way, to feel his skin, the rasp of his dark body hair, the strength of his muscles beneath her hands. She tried to take her mind off what she was doing, gathered her courage to ask him the question she'd wanted to ask since she'd seen he was wounded. "If you dinnae mind my askin', how did this happen?"

"I was attacked by two French trappers. I killed them, but not before one of them tried to hamstring me."

The way he spoke of killing, as if it were nothing, sent a chill down her spine.

He seemed to read her mind. "They tried to murder me as I slept."

Bethie said nothing, afraid her voice would reveal her fear and doubt. Instead, she bent over his injury to examine it. Blood still oozed from deep within despite the tourniquet, pooling red in the gaping wound. She parted the flesh with her fingers, felt her stomach lurch. He was cut almost to the bone.

She could not stitch this.

She stood, took deep breaths to calm her stomach, washed his blood from her hands. "I . . . I'm sorry. But I'm goin' to have to . . . to cauterize it."

He turned his head, looked back at her over his shoulder, held out his hunting knife. "Then do it. Use my knife."

She hesitated for a moment, struck by his seeming indifference to the prospect of so much pain, then took the knife. She walked to the table, thrust the knife blade into the hottest part of the fire, waited for it to heat.

Worries chased one another through her mind. She didn't want to do this. She'd never done it before. And she was afraid—afraid of doing it wrong, afraid he would thrash about and hurt her, afraid he would blame her for his suffering.

She turned to look at the strange man in her bed. He appeared to be sleeping, his face turned toward her, long dark lashes softening his otherwise starkly masculine features. She did not trust him, knew he was dangerous. But she did not want to hurt him.

Then, an idea half formed in her mind, she crossed the room to the cupboard, took out her bag of medicines and the jug of whisky Andrew kept for cold nights. Careful to turn her back to him, she poured a stout draft of whisky into a tin cup, added several drops of herbal tincture, sure the alcohol would mask the taste.

His voice broke the silence. "What's your name?"

"Bethie." Startled, she answered quickly, without thinking, then corrected herself. "Elspeth Stewart."

"Check the blade, Mistress Stewart. Surely it's hot by now."

She turned toward him, cup in hand, walked to the bed and offered it to him. "You'll be needin' this."

He lifted his head, his brows knitted in puzzlement, looked into the cup, grinned darkly. "Corn whisky? You'd best save that to clean the wound."

"But it will help to dull your pain."

He shook his head. "A cup of whisky cannot help me. Besides, 'tis only pain."

Only pain?

She gaped at him. What kind of life had he led that certain agony meant nothing to him? "Fine. Suffer if you like, but I cannae hold you down. What promise do I have that you willna thrash about or kick me?"

He laughed at her. "I give you my word I will hold perfectly still."

"But your sufferin' will be terrible! Should I no' at least bind you to the—"

"No!" There was an edge of genuine anger in his voice now. "I've given you my word. Now let's get this over with."

Sick to her stomach and trembling, Bethie set the whisky aside and retrieved the knife. Wrapping her apron around the hot, wooden handle, she carried it to the bed.

The blade glowed red.

She stood next to his injured leg, dreading what she must do, and tried to figure out how best to apply the heat.

"Do it!" The man reached above his head, grasped the carved rungs of the headboard, his large hands making fists around the wood.

She took a deep breath and pressed the red-hot steel into the wound.

The hiss and reek of burning flesh.

His body stiffened, and his knuckles turned white, but he did not cry out. Nor did he thrash or try to pull his leg away.

The hissing faded.

Bethie pulled the blade free, stepped back from the bed, drew air deep into her lungs, afraid she might faint or be sick. Stray thoughts flitted through her mind like wild birds. Had it worked? Was he still bleeding? Would his leg fester? How had he managed to hold still through such torment?

Gradually her breathing slowed, and the dizziness and nausea passed. Gathering her wits, she carried the bucket and what was left of the fresh water to the bed.

She sat beside him, expecting him to be unconscious, but he was not. Beads of sweat glistened on his forehead, and his face was even paler than before, if that were possible. But his eyes, though glazed with pain, were open, and he watched her.

"I-I'm sorry! I didna want to hurt you." She dipped the cloth into the bucket, pressed the cold, wet cloth to his brow and cheeks.

"Has the bleeding . . . stopped?" His voice was tight, ragged, betraying his pain.

Almost afraid to look, Bethie bent over the wound. What had been a raw, bleeding gash was now burned, blistered flesh. But there was only one way to know for certain. She took up a knife and, after a moment's hesitation, cut away the tourniquet. "Aye, the bleedin' has stopped."

"Pour the whisky in."

"Are you cert—?"

"Aye. Do it!"

She hurried to the cupboard, withdrew the jug once more, then returned to the bed. With a jerk, she pulled the cork free, then poured fiery liquid into the wound and set the jug aside.

Not so much as a sound escaped his lips.

She took a fresh strip of linen, sat beside him, blotting up the excess.

"A pouch of ointments . . . in my saddlebags. The big pocket. Fetch it." He sounded weaker.

"Aye, in a moment. Should you not first have something to strengthen you? You've lost a lot of blood." She reached for the tin cup with the whisky mixture, lifted his head, held it to his lips. "Swallow."

To her great relief, this time he drank.

The sight of her eyes—lovely eyes almost the color of violets—would be the last thing Nicholas remembered.

Chapter Three

He was on fire. Every inch of his chest, belly and back seemed to burn, pain ripping even into his sleep. The ropes chafed his wrists and ankles, imprisoned him, made his right leg ache.

Lyda was again cleaning his wounds, rubbing ointment into his burns, her fingers like glass shards against his tortured skin. He would have killed her, would have broken her neck had he been able to free himself.

But she knew that, and so she kept him bound.

How long had he lain here, drifting in and out of consciousness, half mad with pain and fever? Hours? Days? Weeks? And why was he still alive? Why had they spared him?

Screams.

Josiah and Eben! The Wyandot were burning them, tormenting them. But they were already long dead, weren't they? Why, then, could he still hear them?

"Nicholas! For God's sake, help us!"

* * *

Nicholas awoke with a jerk, caught between the nightmare and wakefulness, his heart pounding, his body covered with sweat. He struggled to open his eyes, found himself lying on his stomach in someone's bed, his head on a pillow. His right leg throbbed, burned. His head ached. His throat was parched as sand, and a strange aftertaste lingered in his mouth.

From nearby came the swish of skirts, the sound of a log settling in a fire, the scent of something cooking.

Where was he?

Through a fog he tried to remember. He'd been attacked. The Frenchmen from the fort. He'd lost a lot of blood, had ridden in search of help. The cabin. The woman.

Bethie was her name. Elspeth Stewart.

She'd helped him, cleaned his wound, cauterized it—not altogether willingly.

Nicholas lifted his head, started to roll onto his side to take in his surroundings, found he could not.

His wrists and ankles were bound to the bedposts.

Blood rushed to his head, a dark surge of rage, of dread.

"You're awake." Her voice came from behind him. "You must be thirsty."

"You little bitch!" He pulled on the ropes, his

fury and dread rising when they held fast. "Release me! Now!"

"I-I cannae do that—no' yet. I've made broth. It will help you regain—"

"Damn your broth, woman! Untie me!" He jerked on the ropes again, outraged and alarmed to find himself rendered powerless. Sharp pain cut through his right thigh.

"Stop your strugglin'! You'll split your wound open and make it bleed again."

Infuriated, Nicholas growled, a sound more animal than human, even to his own ears. He jerked violently on the ropes, but it was futile. He was still weak from blood loss, and the effort left him breathless, made his pulse hammer in his ears.

Damn her!

He closed his eyes, fought to subdue the slick current of panic that slid up from his belly, caught in his throat.

She is not Lyda. This is not the Wyandot village.

His heartbeat slowed. The panic subsided, left white-hot rage in its wake.

"Why did you do this? I told you I meant you no harm!" He craned his neck, saw that she stood before the fire, ladling liquid into a tin cup, a brown knitted shawl around her shoulders.

"Is that no' what the wolf always says to the lamb?" She carried the cup to the bed, sat. "Drink. It will help to replenish your blood. Careful. 'Tis hot."

Tantalized by the smell of the broth and suddenly aching with thirst, Nicholas bit back the curse that sat on his tongue. He drank.

Bethie held the cup to his lips, watched as he swallowed the broth, her heart still racing. For one terrible moment, she'd feared the ropes would break or come loose. She'd known he would be angry with her, but she hadn't expected him to try to rip the bed apart.

Truth be told, she feared him despite the ropes. Although he'd given up for the moment, she could feel the fury coiled inside him. She could see it in the rippling tension of his body, in his clenched fists, in the unforgiving glare in his eyes. He made her think of a caged cougar—spitting angry and untamed. He was not used to being bested.

The arrogant brute! Did he imagine she would grant him warm hospitality after the way he'd treated her? It served him right to be bound and helpless!

As if a man of his strength were ever truly helpless.

Her gaze traveled the length of him as it had done many times while he'd slept, and she found her eyes focused of their own will on the rounded muscles of his buttocks where the butter-soft leather clung so tightly.

Mortified, she jerked her gaze away, felt heat rise in her cheeks. Her stepfather had always said she was possessed of a sinful nature.

"More." His boorish command interrupted her

thoughts. He glowered at her through eyes of slate.

"Aye." She stood, hurried to the fireplace, ladled more broth into the cup, uncomfortably aware that he was watching her.

"How long do you intend to keep me a prisoner?" His voice was rough, full of repressed rage.

She walked back to the bed, sat, feigned a calm she did not feel. "'Tis your own fault you lie bound. You cannae be expectin' to be treated as a guest when you behaved like a felon. Drink."

He pulled his head away, his gaze hard upon her, held up the ropes that bound his wrists. "This isn't necessary."

"You threatened me, held your pistol to my head, forced me to do your will and admitted to killin' two men. Do you truly expect me to trust you?"

He frowned, his dark brows pensive. "I didn't mean to frighten you."

"As I recollect, you seemed quite bent on frightenin' me."

"I didn't have time for social graces. My need was dire."

"So is mine!" She stood in a surge of temper, met his gaze. "I cannae risk you regainin' your strength and then, when you no longer need my help, hurtin' me or my baby or takin' what is ours and leavin' us in the cold to starve! I dinnae even know your name!"

For a moment he said nothing. "Kenleigh. Nicholas Kenleigh."

She repeated his name aloud.

"Now that we've exchanged pleasantries, Mistress Stewart, you *will* release me."

"Nay, Master Kenleigh. I willna—no' just yet." She lifted her chin. "You'll stay as you are till I'm certain you pose no threat to me and my baby."

He gave a snort. "And how will you determine that?"

"Drink." She held the cup once more to his lips. "Perhaps I shall have you swear an oath, a bindin' oath."

He drained the cup, looked up at her. "And if I am a murdering liar, a man with no honor, the sort of man who would harm a woman ripe with child, how would this oath prevent me from doing whatever I want the moment you cut me free?"

Bethie stood, walked back to the fireplace to refill the cup once more, the truth of his words dashing to pieces her sense of safety. "Are you sayin' I should never set you free, Master Kenleigh?"

"No, Mistress Stewart. I'm saying that unless you plan to keep me a prisoner forever and care for me as if I were a babe untrained in the use of a chamber pot, sooner or later you will have no choice but to trust me."

She walked back to the bed, felt her step falter. In truth, she hadn't thought about how or when she would release him when she'd bound him to the bed. Nor had she considered what keeping him bound would mean. She'd been thinking only of a way to restrain him and deprive him of his weapons, and she had accomplished that.

A babe untrained in the use of a chamber pot? Good heavens!

She reached the bed, sat, held the cup once more to his lips. "Very well. I shall cut you free. But you shall first swear to me by all you hold sacred that you willna do anythin' to harm me or my baby or to deprive us of our hearth and home."

He swallowed, licked broth from his lips. Then a queer look came over his face. He stared at the tin cup, then gaped at her. "You drugged me!"

How did he know? "I-I gave you medicine to ease your pain—and make you sleep."

He laughed, a harsh sound. "You drugged me so that you could bind me and take my weapons."

He stated it so plainly that Bethie could find no words to soften the truth of what she'd done. She rested a hand protectively on her belly, felt her baby shift within her. "Y-you left me no choice."

Nicholas saw the defiant tilt of her chin, noticed the pink that crept into her cheeks. He noticed, too, the way her hand softly caressed the swollen curve of her abdomen as if to calm the small life inside her.

What would I have done in her place?

He dismissed the question—and the irritating impulse to defend his previous actions toward her. There was only one rule in the wild—survival.

He'd only done what he'd felt he had to do to stay alive.

And so had she.

"Very well, Mistress Stewart. I swear that I will not harm you or your child or try to take from you that which is yours." His next words surprised him. "And for the short time I shelter under your roof, I swear to protect you from any man who would."

What in hell had inspired him to say that? She was not his problem. Clearly, whatever potion she'd given him had addled his mind.

For a moment she stood as still as a statue, her gaze seeming to measure him in light of the words he had just spoken. "Very well, Master Kenleigh."

She took up his hunting knife, which had lain on the table, then disappeared out of his range of vision. He felt her fingers pulling on the rope that bound his left ankle, felt the cold blade of his knife slide between the rope and his skin. A few tugs later, his left ankle was free.

In a matter of moments, only the bonds around his left wrist remained. He rolled onto his back, watched her as she rounded the bed with agonizing slowness. He could feel her doubt, her trepidation. Her violet eyes wide, she watched him as if he were a wild animal that might attack at any moment.

"I promised not to harm you. I am a man of my word."

The cool touch of a blade. A few sharp tugs.

His wrist was free.

Quickly she backed away from the bed, out of his reach, his knife still in her grasp.

Nicholas pushed himself up onto his elbows. Outside the parchment window, all was dark. Nighttime already?

Slowly he sat, let his legs fall over the edge of the bed, touched his feet to the wooden floor. The muscles in his right thigh screamed in angry protest. Dark spots danced before his eyes. The cabin swam.

Nicholas drew air into his lungs, felt the labored beating of his heart. He cursed his weakness, knew he had come terribly close to dying. It would take days, perhaps even weeks, for him to regain the blood he had lost and, with it, his strength.

"You see, Mistress Stewart? I'm in . . . no shape to harm . . . anyone."

And then, as if to prove his point, he slumped to the floor in a dead faint.

Bethie knelt beside him, touched his forehead, let out a long sigh of relief to find it still cool. He stirred in his sleep, his brow furrowed as if in response to her touch. Asleep like this, his long lashes dark upon his pale cheeks, his brow relaxed, he seemed harmless, not at all the kind of beast who'd hold a pistol to a woman's head.

He lay on the floor much as he had fallen. She could not lift him, or even drag him, without risking harm to her baby. She tucked a pillow beneath his head and draped his heavy buffalo-skin coat over him to keep him warm, but there was little more she could do for him.

Slowly she stood, one hand held against her lower back, the other stifling a yawn. She had already stoked the fire, paid one last visit to the privy house and drawn in the door string. There was nothing left to do but go to sleep.

But how could she sleep with this huge Englishman, this rough and wild stranger, in the same room?

"He cannae hurt you, Bethie, you silly lass. He cannae even—"

Her words were interrupted by another yawn. 'Twas surely near midnight. She needed to sleep.

She picked up his pistol from the table where she had left it after she'd primed and loaded it, carried it with her around his prostrate form to the other side of the bedstead. Then she drew down the covers, crawled into their warmth.

The baby kicked restlessly as Bethie settled onto her pillow. "Quiet now, little one. You wouldna want to keep me awake, would you?"

But despite her exhaustion, sleep would not come, and the baby was not to blame. Each time she began to drift off, something woke her. Several times she abruptly found herself sitting up, pistol in hand and pointed into the darkness. Once it was a log settling on the fire. Then it was the howl of a wolf in the distance. And then the stranger shifted in his sleep, bumped one of the chairs.

Twice Bethie arose, checked him for fever, made certain the door string was pulled in, added wood to the fire. And when she had to use the chamber pot, as she seemed to have to do constantly these days, she found she could not—not with him in the cabin. Quietly she crept outside and saw to her needs under a cold canopy of stars surrounded by furtive noises and the impenetrable darkness of the forest.

With unbearable slowness, the hours drifted by. The fire burned down to embers. The silence of the night, filled with dark possibility, deepened around her.

The first thing Nicholas noticed when he awoke, besides the relentless pain in his right thigh, was the underside of a pinewood table. It took him a moment to remember where he was and why. But how had he come to be on the floor?

He remembered Mistress Stewart cutting his bonds. He remembered trying to sit. And then?

Had the little wench drugged him again?

No. He had passed out.

He cursed under his breath, felt his tongue stick to the dry roof of his mouth. He needed water. A waterskin full of it.

It was then he noticed the pillow. She had placed a pillow beneath his head and had covered him with his buffalo-hide coat while he slept. The thoughtfulness of her gesture left him feeling annoyed. He didn't need her compassion.

Slowly he sat, waited to catch his breath, his heart drumming.

Although the sun had risen, she was still asleep. Even in the dim light, he could see dark circles beneath her eyes, and he knew she'd slept poorly out of fear of him. If his gut hadn't told him this, the pistol she clutched tightly in her hand—his pistol—certainly would have.

She looked helpless, very young and utterly innocent. Her smoky lashes rested on her creamy cheeks. Her long braid had come unbound, leaving her hair to tangle in thick, honey-colored coils against her pillow. She had slept fully clothed, as if to be ready for anything at any moment. Her blankets were twisted in disarray around her thighs, proof she'd had a restless night.

It wasn't his damned fault if she was still afraid of him. He'd given her his word. What more could he do?

He fought to ignore the pricking of his conscience, was about to drag his gaze from her when he noticed something that stopped him. Beneath the plain gray cloth of her gown where it stretched across her rounded belly, he could actually *see* her baby move. At first he thought he'd imagined it. But as he watched, it happened again—an abrupt movement, almost like a twitch, beneath her gown.

Without thinking, he pressed his hand against the surprising hardness of her abdomen. And there it was—a light pressure against his palm, faint at first, then stronger, as if the child could feel his touch and was pushing back. His throat grew tight with unexpected emotion.

A baby. His baby.

Conceived in hatred, it had died before birth. He had killed it, as surely as he'd driven its mother to her death.

Nicholas fought to push the unwelcome memories from his mind, tried to force them back behind the carefully forged steel wall that separated him from his past.

The gentle pressure against his palm increased, undeniable, persistent, as if in tender mockery of his attempts to forget. It held him in thrall.

A gasp. A flurry of blankets and gray skirts.

And Nicholas found himself staring down the barrel of his own pistol.

She is lost. Blinded by the swirling storm, Flame knows that she cannot give up if she is to survive. Her memory gone, the lovely firebrand awakes to find that the strong arms encircling her belong to a devilishly handsome stranger. And one look at his blazing eyes tells her that the haven she has found promises a passion that will burn for a lifetime. She is the most lovely thing he has ever seen. From the moment he takes Flame in his arms and gazes into her sparkling eyes, Stone knows that the red-headed virgin has captured his heart. The very sight of her smile stokes fiery desires in him that only her touch can extinguish. To protect her he'll claim her as his wife, and pray that he can win her heart before she discovers the truth.

___4691-1 $5.99 US/$6.99 CAN

Dorchester Publishing Co., Inc.
P.O. Box 6640
Wayne, PA 19087-8640

Please add $1.75 for shipping and handling for the first book and $.50 for each book thereafter. NY, NYC, and PA residents, please add appropriate sales tax. No cash, stamps, or C.O.D.s. All orders shipped within 6 weeks via postal service book rate.
Canadian orders require $2.00 extra postage and must be paid in U.S. dollars through a U.S. banking facility.

Name_______________________________________
Address_____________________________________
City_____________________State_______Zip___________
I have enclosed $ _________ in payment for the checked book(s).
Payment must accompany all orders. ❑ Please send a free catalog.